BORDERLANDS

Tales of Mystery & Imagination

Ken Pelham

LITTLE
BIG
ECON
PRESS

Borderlands: Tales of Mystery & Imagination.

The stories contained herein are works of fiction. Names, characters, places, and incidents are a product of the author's imaginations. Real locales and public names are sometimes used for atmospheric purposes. With the exception of public figures, any resemblance to actual people, living or dead, or to businesses, companies, events, institutions, or locales is completely coincidental. Any historical personages or actual events depicted are fictionalized and used only for inspiration. Any opinions expressed are completely those of fictionalized characters and not a reflection of the views of public figures, the author, or the publisher.

Little Big Econ Press, Copyright ©2022 by Ken Pelham.

Cover designed by Jen Pelham.

ISBN: 979-8-8411-3180-9

Image Credits and Sources

All images used herein are either in the public domain or used with the permission of the creators, and credited as follows:

Cover Illustration: RobertBreitpaul (iStock).

Story Illustrations:
"The Wreck of the *Edinburgh Kate,*" William Lionel Wyllie, *Dawn After a Storm* (1869), Public Domain, CC0 license per Wikimedia Commons.
"Familiar," Miezekieze (Pixabay).
"First World War," lolloj (Shutterstock).
"The Tower House Prisoner," ambquinn (Pixabay).
"The Rum War," United States Coast Guard Historian's Office, Public Domain.*
"Itchy," geralt, through Pixabay.
"The *Medusa* Jump," Théodore Géricault, *The Raft of the Medusa*, (1819), Public Domain, CC0 license per Wikimedia Commons.
"Great Minds Think Alike", jackmac34 (Pixabay).
"When the Hurly Burly's Done," xusenru (Pixabay).
"The Light Keeper," United States Coast Guard Historian's Office, Public Domain.*
"The Queen Beneath the Earth," sqback (iStock).
"Empty Suit," Anton5146, VasilyevD (iStock).
"Double Effect," thuanvo (Pixabay).
"Myrna," NeangArt (Pixabay).
"The Valkyries of Leningrad," LifeJourneys, (iStock).
"Under the Whelming Tide," Sdecoret, Superstar (Shutterstock).

*The appearance of U.S. Department of Defense visual information does not imply or constitute DoD endorsement.

All images have been digitally altered using Adobe Photoshop.

Publishing History

"Itchy" first appeared in *Pleiades Magazine* in 1988.

"Myrna" first appeared in *Stellanova* in 1988.

"Great Minds Think Alike" first appeared in *No Idea* in 1989.

"Familiar" first appeared in *Black Petals*, 2004. Later published in *In Shadows Written: An Anthology of Modern Horror*, Blue Beech Press, 2017.

"Double Effect" was first published in a collection titled *Treacherous Bastards* in 2013.

"The Wreck of the *Edinburgh Kate*," "The Rum War," and "The Light Keeper" were first published in the collection *Tales of Old Brigands Key*, in 2014.

"First World War" was first published in the Alvarium Experiment anthology, *The Prometheus Saga*, in 2015.

"The Tower House Prisoner" was first published in the Alvarium Experiment anthology, *The Prometheus Saga 2*, in 2015.

"Under the Whelming Tide" was first published in the Alvarium Experiment anthology, *Return to Earth*, in 2016.

"The Queen Under the Earth," was first published in *Shadows and Teeth, Volume 2*, Darkwater Syndicate, 2017.

"When the Hurly Burly's Done" was first published in the Alvarium Experiment anthology, *The Masters Reimagined*, in 2019.

"The *Medusa* Jump" first appeared in the Alvarium Experiment anthology, *The Masters Reimagined Vol. 2*, in 2020.

"Empty Suit," was first published in the Alvarium Experiment anthology, *The Light Fantastic*, in 2021.

"The Valkyries of Leningrad" is published for the first time in this volume.

Awards

"The Wreck of the *Edinburgh Kate*," 2014 Royal Palm Literary Award.

"Under the Whelming Tide," 2017 Semifinalist, Royal Palm Literary Award.

"When the Hurly Burly's Done," 2019 Royal Palm Literary Award.

"The *Medusa* Jump," 2021 Royal Palm Literary Award.

Acknowledgments

Many thanks to the writers of the Alvarium Experiment, with special thanks to my editors in that fun bunch for "The Tower House Prisoner," the talented authors Kristin Durfee and Charles A. Cornell. For "When the Hurly Burly's Done," thanks to Kristin Durfee, John Hope, and Scott Michael Powers. For "First World War," thanks to Daco S. Auffenorde and Doug Dandridge. For "Under the Whelming Tide," thanks to Bard Constantine and Kristin Durfee. For "The *Medusa* Jump," thanks to Kristin Durfee, Charles A. Cornell, and Jade Kerrion. For "Empty Suit," thanks to Scott Michael Powers, Parker Francis, and Daco Auffenorde.

Thanks to Elle Andrews Patt for editing the never-before-published "The Valkyries of Leningrad."

Thanks to James T. Shirley for help with 19th-century maritime salvage law, so vital to "The Wreck of the *Edinburgh Kate*."

Thanks to Antonio Simon, Jr. and Darkwater Syndicate, for editing and publishing "The Queen Under the Earth" in the outstanding horror anthology, *Shadows and Teeth, Volume 2*.

Special thanks to Jennifer Pelham for the cover design.

And as always, thanks to my wife and daughters for their encouragement, support, and thoughts on the work.

—KP

For Laura

Contents

Introduction

When I was a kid with just nickels to my name, I prowled used-book stores for novels by my favorite authors, and always on the lookout for new authors. I gravitated to novels that promised suspense, regardless of genre. Mystery, thriller, science fiction, horror, fantasy, adventure. Didn't matter, as long it delivered the page-turning, or looked like it would.

I was also drawn to short story anthologies and collections that promised the goods as well. And I found that top-drawer anthologies sometimes surpassed good novels. But the anthologies almost invariably centered on a single genre. Science fiction. Fantasy. Horror. Mystery. With little or no overlap.

Then one day I bumped into a few anthologies with Alfred Hitchcock's name on them. *Stories to Be Read with the Lights On. 14 of My Favorites in Suspense. Stories for Late at Night.* I plunked my nickels onto the counter and hurried away with my tattered new paperbacks.

Although the mystery dominated these slim volumes, they weren't entirely exclusive to that. You have Daphne du Maurier's horror novella "The Birds." Then there are Anthony Boucher's "They Bite," and a pinch of science fiction with the horror in George Langelaan's deliciously creepy "The Fly."

Borderlands was inspired by those anthologies. Some of the stories here are pure science fiction, horror, mystery, or thriller. Some have feet in multiple camps. Some are linked, such as the five set on my fictional island of Brigands Key. Two more are linked by an immortal android.

The common denominator is suspense.

Edgar Allan Poe, so commonly associated with the macabre, dabbled in science fiction and invented the modern mystery. His collected works were published posthumously in 1902 as *Tales of Mystery & Imagination*, which I've nicked for my subtitle. Call it theft if you will; I call it homage.

So check the locks, draw the curtains, brew the coffee, spike it in moderation, and settle in to read long into the night.

—*Ken Pelham*

A stormy sea. A ship runs aground, a frenzied group of salvagers rushes to plunder it. But what if the ship transports not wealth from England, but horror?

The Wreck of the *Edinburgh Kate*

Brigands Key, January, 1890

Deputy John Fells Sanborn watched Emma's economical, sure movements as she ladled bean soup into his bowl, avoiding eye contact. He wrestled with what he wanted to say, and how best to say it. He couldn't seem to find words that would be gentle.

The fireplace blazed, keeping out the winter chill. Outside, a slow cold rain, the remnant of the storm of the previous day, settled in and showed no intention of leaving.

Sanborn dipped his spoon and ate the soup slowly and deliberately, delaying the unhappy conversation. Emma settled into her own chair, unfolded her napkin, and placed it into her lap. She glanced up at him, and glanced away again. They ate in silence for long minutes. At last, he said, "The storm has just about blown itself out now. I should be back on the water fishing in the morning after I make my rounds."

"How is Percy doing?"

"He's about healed. He came back onto the boat on Monday."

"That's good. I'm so sorry he lost the fingers."

"He is lucky. The infection took swiftly, and he could have lost the whole arm."

"I don't call that 'luck.' Oh, John, it's not worth it. Do you think the sheriff might increase upon your wages, as he said?"

No, it's not worth it, he thought. "It's as I've told you, I'm a caretaker at best here. If the fishermen profit, the tax coffers fill. If not, the sheriff guards his budget jealously and allocates it across the county according to the jurisdictions' collections. The fish are scarce this year; therefore so are salary increases. And if the fish were bountiful, these scoundrels wouldn't report it."

"It's not like Massachusetts."

"We're not in Massachusetts."

"I didn't mean—"

"I know what you meant. The roof leaks. The parlor window is broken. The fuel oil is low. I'll take care of them and then it'll be something else we can't afford."

"Oh, John, it's not that way at all. I don't miss Boston. I love our home here."

It pleases me that you love it so, he thought. He wished he felt the same. Two years here, and he still felt like a stranger. His stipend as a part-time deputy-sheriff barely covered anything, and despite his working alongside them on the fishing boats in order to make a living wage, the locals roundly despised him as a Yankee interloper.

He thought about his letter of introduction and inquiry to the Chief of Police in Boston. Emma knew nothing of it. The response would be due any day now, and most likely would contain an offer of employment. And he would take it. Alone. He needed a new start, unencumbered.

A new life.

He pushed his soup away and rose from the table. Without a word he moved into the parlor and took a seat at the piano. He rubbed his hands, stretched his fingers, and began playing Moonlight Sonata. The music pushed down his anger, if just for a little while.

He imagined his future, and the island's future. The town teetered on the brink of dissolution, the victim of a dying fishing ground, troubled by four straight years of red tide, and a hurricane that had swept aside miles of oyster beds. Fishing held little allure for him even in the best of times, and these were far from the best of times.

He was respected in town by a few as a man of culture and fortitude, but never as authority figure nor working man. He dwelt outside that circle, and would remain outside until he left or died.

Leaving seemed the easier of the two.

Leaving alone.

He glanced up. Emma stood in the parlor doorway. He wasn't sure, but he thought her eyes glistened. He looked back to the piano keys. Perhaps this was the time to tell her.

A sharp rap came at the front door. Emma hurried to answer it. John remained seated, glad for the interruption.

A moment later, Emma returned, followed by Percy McVee. He was dripping wet. He removed his hat and held it against his chest. His left hand, missing two fingers, was hidden in a heavy leather glove. John was grateful that he couldn't see it.

"Deputy John, there's a ship on the Gulf, run aground in the flats. Some men have already put out boats for a look."

"Are they behaving themselves?"

"They've got a look in their eyes I don't like."

"And the sea?"

"It's dying; waves won't swamp us if we go careful."

"And the ship? Is she signaling?"

"That's the thing. Sergei's been watching through a spyglass from atop the lighthouse. Hasn't seen a thing move on her, but she's more'n three miles out. We think she's abandoned."

"Damnation! Do the others know this?"

McVee nodded. "That's why they're in a hurry. They smell a big payday."

"Very well, then. Let's get moving."

"My boys are getting the skiff ready. Soon as you get your hat— and your gun—we can go."

Sanborn pulled on his coat and boots, and buckled his gun-belt. He looked for his cap beside the door, but it was missing.

Emma stood at the door, holding John's cap. She extended it to him. "Please be careful, John."

He took the cap from her and moved past.

* * *

McVee's young sons, Robert Lee and Jeb Stuart, readied the skiff, piled in gaffs, ropes, and oars, and rigged the small mainsail and jib. John thanked them and tossed each a penny. McVee scowled at the boys for accepting the money, but John knew the man was pleased.

McVee and Sanborn piled in and shoved the boat away from the dock, the boys leading with lines and giving them a boost. McVee leaned into a pair of oars, his powerful shoulders and arms pulling the wooden boat out from the dock, while Sanborn manned the tiller. Once clear of the moored fishing fleet, McVee looked inquiringly at John. John nodded. McVee raised his oars and settled them inside the gunwale with a clatter, and raised the mainsail. The breeze fluffed the canvas and the boat shot out into the channel. Sanborn tacked the small boat starboard to port and back again, zigzagging through the narrow channel, wherein most sailors, and protocol, demanded that the boats be oared clear of the island before going under sail.

But they didn't have time for that.

Three skiffs had already cleared the north end of the island, passing the great tower of Hammond Lighthouse, and moved onto the choppy Gulf of Mexico. Each was overcrowded, slowing them considerably, but the men aboard them strained mightily at oars, propelling the boats ahead into the waves with great determination.

Sanborn glanced up at the lighthouse as he passed. Before its construction, ships ran aground on a frequent basis, spurring the salvage "industry" on Brigands Key. The plunder reached frightful proportion in those days, but the tower and its great beacon became the savior of mariners, and ships no longer ran aground in the shallows about the island, and that source of easy wealth vanished. But stories and lust still ran in these men's veins, and surged in a torrent with the unlikely wreckage of the night.

Sanborn's skiff glided across the water, angling into the waves, swinging far to starboard of the trailing boat.

Out to sea, like a ghost in the mist of the rain, the ship rested unmoving in the shallow flats, heeled fifteen degrees off vertical.

Sanborn tacked to port and they caught and slid past the boat before being spotted.

Guy Fawcett, manning the tiller, shook his fist. "Damn you, John Sanborn! Do not interfere with this enterprise. That ship is three-and-a-quarter miles offshore, outside the territorial limit. And damn sure outside your jurisdiction. The law is on our side."

"Three miles! A line determined by a cannon shot. I indeed know the law. A shipwreck is fair game to salvagers, with the permission of the crew. I presume you intend to secure that."

Fawcett said nothing.

"I thought not," Sanborn continued. "Well then consider this; the crew is bound by duty to protect the vessel from plunder. They will fire upon you, and with my blessing."

"I reckon they would. But we don't think there's a soul alive on that ship."

The skiff slid past them, and caught and passed the other two boats. The crewmen heard every word of the exchange, and offered a few oaths of their own, and lapsed and glared at John in silence. He acknowledged each in turn as he slipped past.

* * *

The stricken ship was a topsail schooner, and a shambles of one. The sails hung limply, tattered, flapping inconsequentially in the breeze. The foremast was broken midway up and the upper portion hung down at an angle, tangled in rigging. Sanborn judged her more than ninety feet bow to stern, twenty-some-odd beam to beam. He hailed loudly as the little skiff pulled alongside. Only a ghostly silence came in answer. He shouted again, and again received not the slightest call in answer. He piloted the skiff expertly aft of the schooner, and rounded the stern. Painted handsomely in red and gold was the vessel's name, *Edinburgh Kate*. She bore no visible armaments or gunports; clearly a merchant vessel; ideal pickings for the scoundrels of Brigands Key.

And nary a soul in sight.

Sanborn tacked back across the wind and came about, still calling out.

He glanced at the salvagers, closing in steadily. He wasn't sure how to prevent the plunder of the schooner, except to board her in haste and find a captain, or whoever might be in charge, and beseech him to forbid the ransacking of his ship. At best, it might buy some time.

Time for what? The captain's prohibition would render any breech a federal crime, and quite probably boost it into the realm of piracy, punishable by hanging.

A thought struck him; if a looting took place, the guilty could not have witnesses. He had placed himself and McVee in an untenable position. Had he ensured their deaths?

With his free hand, he reached down and felt his revolver.

"I'm bringing us alongside, Percy," he said. "Amidships starboard. Make ready."

"Aye." McVee lifted a long rope and grapple and stood in the boat, legs spread and bent. He hefted the steel hook.

Sanborn tilled the boat close and eased it into the hull of the *Kate* with the slightest bump. McVee swung the hook once in a circle and let it fly. The hook clattered over the gunwale, adjacent to the gangway. McVee drew the line tight, tested it, and nodded to Sanborn.

"Stay with the skiff," Sanborn said. He turned and looked up to the gunwale. "Ahoy the ship! Permission to board?"

Silence.

He gripped the rope and scrambled up, hand over hand, pulled himself to the gangway and threw a leg over it, and drew himself onto the sloping deck.

He looked about, listening intently, ready for anything.

Debris lay scattered about, tangled in uncontained lines and netting. Black mold and filth streaked the deck. A few small barrels and boxes lay wedged here and there, their sides stove in.

Dread grew in him. The ship was not merely abandoned. It appeared to have been unmanned for a great many days, possibly weeks or even months, and the relentless battering sea, the rains, the beating sun, the salt, had taken their toll.

A large swell rolled in, rocking the ship gently. The *Edinburgh Kate* seemed to breathe in and out as the roller passed. A white object moved and clattered in a far corner, its shape and appearance registering immediate recognition in him. He moved closer.

A human skull lay there, its dark eye sockets staring. The jaw was missing. He picked it up and stared into it.

He heard a clatter upon the deck behind him. He turned. Guy Fawcett's face appeared in the gangway, his perpetual scowl glinting with something else, something hungry and excited. Fawcett scanned the deck and fixed upon Sanborn.

Sanborn held the skull up.

The man's scowl melted, and his eyes widened. He clambered onto the deck, his eyes still upon Sanborn and the skull.

Sanborn returned the skull to its resting place. He withdrew his revolver and checked the chamber, reassuring himself it was fully loaded.

"You plan on using that on me?" Fawcett growled. It was the first time Sanborn ever heard the man speak in something less than a shout.

"That had not been my intention, Mr. Fawcett. Should it have been?" He turned toward Fawcett, the pistol cradled in both hands, not exactly pointing it at the man, and not exactly not. He returned the gun to his holster, and stooped to find another bone. A femur, he believed. He looked at it closely, and wiped grime from it. "God in Heaven," he murmured.

Fawcett drew near. "Let's hear it, man. What has got you?"

Sanborn held up the bone. "Look closely."

Fawcett leaned closer, reached out tentatively, and withdrew his hand.

"It's scratched," Sanborn said.

Fawcett shrugged.

"Butchered," Sanborn added.

"Lord a Mighty." Fawcett drew his gun and waved it loosely around in a semicircle.

"Easy, fellow."

"Easy? This here's a ghost ship, all right, but ghosts don't butcher men."

More men clambered aboard. Seven now gathered around, with three more staying behind with the small fleet.

Sanborn showed them the bones. "You men despise me, that much is certain. So be it. However, it serves us best to work as one mind on this ship. Something is horribly wrong. If the ship is indeed abandoned, you have a legitimate lien on the vessel and all property, and Blackwall Rules govern your share. I shall take no share. A schooner this size was probably crewed by not more than ten. If the

But he did.

* * *

The captain teetered on the edge of death for seven days, slipping in and out of consciousness, and began a slow climb up from the grave's depths. He spoke not a word during those seven days, and indeed only mumbled, guttural, incoherent, and disjointed.

Doctor Jameson tended to the man and fretted over him almost hourly.

On the eighth day, Sanborn checked in on him as he always did. The man sat upright, his eyes clear for the first time. His lips remained broken and cracked, and he was gaunt as ever, but color had crept back into his cheeks.

"Where am I?" the man said, in a voice like dry wind.

"Brigands Key, sir. On the Gulf Coast of Florida. We removed you from your vessel. You were quite near to death."

The man seemed to consider this. "I . . . thank you for your kindness, good sir."

The voice came ragged and weak, but the British accent was unmistakable. It was an accent few if any of the townsfolk would have ever heard. Sanborn had heard it many times in Boston. "You are most welcome. I feared we would never have the opportunity to speak."

"It is indeed fortunate. I suppose that I have been more dead than alive these past days. Are there . . . any others? Survivors?"

"None but you."

A great sadness seemed to enter the man's face. He sighed, and closed his eyes and lapsed into silence for a time.

Sanborn waited, and asked, "What is your name, sir?"

After a long moment, the man opened his eyes. "Captain Henry Dunham. Of London."

"Mister Dunham, I—"

"Captain Dunham, if you please."

Sanborn held him in his glance. His forefinger tapped lightly on his knee. "Mister Dunham. You have been out of sorts for a spell. During that time, I've made good use of telegraph. Your schooner, it seems, is indeed of British registry, well-known in Boston, and captained by Henry Dunham. However, Dunham is described to me as a small man. Not more than five and one half feet in height. You however, are well over six feet in height. Privation tends to make one grow thinner, not taller, in my experience."

The man sighed. "Very well, you have found my lie. But you must understand the reasoning behind it. In my sorry state, I felt it best to present myself as a man of stature in order to better my chances of attaining aid. I apologize; it was a grievous error in judgment."

"Perhaps you should tell me who you really are."

A pause. "Andrew Millstone. First mate."

"Ah. That much is confirmed, at least in part, by the telegraph. Can you tell me why your accent is British, from an educated background, yet ladled atop an obvious American accent?"

"Ah, a student of linguistics. I am indeed originally from Richmond. I served in Lee's Army of Virginia during the war, as apprentice to a field surgeon. I survived the war and fled to England."

"Why did you, sir?"

"Put yourself in my shoes, although by the fall of Richmond, I wore none. I was a lad of just nineteen years, yet witnessed the unholy carnage at Antietam, Chancellorsville, Gettysburg, and Spotsylvania, and presided over the deaths of hundreds. Can you imagine the parade of death? Do you know how 'sawbones' came to be slang for a doctor? Dismemberment was the prescribed treatment, without anesthetic unless whiskey was at hand. Germ theory was unknown in that time. I spent the war steeped in blood and death, more than a grown man should face, and far more than a boy." Millstone paused, and his eyes focused on something faraway and unknowable. "You can't go through that, and it not tear at your soul. You can't. As soon as the war ended, I got as far from it as I could. I worked my keep on an Atlantic steamer and ended up in London. And I made her my home."

"You must understand, of course, that there will be an inquiry."

"Of course."

"I do not judge you for your survival. But tell me; what became of your ship?"

"A frightful series of events, sir. The *Kate* is a merchant vessel, of course. We disembarked London for Buenos Aires, loaded with European finery, of which the Argentines cannot get enough. Eleven days out, a ferocious storm took us, rather by surprise. Before we could get the blasted sails reefed, the mainmast snapped. We still managed to keep the second intact and functioning, and limped along. We counseled Captain Dunham to return to London, but the man was stubborn to a fault, a true British captain. He would not hear of it and insisted upon a delayed arrival in Buenos Aires, whereupon we would refurbish the ship with our earnings. But the fool took us into the horse latitudes, and we were becalmed and adrift for endless days on a slack, still sea, our supplies running short."

A soft rap came at the door. Sanborn looked up to see Emma peer in, and enter with a tray of tea and milk. "I thought perhaps our guest could use this," she said.

Sanborn nodded. "Thank you. Leave it here." He glanced back at Millstone.

A chill struck him.

Millstone stared at Emma, his eyes suddenly alive and burning. He seemed oblivious to the world, as if only two things existed, himself and Emma. Despite his frailty and weakness, he no longer appeared the same man. The victim of numbing tragedy disappeared, replaced by—what?

Something monstrous and voracious.

And it had spotted prey.

Emma froze in his glance, her eyes widening with terror. She turned quickly away and fled the room.

Millstone continued to stare in her direction, his breath quickening. At last he tore his eyes away.

Sanborn had seen enough. He shivered with certain, sudden dread. "Sir, you perhaps are still far too weak. No matter; you must leave. Now."

Feeble as the man was, something flashed in his eyes, something dark and furious and unfathomable, something from hell. The man seemed on the edge of an uncontrollable rage. He trembled for long furious seconds.

It passed as quickly as it appeared.

"I have no desire to remain, yet I shall leave when I am prepared to do so," Millstone said, his voice crackling dry and distant. His gaze drifted to the window and to the waterfront nearby. "I left Whitechapel when I was ready, not when they wished, those arrogant English pigs." He looked suddenly back at Sanborn. His eyes narrowed. "Never you mind," he said. "Perhaps I shall leave now, after all."

Sanborn's mind raced, trying to piece things together. London. Whitechapel. Millstone sailed from the world's greatest city at the close of 1888, just two years before. At the time the great horror that stalked the city's dark slum suddenly ended.

Could it be?

The men aboard the *Kate*, all dead. Butchered like livestock, and eaten.

"A first mate is a capable seaman," Sanborn said. "Albeit with great difficulty, he could navigate and sail the damned ship all by himself. He would not be lost and adrift forever."

"Ah, so you presume I had a choice, then? That I could simply sail the stricken *Kate* confidently into port?"

"No sir! I presume that your lies exceed your ingenuity. We have already established that you were never the captain. I suspect you indeed were never the first mate, nor any member of the crew. You were in fact a stowaway, completely ignorant of seamanship. The nets of Scotland Yard drew ever closer, and you fell into a desperate need of escape. The first exit you could find was a vessel outward bound for anywhere. Once discovered, they threatened you with servitude and delivery to the first British colonial jail, perhaps in Bermuda or Jamaica. Rather than submit, you slaughtered the lot of them, and feasted upon their remains to stay alive."

"Clever man. Do you think it wise to be so clever with me?"

"Perhaps not. But I shall see that you are brought to justice." Sanborn eased closer to the door. "Emma! Go quick to the neighbors, fetch as many able men as you can. We cannot let this devil leave."

Emma entered the room, her face lined with worry. She glanced from one to the other. "John, what is the matter?"

John frantically motioned her away. "Just go and be quick, Emma!"

She darted from the room.

A sudden movement caught his eye. He whirled back to face Millstone, but the man was upon him. A butcher knife appeared in his hand, slashing savagely. Sanborn dodged and reflexively threw an arm up to ward off the blow. The blade sliced through his forearm, laying open his flesh to the bone. He glanced at the wound; blood welled up and splashed to the floor in frightful quantity.

Sanborn staggered back and the man, despite his extreme frailty, pressed his attack, as though madness and bloodletting fueled him with inhuman strength.

Sanborn blindly seized the pitcher of water and struck back, smashing the man in the face, shattering the pitcher. The man hissed, a line of blood appearing on his cheek, and threw himself upon Sanborn, his knife rising for a blow. Sanborn saw the blade and shot his hand out, seizing the man's wrist and pulling it laterally across and between the two of them, so that the only course of the next blow would be a weakened backhand. Sanborn struck the man with his free fist, and again, and again.

The man staggered.

Sanborn felt his mind darkening, and dizziness took him. He stumbled to one knee, and dimly realized that he had released the man.

The creature now crept upon him, knife raised and ready, a diseased look in his eyes, a look borne of a wretched, perverse soul.

Blackness like a death shroud drew quickly in from the edges of the world.

* * *

The blackness became gray and then white. Warmth caressed Sanborn's face.

He opened his eyes.

He felt weak and drawn. He looked about; he lay in his own bed, covers pulled up. Golden sunlight angled from the window, the sunbeam kissing his face. A cardinal sat chirping on the windowsill.

He was alive.

He drifted off again, and was roused by a click. He opened his eyes again. Emma entered, carrying a tray of tea and soup and bandages.

She saw that he was awake and a smile brighter than the morning sunlight lit her face. "My darling, I nearly lost you." Tears welled in her eyes.

"Where . . . is he?"

"Shush, darling. There was no time to fetch help, so I ran to the parlor and withdrew your pistol and got back just in time. That monster was poised over you, his knife at your stomach. He stopped and turned to me. I've never seen such a look in the face of a human being in my life. He came at me. I shot him twice, in the shoulder and back. He fell away, swinging wildly with that wicked blade, and bolted for the window and fell through, crashing through the branches of the magnolia. I ran to the window and fired again, but could not get a clear shot through the branches. Mister Fawcett and Mister Beckett arrived but he was gone. A trail of blood led to the waterfront and there it ended."

"He . . . fell into the channel?"

"We don't know. He's just . . . gone."

Sanborn sighed and closed his eyes again. He felt himself drifting again, and felt Emma's delicate, loving hands on his face.

"You have a letter from Boston," she said. "Shall I open it for you?"

He remained silent for a moment. "No. Toss it in the fire. Emma, my love, let's turn the garden tomorrow, and begin the tomatoes. This will be a wonderful year."

Notes

The ghastly crimes of Jack the Ripper still haunt the Western psyche, more than a century after the horrific slayings in Whitechapel. The murders went unsolved, the killer never caught, yet the reign of terror suddenly ended. Why? Might he have fled? And fled to his homeland?

The identity of the Ripper remains a mystery, although many enterprising authors claim to have uncovered the truth about him. Yet they can't seem to agree on who he actually was. If they have somehow succeeded in identifying him, it's probably more by accident and luck than anything else. One-hundred years after the fact makes for an almost insoluble cold case. And even though several claim to have identified him through the miracle of DNA analysis, real CSI types will tell you that DNA is far from reliable when the evidence gathered has been contaminated umpteen times over by persons born a century before the term DNA even came into being.

I much prefer the identity I gave the Ripper. A purely fictional one.

After my novel, *Brigands Key*, was published in 2012, I couldn't get the little fictional island out of my head. The place begged for more, so a series of five short stories, each set in a different year of the island's past and all included in this collection, helped scratch that itch.

Today, the word "familiar" brings us a cozy feeling of reliability and comfort. Once upon a time, though, it had a darker connotation and was often used as a noun. And familiarity did not then breed content. It bred fear.

Familiar

Warmth washed over Nikki.

It felt good to be warm. The night had been so cold. Now there was only the warmth. And tickling, that felt good. Everything was right. Gerald was right. She thought of Gerald. He seemed happy, too.

This was the way it was supposed to be. Nikki happy. Gerald happy. And good to her. And the warmth . . .

It was not this way before, not for a long time, maybe not ever.

She remembered how it was before.

* * *

"You're not going to take so damn long, right?"

Nikki hesitated, lingering in the doorway, considering her response. Gerald's question wasn't so much a question as a command, she knew. She began to speak, thought better of it, and twisted the doorknob softly for a moment.

Gerald appeared from the kitchen. "Didn't you hear me?"

"Yes. I heard." She continued to look at the doorknob, avoiding his eyes. His eyes would not be angry, nor would they be cruel. Worse, they would be in control.

"Well? You stay gone too long. You need to be more of a presence here."

"Gerald, honey, it's a job. I don't do it for fun. It pays the rent."

"You get off at ten but you don't get home until 10:45. It doesn't take more than twenty-five minutes. I timed it."

"You're timing me?"

"Don't get defensive. Boston after dark is not exactly a monastery. I'm concerned about your safety."

Right, she thought. My safety. All she said was: "I'm not defensive."

"You know, Feingold is still missing. Two days now, no explanation. Didn't leave a note with the lab or anything."

"Oh please. Feingold's a drunk. He's stumbled through lost weekends before."

"He's too finicky and cautious to not let on where he is, even when he's getting hammered. Baxter didn't come in today either."

"Baxter is Feingold's drinking buddy and sycophant. Soon as the wife goes on a business trip, he starts missing work."

"Are you avoiding me?"

The sudden change caught her off guard. Classic Gerald. "No."

"Don't you believe me when I say I'm concerned?"

"I don't know. Yes."

"Then you need to listen and you need to be here. It's not that difficult."

"I'll hurry home. I have to go now."

"Nikki, don't hurry on my account." He suddenly looked petulant. "I might as well go to the lab and get some work in. Maybe I'll get stoned."

Nikki slipped out, still avoiding his eyes. She wanted to slam the door shut.

* * *

Contrary to Gerald's timed efforts, the drive from Boston into Salem never took less than a half-hour, even on the best days. Nikki turned the conversation over in her mind a dozen times on the drive. He timed me? Unbelievable. She shook her head, switched on the radio, stabbed the presets, and switched it off. She set her jaw and went over again the things she wished she'd said, or done, and knew that she would keep not saying and doing, and her face grew flush with anger. Why couldn't she say something—anything—when she really needed to? She gripped the steering wheel with whitening hands, and realized suddenly that she was gritting her teeth. The Northeast Expressway traffic tugged at her nerves, doing them no great service, and with relief she took Exit 107 near Rumney Marsh and approached Salem from the back roads. What the hell.

She rummaged in her purse for a moment, one eye on the road, found a small bottle, popped it open, and swallowed a pill. A little something to relax.

A light rain began to fall, misting the air and casting a sheen on the road in the darkness. Raindrops danced off the pavement like silver fireflies in the light. The skipped stripe in the center of the road ticked past in a mesmerizing rhythm. Nikki forced her attention from the stripe and shook her head, trying to concentrate.

A small dark thing—an animal, a cat probably—darted across the road just in front of her. She jerked the wheel hard right and jammed the brake to the floor, but the loud thump and jolt told her unmistakably that she'd struck the animal. The tires shrieked and loosed their grip on the pavement, and the car slid broadside across the road, the tires sluicing a great arc of water into the air, and came to rest on the shoulder.

Shaken, her heart pounding, she inhaled deeply and unlatched the car door.

The rain picked up, clouding her vision. The small black figure lay motionless in the road. Although it could not have survived, she approached cautiously.

The death of any animal was horrific to her, and this was worse.

This one, she caused.

The street was an untraveled one, for north of Boston anyway. It ran dark and hushed, feebly lit, and lined with small, huddled houses. In the distance, the pitch-black expanse of Rumney Marsh shouldered ominously against the yellow lights of the houses. She thought for a moment about knocking on the nearest door to report that she'd killed someone's pet, but made no move to do so. The idea of a shrieking, heartbroken child was more than she could deal with.

She glanced toward the dead animal, felt for her phone, and shakily dialed home. No answer, Gerald had already left. He couldn't help, of course, but she needed a calming voice. Her breathing was coming much too rapidly. She shut her eyes and forced a slow, deep breath. There. That helped a little.

She opened her eyes and looked again at the animal.

It was gone.

She scanned the darkness quickly. Could it really have lived through that? Surely not . . .

A pair of shining eyes, feral and yellow, blinked from the blackness of the marsh.

She tried to focus on it, but could make out nothing. A second and third pair of eyes appeared near it. She heard a soft purring sound. The purring grew slightly louder, entwined, harmonizing voices in a drowsy songlike hum. The sound sapped her fear, and she took a step toward it. The purring increased.

It soothed and calmed her jagged nerves.

A burst of white light and a crash of thunder stopped her and jolted her to alertness, as if being shaken from a daydream.

The pairs of eyes vanished into the darkness. She shook her head, clearing it. The pill had kicked in quicker and juicier than expected. She returned to her car and headed down the road, and stopped at the first convenience store for a cup of burned coffee.

* * *

Nikki reached the shop in Salem, calmer yet wired with caffeine, and pushed the door open. The little brass bell hanging on a string clattered noisily against the door glass. Genevieve was leaning against the countertop, reading The Boston Herald on her tablet, and looked up. "Hey, girl," she said. "Haven't dumped him yet, huh?"

Nikki ignored it. "Sorry I'm late. A little slow getting started."

"There is no 'late' in this shop. This crap is not exactly flying off the shelves."

"I'm sorry anyway. You know how it is sometimes."

"More like all the time." Genevieve looked her over. "You know, sometimes a change is in order."

Genevieve's glance lingered, and Nikki looked away uncomfortably. "Any business yet?"

"Right. Business." Genevieve sighed. "No, it's slow again. Too early for summer tourists. You know, Nik, you need to relax a little."

"Maybe. Maybe not. Not now anyway."

"Gerald's playing man-of-the-house again?"

"I'm not going to get into it with you."

"What a pinhead. He won't marry you and he won't come up with the rent."

"MIT is tough. Really tough. He hasn't got time for a job outside his grad work."

"Was he studying when you left, or was he watching TV?"

Nikki didn't answer. She squared up some fliers on the countertop.

"Dump the creep, Nik. Grow a backbone already."

Still she didn't answer.

"It's okay for you to take a full load at MIT and work part-time though, isn't it? Gerry Baby doesn't see a problem there, I'll bet."

"Gen, we've been over this. Can't we skip it for once?"

"It's your life." Genevieve returned her attention to her tablet screen. Gen really was the ideal employee in a town like Salem. She looked the part here, even though street corners and malls throughout America abounded with girls just like her. The jet black hair, the black lipstick, black eyes, black clothes, set against pale, sallow skin. It was a facade. The girl was intelligent, well-read, and sweet, even if a little gloomy. She tried hard to be undead, but it didn't quite fit. She was a country girl from the South Carolina low country, with a twang in her voice she tried hard to hide. She'd moved to New England to get away from a thug with a temper, and had been crushingly alone until she found peers with a mutual fascination for eye shadow.

"What a load of crap," Genevieve said, tapping the screen.

"What?" Nikki asked, grateful for a new subject.

"Exploding raccoons."

"Beg your pardon?"

"The police claim these little incidents we've been getting around here are because of an explosion in the raccoon population."

"Oh, that." Nikki nodded. A slew of stories reported small wild animals making nighttime nuisances of themselves the last two weeks. Spilling trash cans, maiming pets, darting across traffic. Nikki thought about mentioning the animal she'd struck not twenty minutes ago. "I take it you disagree."

"Read the story. They say 'raccoons', but they don't describe 'raccoons'."

"What then?"

"Familiars."

"Beg your pardon?"

"Familiars," Gen repeated. "Damn, girl, this is Salem. Do a little research for once. Familiars were creatures witches consorted with.

Imps. Demons. Cats. Rats. Accomplices to his or her evil works. Sometimes the familiar went on the master's errands alone, but they always returned to the master, not out of love or loyalty, but out of familiarity."

"Black cats?"

"Well, that's the most common form, but it could be any kind of animal. Mostly bedtime story crap, but the locals really bought into it. You know, when your neighbors want to catch and torture a witch, they don't need much evidence."

"You're not offering much evidence of these familiars yourself. Just an idea."

"I told you it's bedtime story crap." Genevieve smiled. "I'm a Goth. I'm entitled to indulge."

It was a slow business night, it being early spring, and cold, and still raining. The Cauldron, like dozens of other gimmicky gift shops in downtown Salem, relied on morbid cheesiness and a guarantee that a certain percentage of the buying public was devoid of taste and common sense. The shop peddled hokum in the form of masks, potions, incantations, totems, and any number of other popular items that held absolutely no historic relationship to the brutal murders of innocents centuries before, just a few feet away from this very shop. Nikki sometimes wondered if she profited from the murders. But a job was a job.

"Gen," Nikki said suddenly, "why did you say they're not describing raccoons?"

"First off, they've found three roadkill raccoons in the last two weeks. This is what the Salem constabulary calls evidence."

"You think they'd lie about dead raccoons on the roads?"

"No, that's not the point. Three dead raccoons? Big deal. Do you ever remember a time when you didn't notice dead raccoons on the road? Just to shoot holes in this theory, I called City Animal Control this morning and asked how many dead raccoons the spring of any given year they would scrape off the pavement in a two-week span.

The guy says, 'I don't know, anywhere from two to seven.' I asked if this year was any different. He says, 'Only if you want it to be, like the cops'."

"The police must have some good reason for saying it's raccoons."

"Yeah, because they're lazy and they're idiots and because raccoons are conveniently small and nocturnal, which is what people are bitching about. But listen to the descriptions: 'small, black, extremely quick'. They dart about."

"And?"

Raccoons are small, but they're not black and they're not that quick. They don't dart. They kind of roll along, like ambling bags of intelligent jelly."

"They look black in the dark."

"Maybe. But of dozens of complaints, not one has specifically mentioned a raccoon. Just a critter."

"I hit a cat on the way in," Nikki said. "I think it was a cat."

Gen looked up. "Maybe a cat, but not a raccoon."

"No. Not a raccoon."

"Well, didn't you stop to see?"

"Yes. It ran away before I could check on it."

"Pretty tough cat."

"I think it was a cat."

* * *

Nikki said 'night to Gen and locked up behind her. The rain had stopped and a cool breeze blew in from the east, carrying with it the fragrance of the ocean. She climbed into her car and started the engine, and sat for a moment thinking. Gerald had a way of getting under her skin. He was a control freak, jealous and manipulative. Had to have the upper hand. She half-decided to cut her losses before she regretted the rest of her life, before she became even more dependent upon him. Even before she'd left for work today, he'd worked his little game. But at the same time, he showed real concern for her safety. He was like that. Just when she was on the edge of a blowup, he'd show a loving side. He loved her. She knew he loved her.

She punched up the lab on her cell phone. Gerald's voice answered, rather subdued.

"Gerald, honey, listen, I'm off now. I was thinking about our situation."

"Oh. Don't worry about that. Don't worry. It's okay."

"No, I'm sorry. You were concerned for me. I get a little tense sometimes."

"It's alright, Nik."

"You sound tired."

"Yeah, I've been working hard. I'm pretty tired."

"Are you on your way home, too?"

"Think I'll stay a while. Yeah. Too tired to drive home. Might nap on the couch a little while, then drive. Just too tired."

"What if I come by? I'll drive you home. Your car will be fine until morning."

"No, don't come by. I'll just nap, I'm fine. Just a little sleepy. Really just need some sleep. Got to go now, Nik."

The phone went dead. Nikki headed back toward Boston, taking a wider berth around Rumney Marsh this time, swinging out onto I-95 and down U.S. 1, stealing a glance at the unbroken darkness of the distant marshes. She shuddered. It was just a marsh, not really anything to note, especially at night. Nothing there to see, nothing at all. This was a better route. Faster, she assured herself.

And better lit.

A flash of movement caught her eye. She peered intently, instinctively pressing the gas pedal a little harder. No, she decided. There was nothing there. Just tricks of light and dark.

She arrived at their house and parked in the garage. The drive had taken forty-five minutes, despite Gerald's stopwatch. He left the porch light on, and the windows threw pools of yellow light out into the yard. He really did care, she thought.

She restarted the car and drove to the lab. Gerald shouldn't have to nap in that cold, dreary place.

Huddled unassumingly in the corner of the MIT campus, the genetics lab was a practical, unattractive building. It was direly in need of renovation, and the campus building revival had seemingly ignored it. The research done within had not exactly been of the limelight, prize-winning type, although Gerald claimed for it and himself minor successes. The old lush, Feingold, broke new ground with his work a decade before, but he was at least half a decade removed from anything of note, his personal habits having robbed him of ambition and inspiration, not to mention hygiene. Gerald pretty much carried the lab lately, molding it to his own vision.

Gerald's Suburban stood glistening, the only car in the dimly lit parking lot. The light from within the lab glinted through narrow slits around the blinds. Nikki parked beside the Suburban, her compact dwarfed by it. She flicked on the car security switch, and hesitated, scanning her environs nervously. Boston could be scary at night, big, blustery, and ancient, with all its ghosts of past heroes and battles and murderers. Caution was always the order of the night, even in a bastion of enlightenment and learning like MIT.

Satisfied, she exited the car and walked swiftly to the door. She slid her identification card into the reader, prompting a soft beep and a click as the door bolt shot sideward.

The front office was vacant, as always, after hours. The receptionist's computer screen flickered, dancing to low music. The computer broadcast the music to speakers throughout the building speaker system, and the predominant running battle among the staff any given day was not who's research findings would eventually win out, but who's taste in music would. Tonight, the place deserted, Gerald got his choice; Pachelbel's *Canon in D* drifted through the space, the lilting cello and haunting violins imbuing the somber rooms with life.

Nikki called out. "Gerald? Are you here?"

She heard a murmur from the rear labs. "I thought I'd bring you home," she said. She followed the hallway past the individual offices of the researchers to the main lab. She rapped gently on the lab door and called again. She heard him respond sleepily, and she pushed the door open.

The lab was not the sterile, Spartan lab of Hollywood, but was typical of high-tech research as it really looked; cables snaking the floor, boxes of papers, textbooks lying about, crumpled papers, half-eaten donuts, homemade rough-lumber frames holding delicate instruments, clamps and bolts and washers connecting junk to more junk from the hardware store.

She didn't readily see Gerald, but knew that he would be in the corner, sawing logs on the shabby leather couch the researchers used for naps.

Dozens of cages lined the far wall.

Empty cages.

The cello and violins hung softly in the air.

Rounding the corner, she found him lying on the couch. He looked up at her groggily, and mumbled her name without a smile. "Go," he rasped, barely audibly.

Gathered around him were the cats. No, not cats. Creatures. All black, slender, covered in fur, their eyes both feline and something else, yellow, glowing, watching.

Nikki looked again at Gerald's face. He shook his head, almost imperceptibly. The creatures slowly spread apart to form a semi-circle on either side of him, their movements slow and sinuous.

Gerald had been partly obscured by the creatures. Now Nikki could see him fully.

His right foot was gone, the leg ending at the ankle in a ragged, red stump, blood oozing from it. His thigh, too, lay exposed, the pants leg torn apart from it, the skin and muscle open to the bone.

The creatures licked their lips.

And they began to purr. Nikki's rising hysteria grew suddenly calm. The sound soothed her, and she looked into the warm, luminous eyes of the creatures.

She remembered something Gen said.

They always return to the master.

A familiar approached her silently, on padded feet. On hind feet. It stopped inches from her, and squatted upon its haunches. The purring filled Nikki's mind with its calm hushed rattle. The room dimmed, all but the familiars with those big, luminous eyes. The purring melded with the melody of the music.

The familiar began to lick her ankle. It tickled.

She felt warm and Gerald lay near.

Notes

During a trip to Salem in all its tacky, touristy glory, and listening to a discussion there on witches' "familiars," my wife suggested this idea for a story. I thought about it, turned it over, liked it, and "Familiar" is the result.

The juxtaposition of Boston, arguably America's most intellectual city, to Salem, arguably the home to America's most anti-intellectual event, provides the dualistic backbone of the story. Science or witchcraft, good or evil, it all comes down to how we choose to employ what we know.

The Prometheus Saga
Introduction

The following two stories—"First World War" and "The Tower House Prisoner"—are my contributions to *The Prometheus Saga* anthologies, introduced as follows:

The individual keeps watch on other individuals. Societies keep watch on other societies. Civilizations keep watch on other civilizations. It has always been so. Keeping watch is sometimes benevolent, sometimes malevolent. It is most certainly prudent.

It is not a trait exclusive to the human species.

Out of such prudence an advanced intelligence, far across the vastness of space, delivered to Earth a probe 40,000 years ago, to observe and report the progress of the human species. This probe was "born" here fully formed, a human being, engineered from the DNA of Homo sapiens. It possessed our skin, our organs, our skeleton, our muscles.

And it still lives among us.

The probe is one of us. Almost. It manipulates DNA and stem cells, healing itself as needed. It dies, but remains immortal. It enters human societies, adopting any guise, any race, any gender, any age it wishes, following a three-month metamorphosis. It witnesses the events, great and small, good and bad, that shape our destiny.

Everything it sees, hears, feels, experiences, and thinks, it flashes across a thousand light-years, in real-time quantum-entangled communication with the intelligence that sent it here.

The probe keeps watch. And sometimes it acts.

Homo sapiens reigns as the lone species of human on Earth, but this was not always the case. Other species of hominid, contemporary to yet far older than ours, thrived around the world. With the spread of modern humans, contact with them was inevitable. Only one species remains. What happened?

First World War

Southern Europe, 40,000 Years Before Present

The first time you die is always the hardest.

Bran didn't know that yet. He wouldn't until the next time he died, or perhaps even a few times beyond that. Nor did he know if there would even be a next time. He only knew that this was dying.

He stared at the broken shaft of wood protruding from his abdomen. Blood seeped from the wound, slipping and slithering down his legs and onto the cold ground, to join the black viscous mud of the earth.

Sounds of fury and battle carried over the windswept meadow. Shouts, screams. The sharp strike of wood against wood, stone against stone. The dull thud and crunch of flesh and bone. Death, dying.

Bran touched the shaft of the spear, felt it, tugged at it. His knowledge of human anatomy—of his anatomy—had grown over time, beyond what he had always known, since the first day he'd known anything. He sensed the depth of the spear deep inside him, its mass and pressure against his torn organs. He knew the damage within him would kill. He knew of pain; he'd witnessed it among the People almost daily, and knew that it caused suffering. But pain existed for him as an abstraction. He felt no pain.

He reached around behind his back, and felt the tip of the stone spear point protruding through his skin. The wetness confirmed that the blood spilled from that wound as well.

Bran's skin grew wet and hot. Sweat slicked his face and dripped into his eyes. He placed a hand over his heart, felt its beat. It raced faster than ever before. His vision blurred, and cleared. His mind seemed to drift and grow dull.

The body needs repair, the mind needs to repair it. But the severity of damage to the body required different levels of repair. Every wound he'd ever incurred—the bruising and cuts of daily life—healed speedily.

He sheltered in a snow-covered thicket that clung to the hillside. He'd staggered from the battlefield, urged from it by the whispers, and collapsed. The world around him teetered and grew indistinct. He tried pulling himself up. He needed to see what was happening in battle.

No. Remain hidden. Secure your safety, a voice in his mind whispered.

Bran hesitated. The voices in his mind reliably steered him through life. They seemed to be infallible guides, directing, advising, suggesting.

In his first one-hundred and sixty-two years of life, he'd wondered about the nature and origins of the voices. Now, he no longer wondered. He'd come to accept them. They'd come unbidden, rarely, to be sure. But often enough.

Remain where you are.

When he had incurred the wound, the voice became insistent, urgent.

Leave now, remove yourself from this battlefield. Protect yourself. Protect your purpose.

He'd obeyed the voice unquestioningly. Experience had taught him well. And so he'd stumbled from the bedlam, watching the People slaughter and be slaughtered.

He puzzled over how this came to pass, the prelude to the carnage replaying in his mind . . .

* * *

The People had slipped down out of the mountain forest from the east, silent as mist. Bran accompanied them, driven by his insatiable curiosity. His need to watch and learn mystified him, yet compelled him to remain near the People.

He'd studied their every step, attempting to mimic their stealth, but often found himself slower and falling behind. Stealth seemed to require a certain guile and a proclivity towards subterfuge.

The People, the Tinnarabu, had accepted him into their society two years before. They were the sixth clan he'd joined during his young life.

The voice again . . .

Protect your purpose.

Except Bran didn't know his purpose.

* * *

The Tinnarabu knew that the Gabu followed the bison migration to the sheltered south end of the valley, away from the cold wind that whipped and howled off the Great Ice to the north. The Gabu were a wary people, necessarily so. They would not commonly walk into a trap. The Tinnarabu knew this and planned this day for a year and thirteen days. The ingenuity that went into the planning might have been more wisely used in another manner, but they insisted that they nurtured a vision of the future.

That vision did not include the Gabu, the Ugly Ones.

The Tinnarabu, ever innovative in the pursuit of slaying, perfected a poison. Wrung and stewed from a fungus, they applied it to the points of wood spears. They debated many hours over the merits of using fire-blackened wood points versus the more lethal stone points they normally favored. Wood points won the argument for the simple reason that the spear, after being withdrawn by tether from its victim, would not run the risk of leaving a stone point embedded in the great beast and alerting the Gabu to trickery.

And so when a herd of mammoths passed through the valley, protected by sheer size and numbers, four poisonous wood points found their mark on one great female. After two days, she'd begun to stumble from the effects of the poison. At first, the herd lingered, urging her on. But the good of the herd eventually outweighed her individual value. She'd been abandoned. Her weakness only endangered the herd.

As the Tinnarabu predicted, the culled, sick female, trumpeting her plaintive anguish to the winds, caught the attention of the Gabu. Such a vulnerable and valuable prize proved too much to resist. A hunting party, twelve in all, had sallied forth to claim her vast store of meat.

The Gabu had unwittingly walked into the Tinnarabu trap.

* * *

From the eastern ridge, Etaa the Ugly, daughter of Enaa, watched the subterfuge, the cunning, as it unfolded in the valley below. Hidden among the boulders and scattered grasses, she had studied the comings and goings of both Tinnarabu and Gabu for three days now.

And now, the meaning and horror of it all grew clear.

* * *

In his life, Bran had seen the Gabu on sixteen occasions, always from afar. They kept their distance, kept to themselves, kept to their own game trails. They stayed in a valley or plain that teemed with game for a few years, and moved on. The Tinnarabu, likewise, had long lived as nomads, moving, using, and abandoning. Most clans still favored that existence.

But a new idea took root among the Tinnarabu, the idea of home, within a land of plenty.

Plenty, unfortunately, was relative. Plenty meant enough for one clan to survive.

Home did not work with the sharing of plenty with Gabu animals.

* * *

Bran once approached Setka Bol, the chieftain. Setka Bol was teaching his son, Setka Sil, the nuanced techniques of knapping a flint blade to an edge that would slice flesh with the lightest pressure. Bran asked Setka Bol why he wished war upon the Gabu.

The great warrior cocked his head, a look of incredulity giving way to suspicion. "They are different from us."

Few Gabu stood as tall as the breast of a Tinnarabu, or any other true person. The Gabu's legs were short and thick, their thighs like tree trunks. Their arms hung long, knotted with powerful muscle. Their chests were massive, much broader than the heaviest of the Tinnarabu. Their flesh was covered in short brown fur, though they wore draped, stitched hides, for modesty as much as warmth, it seemed to Bran.

But the face of the Gabu inspired the greatest loathing in the Tinnarabu. The Gabu face was wide, the lower half thrust forward like a beast's. The nose was broad, the nostrils cavernous. The chin was entirely lacking. Fierce eyes peered from beneath heavy, jutting brows, from which the forehead sloped sharply away, the skull elongated to the back.

"Different, yes," Bran said. "But being different, are they lesser?"

"By Arov! Of course they are. Have you no eyes, Bran? They are not men, they are beasts. Listen, my strange friend, they have entered our lands and killed and eaten our game. Would you have us starve?"

"We do not appear to be wanting; how do you suppose we are close to starvation?"

Setka Sil turned and looked into his father's face.

Setka Bol glanced at his son, hesitated, and looked again at Bran, his eyes narrowing. "Ah, the clever Bran. Talk, clever one! But remember that we took you in. Be careful that you do not overstay your welcome."

* * *

Bran glanced once more at the shaft protruding from his abdomen. His thoughts returned to the day of his own birth, many years past. Birth? He had no other name for it. One day he did not exist, the next, he did, and as a fully-grown man. He knew no infancy, nor childhood, nor adolescence. He had known nothing. Who he was. Where he was. What he was.

He remembered his birth in infinite detail, awakening naked on the plain, shivering in the bitter cold. A dusty cold wind howled across the plain.

About him had lain gossamer shards and threads, the remains of a membrane, brittle and cracking. Bits of it clung to his skin. Later, he deduced that that shell had been his first clothing, his protection until birth.

himself upon the warrior who'd struck with the ax. He seized his head and twisted it completely around. A crunch and crack, and when the Tinnarabu's body went limp, he cast it aside. Two spears lanced the old Gabu warrior in rapid succession—one in his belly and one through his neck, and ended his life.

And still, the battle raged.

Bran fell back, stumbling. He looked at the spear impaling him, and at the carnage all about. He took a step closer to the combat nearest him.

No. Remove yourself at once. Do not take part in this fight.

The voice.

You must preserve yourself.

Bran's foot slipped on a rock wet with his own blood. He fell to one knee, dabbed a finger in the blood on the rock, and rolled it between his fingertips, feeling its warmth and slickness.

New sensations. Eyesight blurring. Ears ringing. Skin burning. Heart racing. Hands trembling.

Preserve yourself. Leave.

He turned from the violence and looked up the scree slope. A fog had rolled in and now clung to the top of the slope, hiding it in a blanket of gray. He staggered to his feet. Pebbles slipped underfoot and rolled away, clattering.

He spotted a snow-covered thicket of brush, a sheltering hollow of sparse foliage underneath it. Out of the open, out of the wind. He'd often seen wounded animals seek such shelter, a place to recover or die in peace. And now, he was no different; when the body senses its end, it commands itself to shelter. He picked his way toward the spot. Time passed, the sound of battle behind him diminishing with every step.

A movement from behind and to his side caught his attention. Bran spun. Was someone there? He hadn't seen anyone, but couldn't be sure. It—whatever it had been—had vanished.

He stumbled again, his strength failing, and collapsed and crawled into the thicket. His vision clouded. He raised himself onto his arms. He examined his wound again, and his eyes followed the red trail, which led to him.

A furtive movement. Someone darted across the trail and slinked among the boulders. This time he was sure that he'd seen someone.

The Tinnarabu often spoke in hushed voices of the malevolent spirits that stole fallen warriors that had not fought well and bravely. Legend held that the spirits wouplald torment them for eternity for their sins of weakness and cowardice. An odd belief, although now it didn't seem so strange.

A malformed spirit emerged from the gray mist and slowly crept toward him.

The spirit manifested itself into a flesh and blood thing. A Gabu?

Not one of his Tinnarabu brothers. The figure stood much too small, but stout like a Gabu. Yes, a Gabu, but somehow different.

Bran returned his attention to the spear inside him. Blood continued to seep. He suspected that only the weapon kept it from running like the rivers from the foot of the Great Ice. But his blood would be spilled, whether swiftly or slowly. Swiftly seemed the smarter option; the sooner he removed the damaging implement, the sooner he could heal.

Bran tugged at the spear, pushing it back and forth. The weapon was firmly implanted and resisted movement. He looked about and selected a heavy rock, the size of a man's head. He hefted the stone and placed it against the broken end of the spear shaft. He tapped it lightly at first, then raised the stone to arms' length and slammed it into the end of the spear shaft. The spear point plunged through him, tearing at his organs, until the point extruded from his back. But the shaft remained. Bran reached his arms around his back, gripped the stone point, and pulled.

The spear point came out slowly, tearing flesh as it progressed, and with a final flourish, he wrenched the weapon from his body. Blood splashed to the ground, front and back. He began to shiver. He fell to one side, but managed to pull himself up onto his hands, and paused, trembling.

His vision clouded, and black specks gathered and drew across his vision.

Life slipped away into the gathering blackness.

Gray. Darkening.

He saw the Gabu creeping toward him.

Blackness.

Death.

* * *

Etaa the Ugly eased up to the strange Tinnarabu, wary. In her hand she gripped an antler knife, ready to plunge it into his neck, if need be. If he tried to attack her or uttered the slightest sound, she would swiftly end his life.

Thus far, he remained still, and only seemed to be watching her as if unable to comprehend. His eyes stared, blinked, and seemed to lose focus. His head sagged to one side. Etaa reached out, touched him. He flinched, relaxed, and lay still.

She touched him again. No movement. She pulled open his coat of fur—mammoth skin, she thought—and placed a hand upon his chest. She gently shook him, felt for a heartbeat again, and shook him with force. Still no heartbeat.

The strange, foolish man lay dead.

* * *

Etaa waited until the sounds of battle ceased, and darkness fell. She dragged the man's body from the thicket to her hidden rock enclosure on the far side of the ridge that bounded the valley of death on the east. She didn't fully know why she did this, except that he deserved respect, in spite of his stupidity. The man had waded into the carnage without weapons and without fear.

She kept the ritual vigil over the body, just as her mother taught her. In the gray dawn, she ventured out into the open, slipping between tumbled boulders, darting amongst the boles of trees, and returned to her vantage point over the battleground.

The Tinnarabu had left; no sign of them remained, not even their fallen.

But the Gabu remained, their bodies being torn apart and devoured by scavenging beasts and birds. There could be no ritual vigil for them.

She considered delivering the strange man's body to the Tinnarabu, but that was impossible. She could never approach them. So she would do as the Gabu had always done.

Etaa returned to her enclosure and found a suitable place a few hundred paces from it, on a gentle slope that would face the rising sun on days when the winter gray yielded to spring blue and green.

It seemed a good spot for a grave.

* * *

Life.

The blackness fell away from Bran, pulling aside, changing to gray.

The world resolved itself in a slow dawn of light and dark, the grayness taking form and mass. Blurs grew solid, streaks became lines.

Bran stirred. His body resisted movement, his muscles stiff. He relaxed a moment, and stretched the stiffness away. Dizziness took him, and the darkness drew in once more, and dissipated, the dizziness going with it.

He rolled onto his side and looked around. He was no longer in the snowy thicket into which he had collapsed. He lay in a rock enclosure of sorts, a solid rock pinnacle overhead, the enclosure small and close about him on all sides. Joints between the rocks were sealed with earth.

He realized that he was covered by a soft animal skin. Judging by its thickness and coloration, it was an auroch pelt.

Someone had covered him with a blanket.

* * *

Etaa scraped out the shallow grave for the strange man. She placed a few items in it to ease his journey into Shadow—cordage cut from his own garments, a clay figurine of the earth goddess, a bundle of fragrant grasses, a braided rope, and lastly, an antler knife. It was modest, but it was all she could afford to part with. She studied her work with satisfaction, and nicked her own finger and squeezed a few drops of blood into the grave, spit on it, and rolled the tiny bit of wetted earth into a ball. A tiny bit of the living, to keep the dead company.

She turned from the grave and headed back to her enclosure, hidden by cut foliage. She must remove the strange man's body before his scent began to attract the great hungry beasts. If they appeared, they would devour him, and probably her as well, and two souls would never enter peaceably into Shadow.

She dragged aside the screen of cut foliage that concealed her enclosure, and crawled in through the small opening. As she entered, she gasped and seized her knife.

The dead man stirred and sat upright.

* * *

Bran heard a gasp of soft breath and a quick movement behind him. He shifted toward the noise.

The Gabu female rested on hands and knees, watching him. She scrambled farther away, seized a hand axe, and held it firmly in both hands. She stared, her eyes locked on his.

He watched her, studied her face.

Gabu? Perhaps not.

She had the broad face typical of the Gabu, the heavy brow ridge, the low, sharply angled forehead. But some features revealed more of the Tinnarabu. Her nose, while wide, was not nearly so broad as that of the Gabu. She had a small chin, whereas the Gabu had prominent jaws but no chins. She was sturdy with thick arms and legs, but not as stout as the female Gabus he'd seen. A fine layer of hair covered her body, thinner than typical of Gabu.

Gabu. Ugly People. So unlike the Tinnarabu, the Tall People.

He held up a hand, palm open.

She raised her axe just a bit, held it against her chest, so he lowered his hand. "I shall not hurt you," he said.

If she understood, she gave him no indication.

"My name is Bran. I am Tinnarabu." When she didn't respond, he moved, trying to find a more comfortable position. He studied her without speaking. Neither of them moved, nor spoke. He waited; he had time. Plenty of time.

He listened for sounds outside the tiny enclosure, for the sounds of battle. No sound came, not even the sound of the dying.

He remembered his death. He was sure he had died, and vividly recalled his heart stopping. Curious, he placed a hand on his chest to feel his heartbeat. Strong and rhythmic. He studied the wound in his abdomen; it had closed completely, a faint pink scar marking the entry of the spear. He reached behind, felt his back. There, too, the wound seemed to have closed.

He glanced up to see the Gabu female still watching him closely.

She stirred and raised her axe, brandishing it over her head. Bran remained still. Eventually, she moved closer to him, stopped, and came closer again. She pointed at the scar in his abdomen. She reached behind her and retrieved the broken spear. She motioned again to his wound and set the spear aside.

Bran understood and pointed to his wound.

The Gabu uttered a string of sounds, unlike any he'd ever heard, like a hoarse rasp carried on the breath of the night wind. Not just sounds or noises. Speech. Unlike his own, yet complex in arrangement, clearly a grouping of words, strangely melodic.

He understood none of it. Yet he had known since his first year of life that he possessed a faculty for understanding languages. He became fluent in each of the various tongues of the Tinnarabu quickly after joining a clan, and would be able to understand a smattering within half a day, and be fully conversant within a handful of days. Would it be so easy to understand her?

Bran placed his hand upon his chest and said, "Bran."

The female hesitated, and repeated it, the name coming out as an airy, "Behhh."

Bran tapped his chest again. "Bran," he repeated, and pointed to her.

She stared at him. "Etaa," she finally said, her voice a rustle of wind in pines.

"Etaa," he said, nodding. "Etaa." He found the word difficult to mimic closely. His voice sounded flat and listless.

The Gabu's face contorted into a grimace, teeth bared.

She was smiling.

* * *

Etaa fed the strange man, accepting his presence in her abode. She wondered if she'd found a man from the spirit world. Bran came not from Shadow, she thought, even though she'd seen with her own eyes his return from death, from Shadow. No, he must be from some spirit realm.

Such a strange man.

His strength returned quickly. In two days, he showed no ill effects from his death. His wounds had closed completely and only the faintest scars remained.

Etaa watched his progress with fear at first, and then awe. When he spoke, she would look away or cast her eyes downward, and, though curious of his attentions, answered his inquiries with shy whispers.

But the man would not be dissuaded, and continued to engage her in conversation. Quiet for so long, Etaa found she liked hearing the voice of another.

Bran pointed to everything in sight and called out its name in his own tongue, and coaxed Etaa to do the same in her own language. Within hours, he had acquired a fundamental understanding of her language, though he failed to pronounce any of it with acceptable quality, much to her amusement. Were all Tinnarabu so pathetic in speech, so tuneless? Surprisingly, she found that she, too, possessed a facility for language, but struggled with the grating Tinnarabu words. She wondered if the differences in the voice-making structures between the two peoples was too great. That hardly seemed fair; he would enjoy the beauty of her speech, while she would have to suffer the hyena-shrieks of the Tinnarabu.

No matter. They could now converse. And with each exchange, his Gabu grew richer.

* * *

A small fire hissed and popped with the drip of juices from a spitted rabbit. The aroma of the cooking meat had that quality that the Tinnarabu claimed to be excellent, although Bran saw little value in such judgments. So he took their word for it. Bran felt no particular hunger. He'd never felt hunger in his life, and was unsure what it entailed. He could see it in others and understood the satisfaction that food brought. The experience, the appeal, the enjoyment, seemed universal among all the races of humanity, even among all animals. He pitied those that endured such an unexplainable feeling.

When Etaa handed him his share of the rabbit, he graciously accepted the tough, burnt meat, and pretended to enjoy it, smacking his lips and uttering grunts of simulated pleasure.

Etaa consumed her portion of meat, tearing off chunks with her teeth, snapping the small bones apart and sucking out the juices, and licking her fingers. She had gathered tender leaves and nuts and crushed them into the meat before and during the cooking of it; this practice gave the meat a different taste, and so he assumed that he must appreciate the difference. And he began to think that he could.

After a time, Bran set his meal aside. Etaa looked up at him, paused. He took another quick bite, and made what he hoped sounded like a sigh of ecstasy.

She grimaced, happily, he thought, but he couldn't be certain. Her language, he'd mastered. Her ways, he wondered if he would ever understand. Was that a universal difference between man and woman? What if he were a woman? Was such a thing possible? He would have to consider that someday.

Bran slowly reached out to her and placed his hand on hers. She flinched, snatched her hand away. He tried again. This time, she did not withdraw. "Etaa, do you live here alone?"

"There is no place in the world for Etaa."

"How did you come to be here?"

"I have always lived here."

"Alone?"

"I had my mother. She died long ago."

"How old are you?"

Etaa's brow furrowed. "I do not understand."

"How many summers have you lived?"

"What is 'many?' I have only lived one life."

"You never counted the summers?"

"A life."

Bran considered this. Her answer felt genuine, perhaps more so than the Tinnarabu insistence upon defining life into sequential pieces. What did it matter to her how many years passed? Her life must consist of an encompassing grind of solitude and survival.

He had begun to look upon his own life in such a way.

He took another bite, smacked his lips, and sighed once more. Etaa shook her head, a ghost of a smile upon her face. He set the meat aside.

"Etaa, you are neither Gabu nor Tinnarabu, and yet you are both. You know this, do you not?"

She stopped eating. "I know this."

"May I look at you closer?"

Silence. A baleful stare. "Why would you?"

"I wish to see you and know you better." He waited for a moment, and slid closer to her.

Etaa set her meal to the side. Her face grew still and hard, her eyes narrowing. But she remained still.

Bran reached slowly and touched her cheek with one hand. She tensed. He caressed her cheek gently, feeling the broad, angular cheekbone. She withdrew from his touch ever so slightly. He paused, and leaned closer, continuing to caress her face, delicately tracing fingers down her cheek, and up to her heavy brow.

He took her face in both hands, studying the lines. "Gabu," he said. "And yet not Gabu. Tinnarabu, and yet not Tinnarabu. What should we call you?"

"Alone," she said. "And to you, I am more Gabu than not. An Ugly One."

He shook his head "Ugly. Beautiful. I am baffled by such descriptions. One might say the Great Ice is ugly, and also beautiful. It is both. You are you, Etaa. But you are unlike any other. You are one of a kind."

She blinked. Her eyes glistened. "Do not mock me, Tinnarabu."

Bran withdrew his hands. "I do not and would not. But I would know more of you. How did you come to be here? Alone?"

"I have always been apart, but not always Alone. I had my mother. Together, we lived here, Alone. Her name was Enaa. A Gabu."

"Your father . . . he was Tinnarabu?"

"I do not know my father, but he was Tinnarabu. My mother's clan was small. They were slaughtered by a Tinnarabu raiding party, all but Enaa. Ugly though she was, the warriors kept Enaa for three days as a reward. Afterwards, she was to be killed. But the Tinnarabu liked drink as much as rape. Enaa was clever; she introduced them to a Gabu drink fermented from grapes. The Gabu kept many skins of the drink in the cave, and Enaa plied the Tinnarabu with one skin after another. During their drunken stupor, she escaped to the Alone. They did not try to find her. She kept moving until she found her way across many valleys to the neighboring Gabu clan and lived with them.

"But it could not last. Mother was pregnant, and gave birth to me. The Gabu were disgusted at the sight of me, and banished Mother and me once more to the Alone. They could not abide one that looked so much like their enemy, nor accept the offspring of an unclean union between Gabu and animal. Mother and I lived in the Alone, but we were happy together. Then one day, while hunting, Mother fell down the scree and broke her leg; the bone pierced her skin. Blood drenched her. She survived the bleeding and the pain, but died thereafter of sour wound. Years ago."

"And you have been Alone ever since? How old were you?"

Etaa considered. "I was small, a little girl. An Ugly little girl."

Bran took her face into his hands. "A beautiful little girl."

* * *

Etaa showed him the rushing, burbling creek from which she drank. After drinking his fill, he motioned for her to join him, and led her to a small pool of still water in a broad bend in the creek. Rushes and grasses abounded in the moist earth there, and lily pads floated near the water's edge. Lavender flowers graced stalks above the pads. She plucked a flower, smelled it, and held it out to him. He studied it for a moment and sniffed its fragrance, nodded, and extended it back to her. She stared at him, puzzled. He tucked the flower into a strand of her long red hair, and pulled her to the edge of the still water. She looked down and saw her reflection, the flower brilliant against her face.

Bran pointed to the reflection. "See? The beautiful little girl grew into a beautiful woman."

She grumbled that there was much work to be done, and no time for such foolishness. But she left the flower in her hair, touching it gently every so often to ensure that it remained in place. After their evening meal, a full moon rose in the darkening sky. Etaa slipped away to the pool of water. There, she sat, gazing upon her reflection, and the lovely flower in her hair.

* * *

In the morning, Etaa went about her daily chores, her means of survival—collecting wood, hunting small game, foraging for plants, mending clothes, replacing the dying foliage screen with fresh foliage.

Her thoughts returned to the pond, the flower, and Bran calling her "beautiful." She now understood the difference between being Alone and being lonely. Though she missed her mother with great sadness, she came to accept her own existence as simple fact. Her fate seemed neither a good nor a bad one.

How wrong she had been.

She knew that Bran, ever curious, watched her go about her tasks, and studied the tricks and nuances of her efforts. He treated her with kindness and generosity. He taught her the Tinnarabu skills for the same tasks. She made extra effort to perform her tasks as best she could.

On the sixth morning after he'd returned from Shadow, Etaa finished grinding a handful of nuts, wetting them with water, and making a paste. She turned to see Bran staring at her.

A strange feeling came over her, a new feeling. Her face grew hot and she looked away. She cast about, and fidgeted pointlessly with a bit of rope, pretending to care about its strength. She tried to push the feeling aside, but couldn't. She thought only of Bran; *he* made her feel this way. Etaa suddenly realized that it pleased her that he'd been watching her. She cast a furtive glance in his direction. He smiled.

Her mother had spoken to her about mating, how it was a thing to be endured, unless one found a mate. Then, mother said, the act could become wondrous, and explained the feelings, the tenderness, the longing for one's mate when he was away. She called this love. The word held no meaning for young Etaa; she would never know love, she would never find a mate. She was Alone.

In the following days, Etaa thought about what her mother had told her. And whenever Bran left her sight for even a moment, she longed for him, missed him.

Etaa the Ugly, Etaa the Alone, had fallen in love.

* * *

Bran was collecting wood and dried dung for the fire in a nearby ravine when the voice in his head returned, startling him . . .

You cannot remain in isolation. Return at once to the Tinnarabu.

Bran wondered at this sudden, unbidden interruption of his thoughts. He had never before attempted to respond to the voices. He only listened, and wondered at their origin.

Return now.

Why should I return? I learn many things from Etaa, things I could not learn from the Tinnarabu.

She is Gabu. Hers is not the destiny of the planet.

She is not Gabu. She is not Tinnarabu. She is neither. She is both. There is much to be learned.

Return to the Tinnarabu at once. Do not waste time on the losing species.

Why must there be a losing species?

It is always the way of technological advantage. Always, and on all worlds.

Why?

Bran waited for an answer that would not come.

* * *

Etaa set the last of five fish traps in the creek, and looked up to see Bran approaching. She quickly dragged her fingers through her hair and tried to comb it out after a blustery afternoon. Anything to look better for him.

"My friend," Bran said. "I must talk to you."

Friend, Etaa thought. Not Etaa, the Beautiful?

"It is not good to live apart or Alone. We should live among others."

"What others?"

Bran hesitated. "I am Tinnarabu. The Gabu will not accept me. You, Etaa, are but half-Gabu. And half-Tinnarabu. The Tinnarabu will accept you if you are with me. I will stand for you."

"And you believe that, Bran?"

"Why would they not?"

She stared into his eyes. "What will become of me there?"

"You will learn their ways—our ways—and they will learn yours. You have much to learn, and much to teach."

"That will not be the outcome. There can only be one winner in the Great War. Half-measures and half-breeds will not be welcome."

"You are wrong. When people are ready, they can be shown the way of life. They will embrace those that are different. They will move forward together."

Oh, Bran, she thought. How can you not see?

Bran touched her cheek, and she trembled, as she always did when he touched her. His touch was so gentle, so caring, so... undemanding. Why could he not touch her in a more intimate way? She thought back to the day they looked at her reflection in the pond. He'd called her beautiful. She'd believed him, but now she questioned the idea.

She had to trust him.

"Yes, my Bran," she said. "I will come with you to your people."

* * *

Bran at first led the way down the rocky hills and onto the steppes, until he recognized that Etaa was far more adept in traversing open country than he or the finest Tinnarabu hunters were. She moved as a shadow, swiftly and stealthily, with Bran following, and slipped from boulder to boulder, through ravines, tall grasses, and into the forest.

Bran surveyed the landscape for the great predators that could end lives, possibly even his own, without hesitation or preamble. Wolves, bears, hyenas, and the great cats prowled the steppes. In the open, if a lion decided to make a meal of either of them, there was no preventing it. He marveled at the resourcefulness that Etaa must possess to have survived.

They crept into the lapsed battlefield. The dead of the Tinnarabu had been removed. The Gabu lay where they fell, though little remained of them. Scavengers had picked the field clean; only a scattering of bones marked their brief existences.

The track of the Tinnarabu led, as Bran expected, in the direction from whence they had come, three hands west of the distant and never-moving Ice Star, far beyond the Great Ice of the north. They left the steppe and ascended a steep, serrated ridge. The day cleared, and the view slid off into the distance.

There, many days' marches away, the Great Ice loomed, a single, unending plateau of white, stretching east and west as far as the eye could see. One-hundred and twelve years ago, Bran had studied the Great Ice. He determined that it towered one thousand two-hundred and forty-two times his own height. He did not share this fact with anyone. He learned early on that sharing knowledge only drew suspicion.

They descended the opposite slope of the ridge, leaving behind a wind-swept expanse of loose rock. At the base, two sentries sprang from behind a jumble of boulders, spears raised and ready. Men whom Bran had long known.

"Ah, Bran!" Moolik Mol said. "You're alive! And you return with a slave."

"Not a slave. A friend."

The sentries exchanged glances, and the glances became smirks. They escorted Bran and Etaa on the last day's march. The Tinnarabu village stood in the open plain, twenty-two homes of mammoth tusks and hides, arranged within the great circle of a wood palisade.

The villagers gathered in a rush, staring and pointing and whispering. Etaa clung to Bran, her eyes downcast. He gently took her by the hand. She shivered, but not from the cold.

Setka Bol strode forward. He glanced around to make sure everyone appreciated his leadership, although Bran knew that leadership was an informal agreement, generated by nodding consent and tolerance more than by ordination. Setka Bol led by the slightest of notions.

"Bran!" Setka Bol said. "You return from the dead."

"You are closer to truth than you realize," Bran said.

Setka Bol studied him up and down. "You are not hurt? I saw with my own eyes the spear that pierced your body."

"The wound was more superficial than it appeared." The lie felt uncomfortable. "I was not mortally gutted," he added. This, both truth and lie at the same time, eased the discomfort of lying. "And I was rescued and nursed to health by my companion." He gently eased Etaa forward. "This is my friend, Etaa."

"She is Gabu," Setka Bol said, matter-of-factly. "Ugly. Not one of us. She cannot be here."

"She is also Tinnarabu. She is the child of a union of the two."

Etaa looked up at Bran and met his eyes.

Setka Bol approached her. "By Amru, she is ugly. Do you speak, Ugly One?"

"She knows some of our words, Setka Bol. Not many. But I can speak with her. I have learned her tongue."

"You learned her tongue?" Setka Bol shot him a look. "How?"

G'meel G'meeka, the matron of the clan, stepped to Setka Bol's side and touched his arm. "It has long been known that Bran learns words quickly. He learned our own within a day."

Setka Bol considered this for a moment. "Perhaps. So, let us hear the Ugly One speak."

Bran turned to Etaa, gently raised her chin, and looked into her eyes. Tears rimmed the edges. Had she understood Setka Bol?

"Etaa, beautiful friend," he said in the tongue of the Gabu. "Speak now and let them hear the song of your voice."

"Oh ho," G'meel G'meeka said. "Bran speaks animal, almost like an animal."

Laughter erupted. The laughter of aggression, not good cheer.

"Speak, Etaa," Bran said.

Etaa, eyes downcast, said in her own tongue, "Bran wishes me to join him with the Tinnarabu. I wish it too." Her eyes flickered up and about, and down again. "I wish to serve the Tinnarabu."

G'meel G'meeka made a sound like a wild dog barking. More laughter.

Bran translated what Etaa had said, and added, "Not as slave. As equal."

"Perhaps as pet," Setka Bol said.

"As equal."

"That will never happen."

"But there is much we can learn from her. Her race has lived here many thousands of generations before us."

"Like bison? I doubt we can learn much from bison."

"The Tinnarabu came here from the warm lands. Etaa and the full-blooded Gabu have changed in form over many generations to dwell in the cold wastes of the north."

"Bran, she is Gabu. The enemy of our people. The world cannot have a good people and a bad people. One must disappear and will disappear."

"That is nonsense."

"The Gabu slew my only son," Setka Bol said, his voice cracking. "And will slay other men's sons as well, without hesitation. They are beasts."

"You twist the world to suit you. Setka Sil would be alive if you hadn't led your people to war against the Gabu. You killed him."

Setka Bol stepped forward and struck Bran in the face, and stood before him, shaking. Bran steadied himself, and wiped a streak of blood from his mouth.

"One will disappear," Setka Bol growled. "And it will not be ours." He signaled with a hand. Two warriors rushed Bran and seized him, pinning his arms back. Two more seized Etaa. She wrenched one arm free and swung a fist into the face of her attacker, sending a rope of blood whipping through the air. The warrior recoiled from the blow, and two more rushed in and drove Etaa face down into the dirt.

She struggled momentarily, and gave up resistance, unable to defend herself.

"Kill it," Setka Bol said.

A warrior approached, raised his stone axe.

"No!" Bran shouted. "You must not kill her. She is a healer of great powers. You saw for yourself that I was down and dying. The Gabu spear ran me through! Have you ever seen a man recover from such a wound? Who do you think healed me? Etaa did. Did you think I healed myself?"

Setka Bol hesitated. He raised a hand to stay the execution. "I do not know how you survived. This is true."

"Neither Tinnarabu nor Gabu possesses such magic," Bran continued. "Yet she, the offspring of the union of the two, does. Do you not see the value of such a great woman?"

"She is not a woman. She is a female. There is a difference."

"Unhand us both. Neither the great Etaa nor I can escape. I shall prove to you her magic."

Setka Bol nodded to the warriors. The captors reluctantly released Bran, and shoved Etaa into the dirt once more before releasing her.

Etaa looked up, her face streaked with red mud. Blood trickled from her nose. Her eyes, shimmering with tears, found Bran's.

The whisper in Bran's mind: Do not attempt this.

Bran withdrew his stone knife and plunged it into his belly, once, twice, three times.

Cries of shock and disbelief arose. A child shrieked.

"Fool!" Setka Bol shouted. "We might yet have let you survive the day."

"And I shall still. The great Etaa will heal me. Even should I die, as I already once have, she will bring me back."

Etaa wailed, the sound of her voice as haunting as that of the cold wind that sweeps off the Great Ice.

Blood poured from Bran's wounds. He looked at Etaa. "Great sorceress," he said in Tinnarabu, "place your hands upon me and heal me." In Gabu, he added, "Etaa, come to me. Lay your hands upon me. I am weakening. I will slip from this world soon, but I will return, alive and healed, within a day."

"I cannot," she said, her voice breaking.

"You must. It is the only way. Do this and you will live among the Tinnarabu as a goddess."

"As a witch."

Bran felt his legs weakening. He stumbled to one knee, steadied himself with a hand on the ground. "Come. Now." He coughed blood, swayed, and fell forward.

Etaa came toward him and steadied him. She placed both hands upon his wounds. Blood seeped between her fingers and covered her hands. She sang and spoke in her beautiful, airy language.

Darkness crept into Bran's eyes, the specks of a dark, black Universe gathering.

Death.

* * *

Life.

Black to gray, gray to light, gray to color. The world returned.

Bran blinked, turned, looked about. He lay on a soft bed of fur in the Gathering Hut. It was the largest of the huts, the most prestigious. Three Tinnarabu women stood near, and gasped, and backed away. G'meel G'meeka shrieked and clapped a hand to her mouth, and fled from the hut, crying, "He lives! Bran lives!" The other women ran after her.

Bran sat up.

Etaa lay next to Bran, but on bare ground. Her eyes were closed, her breathing labored and ragged.

A leather blanket covered her. The sand beneath her was black, and a pungent odor hung in the air. He eased the blanket aside, exposing her naked breasts and body. Blood smeared her body and soaked the inside of the blanket. Her wounds mimicked his own, three deep stabs into the belly.

He gently touched her face. "Etaa."

She stirred, opened her eyes. Dullness, then recognition. A glimmer of joy behind pain. "Bran." Her voice a whisper. "You live."

The flaps to the entrance of the hut billowed and flew aside. Setka Bol stomped in, scowling, an axe in hand. He stopped, staring wide-eyed at Bran. The matron appeared behind him, trembling.

Bran returned his stare. "You've hurt her."

Setka Bol clutched his axe against his chest like a talisman against evil. "I did not, Bran. We did not."

Bran turned to Etaa. "Which of these men hurt you?"

Etaa drew a slow, ragged breath. "I . . . stabbed myself."

"But why?"

Etaa's eyes darted from Setka Bol to G'meel G'meeka, and back to Bran. "Because you died, and my medicine was failing. I ministered, I waited, I incanted, but you only grew colder. At last, the Tinnarabu grew angry and impatient. They were going to kill me, so I performed one last act of medicine. I stabbed myself and bathed your wounds

with my own blood. The women were to stay and observe us both."
She drew a slow breath. "Bran. My love. Can you heal me?"

Bran shook his head. "Not as I heal myself."

"I did not think so."

"But I will tend to your wounds and you will live."

"Do not fear for me, Bran. I know I die today, but I do not die
Alone, and I am at peace. I could not return to the Alone and they
would never have let me leave here alive anyway. They would kill me
and leave my carcass for the vultures. I am Ugly. The enemy."

"You are Etaa the Beautiful. You will be revered as a great healer."

"No. They will hate me even more, and worse, they will fear me."
She closed her eyes, rested for a moment. She opened her eyes again,
and began to shiver. "I grow so cold. Is it darkening?"

Bran turned to Setka Bol. "Leave us now. She dies, and even her
own magic, which she has now bestowed upon me, cannot save her."

Setka Bol hesitated. "Bran . . ."

"Leave," Bran said, his voice a growl. "Do not anger a man of
magic."

G'meeka G'meel hurried away. Setka Bol remained. "Bran, the
Gabu female did not leave your side, and she has taken her own life."

"Then it is as you wished."

Setka Bol looked down at Etaa. He opened his mouth to speak,
paused. "It was," he said at last. He knelt and stroked Etaa's hair
gently. "For that I am sorry. Forgive me." He arose and left the hut.

Bran lay beside Etaa the Beautiful, his naked skin against hers, and
embraced her. He pulled the blanket over her. Her trembling eased,
and she smiled and curled her body against his.

* * *

Bran wedged the last rock in place onto Etaa's grave, high atop a
windy ridge. The grave was deep and would not be scavenged by the
great beasts. He would remain for a moon cycle to see that they did
not.

He wiped the sweat from his brow and sat back to rest and study the view. The village of the Tinnarabu lay two days north. Far beyond that, the Great Ice loomed.

He had left the village, and doubted that he would ever return.

Twice he had died now. Would this always be the way? Something told him it would. He was Tinnarabu; he had their features, their manner. And yet he was vastly different from them, and in ways he was only beginning to comprehend.

He seemed to have a purpose.

Two peoples, two types of human on this world, at least two of which he was aware. Two very different human species. Setka Bol once said, "One must disappear, and will disappear." Bran suspected this to be true and inevitable. And the Tinnarabu already laid plans for yet another extermination raid against Gabu to the east.

Now, however, even Setka Bol began to question the rightness of such a course. Maybe there was hope, but Setka Bol's own warriors now questioned in turn his authority to lead them.

One must disappear, and will disappear.

Perhaps. But Bran began to doubt that the deserving one was winning the first world war.

Notes

The evolution of species has never been a pyramid with us at the top. Think of it more as a bush with millions of leaves, each leaf representing a distinct species. One leaf represents humans. A larger number of leaves represents hominid species that have existed in the past.

Homo sapiens shared the planet simultaneously with at least four other species of hominid (*Homo erectus*, diminutive *Homo floriensis*, discovered in 2004 and popularly called the "hobbit", *Homo luzonensis*, discovered in the Philippines in 2019, and *Homo neanderthalensis*).

Only *Homo sapiens* remains.

A pared-down version of human evolution goes something like this. In the Great Rift Valley of Africa, some 3.6 million years ago, *Australopithecus afarensis*, the first upright primate we know of, appeared. Similar species came and went, but one line evolved into *Homo erectus* and spread from Africa to Europe and Asia. Ultimately, several lines of hominid (with interim species) evolved from *Homo erectus*. One, *Homo neanderthalensis*, evolved in the Middle East and Europe. Another, *Homo sapiens*, evolved in Africa roughly 200,000 years ago. H. sapiens fanned out from Africa and appeared in Europe about 40,000 years ago. And not long after our species arrived, Neanderthal vanished.

But not entirely. Skeletons found in Spain possess traits of both modern humans and Neanderthal, and DNA evidence now shows that 3% of humans of European descent carry a bit of Neanderthal in them. So the evidence is clear that some mating of *Homo sapiens* (called Cro-Magnon in Europe) and Neanderthal occurred.

The image of Neanderthal as small-brained and stupid is, well, small-brained and stupid. By volume, the Neanderthal brain was larger than that of modern humans. The base and back of the cranium, in particular, were larger. Those regions are associated with vision, smell, and memory, so Neanderthal may have had more acute senses and better memory than we have. However, he probably had less capacity for abstraction and planning, and this likely explains the slower rate of technological innovation.

Technological advances crawled for most of human development; a stone tool might go unchanged for hundreds of thousands of years. But about 50,000 years ago, the rate of progress began to accelerate, and humans routinely improved tools, art, and cultural practices (an example being the atlatl, or spear-thrower, described in this story). An alien civilization might decide it would be a good time to keep tabs on us.

The Prometheus android gets caught in the intrigues of an Ireland struggling for an identity of its own, along the borderlands of the Medieval and the Renaissance, with fear of the supernatural running rampant in the land.

The Tower House Prisoner

Ireland, North of Cashel, 1605

Captain William Farnham studied the tower house from the edge of the renegade's dead fields. The dawn's fog dissolved and light came thin and pale, a jaundice afflicting the sun's beams. Farnham took a bite of apple, tossed the core aside, and wiped his mouth on his sleeve. He thanked God and cursed Him in the same breath. Just enough light for killing.

The long, bleak siege, three months in, would soon be over, its end assured this day. His vehement request had been at last granted by plump administrators in Dublin Castle, scratching at carved oak desks, imbibing French wine, and playing at love with whores in featherbeds.

Lord, how he hated Ireland. Step outside Dublin's walls and you sank into an ill-bred, barbaric country. Why King James insisted upon English ownership of such a land baffled him, yet royals throughout Europe scrabbled and clawed for any dirt they happened upon in their mad zeal for colonies. Ireland abounded in no riches, unless rocks be riches. The Irish scurried about as savages, or nearly so, speaking their gibberish tongue and wallowing in fleas and filth.

The only thing worse than an Irishman was an Englishman gone Irish. Like Lord John Merriwether, the little fool that dwelt in this tower house, this pitiful excuse for a real castle. The towers dotted the Irish countryside, looming over all. They rendered English lords godlike in the eyes of Irish bumpkins who themselves dwelt in rude huts and hovels. And though pretend castles fed arrogance and a sense of invincibility, they impressed veteran English soldiers not at all.

Still, Merriwether's two dozen defenders accounted themselves well, repulsing the two frontal assaults ordered at the beginning of the campaign by quill-pushers in Dublin before the fight settled more sensibly into siege. Safe within their sturdy walls, they lost perhaps three of their number, while Farnham lost sixteen men dead, another eighteen wounded beyond use. Men he counted true and brave and worthy.

Farnham turned from the tower house, confident it would remain quiet. It lay outside the ranges of the King's archers, and his siege lines outside those of the tower's.

He signaled his men to bring forward the engine of destruction that would put an end to this campaign. From the wood forty yards behind, his men emerged, a quintuplet leading, and two great horses following and hauling the cannon.

Merriwether had been seduced by the barbaric ways and redhaired charms of his Irish wife. The hearty nobleman of England began sliding into this depravity a good decade ago, slow to collect taxes at first, slower still to install proper English ways, and—most unpardonably of all—siphoning off more than his fair share of revenues.

Marrying local did that to you.

Laxness among the governing lords festered, leading many to lapse into local custom and morals. Impatient, the King commanded Dublin to bring the scattered errant lords back into line, and sent hand-picked emissaries afield to discuss the matter, gently or firmly according to need, with the wayward lords. Some capitulated without so much as a harsh word. Others resisted. Merriwether, a particularly quarrelsome sort, took another, more foolish step.

He imprisoned Catherine Stokes, the King's own emissary.

Dublin did not need guidance from King James in this matter. They knew that if the situation remained unrectified they would soon be dealt with themselves. So they mustered a force barely large enough for the task, positioned the unlucky Farnham in its lead, and sent them to take Merriwether Castle and fetch both rebel and emissary back to Dublin, posthaste.

Captain Farnham knew what to expect. He'd brokered similar situations, peacefully and without loss of life as luck would have it, twice before. Succeed or not, it was unlikely the emissary still lived. Once the Crown refused to pay ransom, food and water to the prisoner became whims of the captor. And when under siege, a lord parcels and conserves his foodstuffs wisely.

Farnham had entreated Merriwether in straightforward fashion. Release His Majesty's agent, he'd told the man. Beg leniency and perhaps be spared, albeit most likely forced into hard labor, or exiled to some hard, foreign shore. At least earn a measure of mercy for your family and servants.

Merriwether grew nervous and claimed that Catherine Stokes and her lone guard came, issued outrageous demands, and left, heading west. That was the last he'd heard of the woman. The traitor then ended negotiations abruptly. He would not surrender.

Merriwether lied, of course; the Crown's spies in the province assured Dublin that the lady entered the tower house and never left. That spoke the worst for the poor emissary. She had likely been cut from rations and left for dead, a common practice among ransoming lords. Or simply murdered and buried.

The sky brightened and Farnham squinted into the distance. Defenders assembled atop the tower to watch the cannon being wheeled into place. Merriwether, Farnham gathered, had never witnessed artillery in action. Most small-minded local lords hadn't, safe in their provincial ignorance. New, fearsome weapons terrorized peasants and royals alike across Europe, rendering useless the old ways of warfare to which even many English clung. Farnham knew better. He'd used the new weapons. Stonework, so reliable a defense for centuries, now afforded merely a heavy tomb in which defenders might be buried.

Merriwether was to receive his first lesson in modern warfare.

The men stuffed the cannon with gunpowder and wadding, rodded it in, and rolled the forty-pound ball into the barrel.

"Light it, Captain?" asked Carter. The gunnery lads drew near, one holding the glowing igniter, eagerness in his eyes.

Farnham shook his head and turned again to the tower house. Merriwether could not mistake what came next. Surely he knew of cannon and what terrible destructions could be wrought by it. But knowing and believing differed. Farnham waited. Moments passed, laden with excitement and dread.

"So be it," Farnham said. "Fire."

The gunner licked his lips and extended the igniter to the touch hole. A hiss, a streamer of smoke.

The cannon roared and bucked and rolled backward. The muzzle flashed orange and a cloud of smoke exploded from it.

The iron ball smacked into the tower, forty feet above the ground, slightly off center. Plaster flew from the wall, and limestone rained down. Cracks spiderwebbed the surface.

"Excellent," Farnham said. "But lower the arc. Hit the tower at its base and let the great weight of stone above help bring it down. Sponge, prime, reload, and ram."

Carter nodded. The exercise repeated, and Farnham again gave the order to fire. The roar and flash, the smoke, the metallic strike of iron on stone. The cascade of dust and rock from the tower house wall.

The pause. The wait for an answer.

None came. Perhaps Merriwether believed Farnham would exhaust his powder and shot and give up. He would be wrong.

The cannon roared again. The cracks in the tower house spread. Sections began to slough off in great masses. If the barrage kept on, the tower would soon collapse and kill all within.

From a window in the top floor, a pike extended slowly, a white banner hanging from it, and waved.

Merriwether had had enough.

* * *

Farnham watched and waited. He'd fought enough battles, seen enough treachery, to learn distrust. And those battles pitched civilized men against civilized foes. He would certainly not rush out with open arms to embrace a barbarian Irish foe, even one who was English.

The listless white flag withdrew. And still Farnham waited.

Carter, next to him, shifted restlessly. "Blast 'em again, Captain?"

"Patience," Farnham said. "They were lost as soon as the gun arrived. It just took them awhile to know it. There's no need to kill them all."

"Captain, they'll all hang, you know."

He knew. But that blood would stain someone else's hands.

* * *

At last, Merriwether exited the tower house, followed by his wife. After them came a redhaired girl of about eleven years, and two old women and an old man limping along on a crutch. Fifteen men followed, poorly armored in the tradition of the barbarians, but unarmed and with hands raised.

The entire body trod through the collapsed gate of the low, surrounding bawn wall towards Captain Farnham. His men trained drawn bows and arrows upon the lot of them. At length, Farnham raised an outstretched palm and said, "Come no closer, traitor Merriwether. Kneel where you are, all of you."

The body paused, watching their lord. Merriwether studied Farnham for a moment and sank to his knees. His entourage followed suit.

"Very good, traitor. Have you weapons, any of you? Speak truly and seek our good graces. If we find even a knitting needle upon you, you will die on the spot."

"We have no weapons, English," Merriwether growled.

"That is good. Do not move while we put your claim to the test."

Farnham's soldiers searched the kneelers. One of the men, Mason, yanked the young girl to her feet. She screamed and he slapped her, knocking her back to the ground. "This one's got a blade!"

Merriwether sprang to his feet. "Get your English hands off her!"

"Stay put, Merriwether," Farnham snapped. "Little girl, withdraw your blade and cast it aside. Mason, careful. Release her and back away."

The girl whimpered and looked from face to face, her eyes wide.

"Do you speak English, girl?"

"Damn you, Farnham. My little girl is Irish, through and through." He turned to his daughter. "A chaitheamh ar leataobh an lann, cailín."

The girl nodded, sobbing. From under her apron she withdrew a long-handled wood spoon and cast it aside.

Farnham sighed in relief. He turned to Carter. "Seize and bind the traitor."

"An' the rest, Captain?"

"Escort them under guard back to camp. Traitor Merriwether, is anyone left in this ridiculous castle?"

"No one that yet lives, ye English lackey."

"And Catherine Stokes? I know for a fact that she never left. Therefore it follows that you have murdered the King's own emissary. An unwise choice."

"Take it as ye will, lackey. Aye, the woman did not leave and does not yet live. If the King sends witches to do his work, he should not expect better."

"What do you mean?"

"The witch lies dead and mouldering in the dungeon, lackey."

Farnham considered this for a moment. Superstition ran rampant through the uneducated underclasses of Europe. Yet it never ceased to amaze him; and this traitor, Merriwether, came from a fine family and estate in Cornwall, and had received a gentleman's education. "Show me to the dungeon, traitor and murderer. The emissary shall be accorded a decent Christian burial. Perhaps you shall join her."

* * *

Captain Farnham advanced step by careful step toward the tower house, his fist twisted into Merriwether's collar, pushing the traitor in front at arm's length, a human shield. He would not chance the possibility of a vengeful rogue or two still lurking about the place, committed to some suicidal last stand.

The swift Irish weather changed, a cold westerly wind sweeping over the land and driving a rain before it. Lightning flickered and the sky rumbled.

Farnham knew well the intricacies of tower house defenses, and Merriwether's stronghold likely incorporated them all. He took a moment to look the castle up and down once more.

Carter, in his youthful, foolish eagerness, strode past, sword drawn.

"Hold, lad!" Farnham snapped. "Caution is the order of the hour. Look up."

Carter stopped and stared upward.

Perched and overhanging the door niche, at the very top of the tower house, a dark rectangle of stone projected a few feet outward, directly above the entrance. The machicolation. Defenders above would simply drop things upon the intruders. Boulders, boiling oil. They could not be avoided, and bloody ends inevitably awaited some unlucky soldiers.

Nothing came raining down from above.

The great oaken door hung upon iron hinges, recessed sideward in a niche in the base of the tower wall. Directly in the back wall of the niche, two slits, one horizontal and one vertical, formed an elegant cross-shaped window that had nothing to do with Christian piety. The vertical slit formed a loop for arrows from a longbow, and the horizontal slit a loop for the launch of bolts from a crossbow. Anyone approaching the door could not avoid the line of fire.

Farnham shoved Merriwether against the crossed loops and leapt to the side of the niche, pressing himself against the wall, swinging his shield up protectively, and looked up. As expected, a dark opening graced the ceiling of the niche. The murder hole. Another ingenious defense against unwanted visitors. If one stood within the niche out of the harm of the machicolation, defenders could stab from above with long-handled pikes.

"I told ye no one left alive remains in the castle, lackey."

"And I trust you implicitly, traitor." Farnham swung Merriwether about and pushed the door open with him. "You still have value, it seems."

A small vestibule lay within, a heavy door on the left of it opening onto the kitchen. He turned to look up the narrow staircase that wound its way up and out of sight. "Up you go, traitor."

They climbed the five levels of the tower house, pausing to inspect each room, finding each untenanted. At last they reached the top room, the entertaining hall. Farnham knew that the dungeon entrance lay in the top room, the most inaccessible in the castle. He shoved Merriwether inside and released him. "The dungeon entrance, traitor. Show me."

Merriwether mumbled some gibberish curse, and crossed to the wall opposite the doorway. A niche, with window looking out, held doors on either side. One would be the entrance into the cavity within the double wall of the tower to the quarters in which occupants relieved themselves. Opposite it, a second narrow door also opened into the double wall. "Here?" Farnham said.

Merriwether nodded.

"Good. Carter, descend into the dungeon and fetch the prisoner."

"You may regret it."

"And why is that?"

"Why? The woman was a witch."

"'Was?'"

"Don't be a fool, lackey. We lowered the witch into the dungeon and left her. Four months ago."

"And I assume you gave her food and water."

"One does not offer sustenance to evil."

"Then it is as I feared. You have murdered the King's own agent and you will hang for it."

"James I is your king, not mine. He is my oppressor and his agents my enemies. I shan't weep over the deaths of enemies."

"And I shan't weep over you as I watch you squirm and kick when you drop from the gallows. Carter, open the trapdoor."

Carter shot him a glance, gripped the iron ring handle of the trap door, and heaved it up and open.

Captain Farnham stepped back, expecting a miasma of death and decay to assail him. Yet no stench of rotting flesh assailed him. Just a smell of ancient, musty nothingness.

"In you go, Carter."

Carter grimaced, a look of fear shadowing his face. "Captain—"

"Oh, come now, Carter, afraid of the dark? You always claimed to be the bravest man in the King's ordnance. Don't disappoint. We cannot simply leave the remains of the emissary in this dungeon. She must be afforded a decent burial."

"Captain, I do not fear dying. But this—"

A sound, a muffled scraping, came from the dark depths of the dungeon. Carter backed from the opening. "Saints preserve us."

The scraping sound ceased, and silence reigned for a moment. And they heard a voice. A woman's voice. "I should like to be free now, if you please. Kindly toss a rope down and we will chat."

Farnham took a moment to gather his wits. "You down there, who are you? How did you come to be sealed with the King's emissary?"

"I am the emissary of His Majesty, King James I. A rope, if you please."

* * *

Dublin

Farnham pushed his way through peasants and laborers outside the gate of Dublin Castle. Thousands thronged and buzzed in anticipation, eyes wide with excitement. The crowds surprised him; but then, this trial stirred peasants and titillated nobles, making it the event of the season, if not the entire year, in Dublin. News of the great witch trial swept the province, and the few facts known and shared had taken on lives of their own. The defendant, it was whispered, prowled and pranced about on cloven hooves. Fur—or scales, depending upon the teller—covered her body, and her tail writhed and twisted like a serpent.

Farnham presented himself to the scowling guards. After whispered discussion, one of them ushered Farnham inside and escorted him into a broad, high-ceiled room, the great banquet hall. The room bustled with the movement and animated conversations of three hundred men and women. He spotted his wife, Mary, and nodded to her. She smiled weakly in response, her face drawn and pale.

The guard waved Farnham to the front of the crowd and off to the side. A vast table of oak occupied the center, with three high-backed chairs, all empty. After a few minutes, a quartet of soldiers marched in and positioned themselves, two to a side at the ends of the table. Three men swept in behind and took their seats at the table, and the crowd fell silent.

Farnham knew the men. To the left and right sat Sir Hugh Colby and Sir Charles Lytton. Between them sat Sir Edmund Godfrey, a small man made large by virtue of heavy red robe, black mortar cap, and permanent discontent. Godfrey motioned impatiently to a boy, who hurried to hand him a parchment. Godfrey placed the document upon the table before him and studied it at length, his face darkening. Presently he looked up. "Fetch the prisoner," he said.

Two soldiers hauled a woman in filthy rags before the table and pushed her onto her knees. Her blonde hair hung limp and tangled, and dirt smeared her face. Yet beneath the young woman's squalid exterior, her eyes belied a quick, observant intelligence. Catherine Stokes. The tower house prisoner.

Farnham glanced about. As half-expected, no one seemed to represent the prisoner. Her surname bespoke humble origins; most certainly she was not high-born and of generous means. Yet somehow this tradeswoman had been selected by His Majesty to represent his government abroad. That the King had selected a woman to send on such an errand was unheard of. That meant something, so one could not underestimate the woman.

Godfrey studied the prisoner, read a bit more from his parchment, and looked again at her. "Catherine Stokes, you stand accused of witchcraft, a most serious crime in the eyes of God and King. Care you now to confess the crime, that we may end this trial and get on with our lives?"

"I do not confess, Sir Edmund."

Godfrey nodded to a scribe, who wrote furiously with quill and ink on a small table to the side. "Very well. Mister Williamson, record every word, omit nothing. This trial's record shall speak truths to future generations." He paused. "I have read the report of Captain Farnham and the statement of the traitor Merriwether. Have you anything to say in response?"

"I have not read those documents. I cannot respond."

"You traveled to the country two day's north of Cashel, accompanied by one of the King's soldiers, to treat with the traitor, at the behest of His Majesty, King James I."

"I did."

"What instructions did the King provide?"

"The King directed me to implore Merriwether to end his reckless behavior and return to loyal service immediately."

"And His Majesty would then grant clemency?"

"His Majesty might then let Merriwether live out his days. In the Tower of London. But Merriwether's family would be spared, stripped of title, lands, and rights, and released to move west and perhaps live as Irish."

"You delivered the message as directed?"

"Yes. And more."

Godfrey raised an eyebrow. "Well then?"

"I delivered it as commanded. But King James had no intention of letting the man escape execution. I added alternative suggestions."

"You offered alternatives to the King's wishes?"

"I am the King's emissary. His diplomat. Diplomats seek ways to end impasses."

"And your suggestions—?"

"That Merriwether accompany me to Dublin and London, to explain to His Majesty that Ireland is not England, that it has its own history, its own heroes and villains, its own language, its own gods and demons, and that it should be treated as an equal partner."

"What unbridled rubbish! Have you not seen this land? It is not the equal of England. It is not even the equal of France, or Spain, or Portugal. It is perhaps, if one uses license, the equal of the savage New World."

"I have seen many countries, known many peoples, spoken many languages, Sir Edmund. It is why I am the emissary and not you."

"Let the record show that the defendant misrepresented the King. Criminally poor judgement at best, treason at worst. Trending toward the latter." He leaned back in his chair and tapped softly on the table. "Bring the traitor forward."

Guards shoved Merriwether closer.

"Traitor," Godfrey said, "understand that you are not on trial. But you will hang. Useful information rendered might, however, ease your journey into the next world, be that one of fire or one of light. God hates traitors to England, but smiles upon those who aid the war against evil. We, and our God, acknowledge that you imprisoned this woman or monster."

"I didn't know she was a witch when she first arrived. I didn't know that until the next day."

"You realize that you draw a breath and elude the hangman only insofar as you may bear witness against the accused witch, do you not?"

Merriwether shrugged. "I am a dead man either way. Timing concerns me little."

"So be it. What became of the soldier accompanying Catherine Stokes?"

"He was killed by one of my men."

"So I have read. Do you care to explain the murder away?"

"When she differed from the wishes of King James, her soldier flew into a rage, drew his sword against her. I commanded him stop, but he swung mightily downward and the emissary fell back to avoid the blow. The blade sliced through her collarbone and two ribs. A frightful injury. My men ran the murderer through and killed him on the spot. The woman was gutted yet seemed not to care. No cry escaped her, though her blood fell in a torrent and she weakened and stumbled. My women bandaged her tightly in great haste, but I did not expect her to live the night. We plied her with whiskey to ease her suffering and provided her warm bedding and locked her in an empty room to recover. Or to die."

"Most hospitable of you."

"There was little to be done for her."

Godfrey motioned to a guard. "Strip the accused's tunic."

The guard tore the garments from the prisoner, exposing her breasts.

Godfrey looked at her and then back to Merriwether. "She hasn't a scratch upon her!"

"Aye, now ye begin to understand."

"You claim she has healed completely in the three months since?"

"Ye don't understand. She didn't have a mark the very next morning."

"Rubbish. No one can heal that quickly."

"Therein she must be attained a witch. And in my terror I committed her to the dungeon."

"And treated her well?"

Merriwether hesitated. "Your king sent a witch with frightful powers to bargain with me. I could think of no reason for James to do so other than to destroy me with black magic at little cost and no risk."

"Answer the question."

"We treated her accordingly."

Godfrey waited, his face darkening.

"I threw her into the dungeon to die," Merriwether finally said. "I did not need the agent of a despot in my house wielding the very powers of Satan against me. We gave her neither food nor water."

"You speak absurdities. The King's view of witchcraft is well known and his righteous attendance to the North Berwick trials bears this out. He will never allow a witch to live in his kingdom."

"Except perhaps to deal with Irish barbarians. A bad outcome for either is a good outcome for your king."

Godfrey scowled. "Captain Farnham. You freed the prisoner from the dungeon. What was her condition?"

"Filthy, yet healthy as now you see her. No signs of starvation or privation. No wounds. No bruises. Not even the slightest scar."

"Then you attest to witchcraft?"

"I attest only to what I report. I freed a woman who bore signs neither of abuse nor neglect."

"How do you account for it then?"

Farnham shrugged. "The simplest explanation is most always the correct one. Merriwether is a traitor to England and beneath contempt, and one must assume him a liar as well. I believe Merriwether treated and fed his prisoner well, and lowered her into the dungeon the very moment he saw our cannon arrive."

Merriwether snorted.

Godfrey tapped his fingers on the table. "And what, pray tell, does he gain by this? If he had treated the emissary as a guest, he might have somewhat mitigated his punishment."

"He is a clever fiend, no doubt. If he has half a brain, he knew defeat was imminent the moment we hauled cannon within range. He then hid the prisoner in the dungeon, bound and gagged, and planned to say that she had visited and left freely, never to return, or that perhaps she never even visited. Both lies are plausible, if we hadn't found the prisoner. Yet I am well-schooled in the architecture of tower houses."

Godfrey turned to Catherine Stokes. "And what do you claim to be the truth of the matter?"

"The good captain is correct, my lord. Lord Merriwether indeed treated me well, though under lock and key. I neither saw nor knew of a dungeon until the morning of the cannon's bark."

Merriwether laughed. "What a lying denizen of hell! What a damnable fiend!"

"But if such is the truth," Godfrey said, "it mitigates somewhat his crimes. He would have no reason to fabricate such a falsehood, so it rings true."

"A test of witchcraft, then! Take your knife. Wound her. Carve a 'W' in her forehead. I promise ye, by this time tomorrow there won't be a mark upon her, and ye'll have your proof."

"Slice up the hand-picked emissary of His Majesty? I think not. I have grown attached to my balls." Godfrey chuckled, and the audience joined him.

Farnham stepped forward. "If I may address this court?"

Godfrey gave the slightest nod of assent.

"I quartered in Scotland those few years ago and attended the North Berwick trials," Farnham said. "I saw the King's justice and wisdom on display. And I have studied at length the King's great work of scholarship, *Daemonologie*." He paused. "We have reached a delicate point. We have one here accused of high treason and another of witchcraft. Which is the worse crime? One is treason against England, the other against God. That is for greater minds than mine to decide." He turned to face the rapt crowd. "My lords, my countrymen, the honorable judge is in a spot. If he finds Stokes guilty, he can by law claim her possessions and wealth as his own."

A silence and stillness filled the great hall. Farnham glanced at Godfrey, who regarded him through narrowed eyes. "This is the great beauty of witch trials," he continued. "A pestilence is stricken from the country and the presiding judge walks away a wealthier man. An enticing proposition. I'm told that the honorable judge has a taste for gaming, yet lacks skill at it, and manages frequently to find himself in substantial debt. Just as he found himself in the gaming rooms of Edinburgh. The North Berwick trials provided lucrative, fortunate timing indeed. Speedy convictions of dozens of witches, and speedy confiscation of property by the judge. Within days, his gambling debts had evaporated."

Godfrey slapped the table. "Careful what you say, man!"

"Yet Stokes is a woman of little means, in spite of her high posting. She seems to have accumulated little wealth during her service to the King. Still, she is bound to have some small amount of money, so even though our fine judge finds himself again in debt, he stands to gain from a witchcraft conviction and much-needed securing of money.

"Sir Edmund Godfrey was dispatched from London for one task alone; preside over the treason trial of Merriwether, gain a conviction, and dispense immediate and harsh punishment. Send a message to the wayward English lords in Ireland. Sir Edmund prepared for the quick trial and conviction, but received a surprise. Merriwether was delivered to him but so was another, this woman Catherine Stokes, the King's own, accused of witchcraft.

"I witnessed the North Berwick trials. They came swift and ruthless, as so many confessions had been wrung from the defendants through torture. Godfrey is not about to torture the King's emissary, who professes her innocence. Yet he cannot sidestep the trial. He is forced, it seems, to find the accused guilty; there are many witnesses, and even though they attest to the impossible, under the King's moral authority their testimonials must be held to be true."

"You approach treason yourself, Captain," Godfrey said. "The King himself presided over Berwick, and you hint that his divine guidance was less than honorable. He shall know of this."

Farnham glanced at Mary. Her face was drawn with fear, her eyes glistening, pleading to go no further with this. He wavered; the path ahead lay fraught with mortal danger, not just for him but for Mary as well. But the past and his own failure as a man had returned to confront him and demand reconciliation.

With effort, he looked back at Godfrey. "Ah, Your Honor, I dare not question the wisdom and motives of the King! I seek, rather, to simplify this case for all." Farnham strode toward Catherine Stokes, and stopped a pace from her. "We have heard the extraordinary claims of Merriwether. Claims of miraculous power." A sudden movement, a glint of metal, and Farnham produced a knife and slashed the face of the accused.

The prisoner winced and cried out. But her reactions missed a beat, the merest of hesitations. Something seemed untrue, as if the wound alarmed the prisoner not at all.

Blood welled and spilled from the cut on her cheek. A deep, scarring cut, to be sure, but not a dangerous one.

The audience cried out. Godfrey sprang to his feet. "Damn you, man! What are you doing?"

"Putting accused and accuser to the test. If the witchcraft be true, by Merriwether's assertion she will be healed by tomorrow. If the accusation be false, she will remain cut deeply. I have given her a scar to bear for life, but in doing so I have given her life. She is no witch. You would try her and convict her on the testimony of a traitor, and burn her at the stake within the week. I stood by and watched this in Berwick; I shall not stand by again."

A terrible quiet filled the hall. Godfrey fixed his dark, narrowing eyes upon Farnham. "Very well, Captain. The court shall reconvene at noon on the morrow to consider the wound of the accused. And know ye this: protecting a witch implicates the protector in the same wicked practices. Interfering in a charge of treason implicates one equally in crime. These are principles of God's natural law, and of all civilized men. You are herewith jailed until your own guilt or innocence may be decided."

* * *

Farnham paced his cell in the New Gate Prison, thinking things through. It did not seem promising. He had put Godfrey in an untenable position, and no doubt the judge was concocting unpleasant outcomes for him even now. He had let the bastard off easy by making the decision for him, yet Godfrey would still demand his pound of flesh. The King would not abide a witch and would be satisfied with her execution. Godfrey could then count whatever small sums he would earn from the extinction of Catherine Stokes. Now, by Farnham's hand, Catherine Stokes stood at least a chance of release—scarred and bloodied, true—but her innocence intact. And if she were executed in spite of it all, the whispers of injustice would spread through the kingdom.

Both Farnham and Merriwether would hang.

So Farnham paced the inky blackness, unable to sleep. He stopped at the massive gate of crossed iron bars and tested it for the hundredth time, pulling it this way and that. It did not budge. Hannibal's elephants could not throw down this gate.

He reached through the bars and felt the keyhole for the lock. There would be no opening it. He withdrew his arm and sank to the floor, thinking of escape, going over the possibilities once more.

He'd searched every square inch of his cell. Useless. If there stood a chance of escape, it would be when someone from outside opened his cell or grew careless. So far that had not happened. The only time the door would be opened would be to escort him to his own trial and execution.

The cell possessed no flaws. In a century, perhaps, as the iron rusted and limestone masonry weakened. But he didn't have a century. He had at best three days.

He harbored no illusions on Godfrey's adjourning statement. The judge's eyes signaled an unsavory end for that transgression. Farnham had cast his lot with the fates of two prisoners. Either, and possibly both, would be found guilty of their crimes, and Farnham would be assigned their guilt as well.

If found guilty of treason, Farnham would be hanged or beheaded. If guilty of witchcraft, he would burn. No workhouse or hard labor punishments awaited, only death.

Why had he thrown himself into this position? His rashness consigned his wife to a life of misery. Poverty and scorn would be Mary's reward, alone in an uncaring world.

Why?

He had served to the best of his abilities. He'd fought the King's wars, spread the King's rule across growing lands and seas.

He knew why.

Scotland. Godfrey and James had presided over the trial of young Katie Williams of Edinburgh, his wife's sweet niece, in North Berwick. She, like James himself, hailed from Scotland. Yet the judge condemned her to the brutal punishments of the times. A mere thirteen years of age, and a witch, they called her!

For the crime of rebuking and revealing Godfrey's advances.

Sweet, innocent, murdered Katie, now a pariah in England and Scotland, cursed and excoriated as Edinburgh Kate.

The moment Farnham laid eyes upon Godfrey in Catherine Stokes's trial, he could not let the man repeat that crime. He'd cast his lot with the condemned, and now stood condemned himself.

The chill of the night crept into the cell and into his bones. A rain had commenced while they hauled him to the jail, and still fell for all he knew. Drops of water plinked onto the stone floor. Despite the cold and wet, he felt his eyelids grow heavy and the world drift from him.

Something, a sound, startled him awake. Had the day arrived, the day in which he would be charged with capital crimes of his own? He shook the slumbers from his mind, tried to clear his thoughts. He needed his wits today.

There . . . the sound again. Down the way, slow and stealthy. He strained to hear. Yes, someone approached, measuring footsteps. That perhaps meant relief. His jailers would certainly feel no need for stealth. Someone else lurked there.

The faintest of light, a glow, appeared down the corridor, and a single candle appeared.

Mary Farnham emerged slowly from the gloom, carrying the candle before her, looking this way and that.

"Mary! I'm here!"

His wife gasped and ran to him, her eyes wide. He reached through the bars and pulled her close. "What . . . how did you get in here?"

She held her fingers to her lips. "Shush, my darling," she whispered. "We must be quiet and quick." She inserted a long key into the lock, twisted it, eased the door open with a grinding of rusty iron, and stepped inside. They embraced and kissed. He felt the tears on her face. She took his hand, squeezed it, and led him from the cell. He crept toward the exit, the direction from which she'd come. She stopped, held his hand. "No. Not that way."

He looked at her. "I know this jail," he said. "It's the only way out."

Again, she pressed fingers to lips. She turned and headed in the opposite direction, pulling him after her.

The corridor turned once, twice. And Mary stopped before a cell. Sitting against the wall, Lord Merriwether looked up, surprise filling his eyes. "What's all this?"

"My question exactly," Farnham said.

"Quiet, the both of you!" Mary turned to her husband. "We must free him."

"Nonsense! Let us make our escape and quit this place at once."

"We must free him. I have promised his wife we would, and we owe your freedom to her."

Merriwether gasped and sprang to his feet. "To my sweet Saoirse!" He pressed his face to the bars, trying to see down the corridor. "Where is she?"

"She is—" Mary hesitated. "She is with the night guard, My Lord. Keeping him busy. It was the only way to draw him from his post."

Merriwether pulled back and looked at her. "She is—" He turned away, and back again. "By the saints, what a woman! This, Captain Farnham, is why I chose my sweet Irish bride. Can you imagine such a love from an English lady?"

Mary turned the key and Merriwether stepped out. "We must hurry," she said. "Saoirse has him occupied but his watch is to be relieved within the hour."

"Well, Captain Farnham. It appears we cannot find common ground, but our wives can."

"That would appear to be the case."

"Come," Mary said. "We must be away now."

"Wait," Farnham said. "Catherine Stokes. Where is her cell?"

Merriwether grunted. "Heavens, man! We must go."

"Her cell?"

Merriwether shook his head. "Very well. She is around the next corner, a few paces farther. And she is a witch and cursed to hell anyway."

"There are no witches, you fool. She won't die for your superstition." Farnham took the key and pushed past Merriwether. In a moment he stood before a dark cell. He could dimly make the shape of a woman against the far wall. "Mary, quick, the candle."

She hurried forward. Farnham turned the lock and opened the door. "Catherine Stokes, you are free. Step lively, woman."

"My thanks, my lords and lady." She stepped forward into the light.

Mary drew a sharp breath.

"Damn you, you see?" Merriwether said.

The hideous, deep cut that yesterday marred the woman's face from cheek to chin, the cut administered by Farnham himself, had vanished. Not the slightest mark remained. Farnham raised the candle to the woman's face, studying her.

"Then it is true," he whispered. "True."

"All that is true, my lord," Catherine Stokes said, "is that I have a remarkable capacity for healing. That is all."

"*All*? That is enough! Are you not a witch then? Are you not mortal?"

"I am not a witch. I am not mortal, either. I am . . . older than I look."

"Enough," Mary said. "Husband, do you bring this woman with us in escape or not? We cannot sit and debate it."

Farnham stared at Catherine Stokes, all certainty crumbling inside him. Magic was afoot here. There could be no other explanation. Yet as he looked into the intelligent, sincere eyes of this attractive young woman, and her impossibly cured face, he sensed nothing evil. Nothing. Just an unearthly . . . difference.

"Husband!" Mary said, squeezing his arm.

He must decide, and quickly.

"Catherine Stokes," he said. "Good fortune shines upon you tonight."

"My gratitude, Captain. I am indeed lucky and have led what you might say is a charmed life, having survived many a certain demise. Yet a burning at the stake would not be survived even by one as...durable as myself."

"Egads, fiend, I should say not," Merriwether said.

Mary waited no longer, and brushed past them all, headed for the way out.

* * *

By the time the guard discovered the escape, they had slipped down a dark Dublin lane, and hurried down the shingled beach of the River Liffey. There they waited silent, tense minutes. A faint tap of two sets of footsteps came to them, stopping in the blackness mere feet away.

"John?" a woman's soft voice called.

"Saoirse!"

Merriwether sprang forward and squeezed and kissed his wife and child.

Mary said, "We have arranged a boat, hidden just ahead. We will be on the sea and under sail in minutes and Dublin will be far behind us by daybreak."

"And where shall we go?" Farnham asked. "England is lost to me."

"Where we land matters not, my darling husband, as long as we are together."

"It matters immensely."

Merriwether stepped closer, pulling his wife and child with him. "It would seem ye are now much like me, lackey. An Englishman no longer welcome among the English. Care to become an Irishman?"

"Not especially." Farnham regarded the man for a moment. Merriwether's treason long preceded any misdeeds visited by him upon Stokes. Guilt covered the man like a shroud. Yet his story of Stokes's magic now rang true. Witchcraft? Perhaps. Or something else? Either way, the truth mitigated in small measure Merriwether's guilt.

"My family will begin anew—as peasants, in truth—in the northwest of Ireland. It is a wild, untamed country there. The tyrant James and his Dublin lackeys are far too busy pacifying the south and middle to worry about that land. Come, join us. Ye'll make a passable Irish man and woman."

Farnham sighed. Ireland. "And you, lady?" He held his lantern to the face of Catherine Stokes.

The strange woman remained quiet and still for a moment, her eyes distant, as if lost in thought, or eavesdropping upon faraway conversation. A smile ghosted her face. "Burnt offerings seem quite the fashionable punishment in Europe for misfits like myself, Captain Farnham. I should like to visit the Americas, I think. Peoples of wildly differing science and philosophy are being thrown together into a cauldron of a wholly different sort."

She paused and looked to the west. "Worlds are in collision. I am compelled to witness them."

Notes

Although the witch trials of Salem, Massachusetts, are rightly infamous in America, they pale in comparison to the persecution and slaughter that raged across Europe. It's estimated that more than 100,000 witch trials took place between 1450 and 1750, and 50,000 persons, three-quarters of them women, were found guilty and tortured and murdered by the authorities.

A charge of witchcraft was hard to beat and witch trials became institutionalized and lucrative for the accusers. An accusing judge could claim the wealth and possessions of the convicted as his own, and build up quite a fortune. So judges were incentivized to find guilt and extract accusations implicating others. Defending an accused witch often meant becoming the next target for accusation. Ireland had its own history with witch trials, the most famous being held in Kilkenny, but by far the greater number occurred on the Continent.

King James I—the very monarch that commissioned the *King James Bible*—did indeed initiate and oversee the North Berwick trials of Scotland in 1590, in which more than a hundred persons were accused as witches (at the time, he was James VI, King of Scotland, not becoming James I until he united England and Scotland in 1603). James built on his witch-killing expertise by authoring a tome titled *Daemonologie*, a work that inspired the witches of Shakespeare's *Macbeth*.

The New Gate Prison (later "Newgate") was an early *gaol*, or jail, originally built around the 12th century as part of the city wall, or gate, a short distance from Dublin Castle. Prisoners on or awaiting trial were usually held there or at a private tower nearby, Brown's Castle, also known as the Black Dog (no relation to the Led Zeppelin song). The first Newgate Prison was later replaced by another completed in 1781.

Europe is dotted with the remains of castles, and Ireland, although never a power on the order of England, France, or Germany, boasts more per square mile than any other country. Tower houses came into vogue as a later version of the traditional castle, designed as much as residences for the local lords as for defensive fortification. Nevertheless, their builders ingeniously planned and constructed them with defensive features—the machiolations, the crenellated tops, the narrow, twisting stairwells, the murder holes, the arrow loops—as described in "The Tower House Prisoner." The dungeon might be a tiny cell in the base or below the castle while its entrance might be in the top floor, making escape impossible. A prisoner might be lowered there, bound, and left without food and water until he or she died. I had the pleasure of spending a few days in 2016 in one such Irish tower house. As a guest, not a prisoner.

Bootlegging is a crime. But to some, it's a means of survival, and a lark and a story to others. The Prohibition and the Great Depression forged dangerous liaisons and unlikely relationships at times.

The Rum War

Brigands Key, Florida, February, 1932

Lou Denton scratched the stubble on his chin and knocked back another pull of Scotch whiskey, watching his boat with a hawk's eye from the second-floor loft of the warehouse, easing the heavy black shutter board aside. Watching his stolen boat.

Each sip of whiskey burned his gut. He didn't particularly care for the stuff, though it paid the bills and had gotten more popular than it had been when it was legal. But he needed it tonight. He needed to be a lot on edge and a little on drunk to go through with what needed doing. This promised to be a hard night, one he might not outlive.

They took his damn boat! *His* boat, his family's boat for fifteen years. Now being defiled by desk boys in the Coast Guard.

Goddamn crooks. They stole it, and with it a small fortune in goods.

He took another drink. This needed fixing, and soon. The window would slam shut and then it would be too late, maybe by tomorrow. The boat would be gone and he'd likely be in jail.

The sons of bitches already had Anna in jail. He shook his head. The girl had tried hard to do a good job, but weren't too damn smart, and not quick enough on her feet to get through a jam. Kind of lacked the Denton brains and mean streak.

But that didn't make him feel any better about it. She'd go to federal pen for a long time, and it was his fault. She couldn't sneak her way through.

He had to act tonight, but he couldn't pull it off alone.

A hand snatched the shutter from his own hand, slammed it shut, and slid a bolt down to lock it in place. "Damn you, Denton," Cleveland Ross said. "This is *my* joint. You ain't supposed to open the window any time, much less when the damn Coast Guard is in town."

"Your bar ain't a boat, Cleve, so the Coast Guard don't care."

"They'll tell the G-men. Jesus, you're stupid. Once more and you're gone."

Lou glared at him but sullenly took a seat. "Fine. Set me up with another Scotch."

"Two dollars, no credit."

"Two dollars! I sold you the damn stuff."

"You wanted whiskey, you should a kept some for yourself. Two bucks."

* * *

Lou huddled alone over a second whiskey, smoking a fifth cigarette. The joint had filled. All the rooms upstairs hummed with vice; this room—the biggest, the speakeasy—hummed the loudest. The other three rooms, peopled by ladies entertaining gentlemen, hummed quietly, with occasional shouts of gusto. Downstairs, all remained dark and quiet, a rusted rat-hole warehouse.

The booze flowed, the tinny piano played, the jokes drew laughs. A fistfight or two. Lou's friends, Pat Johnson and worthless Rabbit Abbott, strolled in, but they steered well clear of him. He couldn't blame them. When shadow business drags you into the light, you're pretty much on your own. You don't expect folks, who done the same things and worse, to stand up for you. They had mouths to feed.

But Lou needed help tonight.

So when two strangers entered, Lou kept a studying eye on them. One, a tall thin sort, a little too precious for dirty work, glanced around the joint with a tight-lipped, pasted grin and jumpy eyes.

The other, now there might be something to him. Not old, but weathered like Lou's old Minor League baseball glove, and built real stocky. A broad dark mustache sprawled across his square head. A little rough around the edges. Maybe just enough. Seemed a little too smart, but that might be a good thing.

The two men sat and ordered, and two glasses of beer soon appeared on their table.

Lou stubbed out his cigarette and sauntered over. "You gents mind some company?"

The dainty one said, "Well, actually, we were only going to linger here a minute or two."

"Settle down, Max," the other said. "Live a little. Sure, mister, pull up a seat." He waved to the bartender. "This beer's on me."

"Obliged," Lou said. "Name's Lou."

"Pleasure, Lou. Call me Ernest."

Lou studied him for a moment. "I seen you two pull a pretty boat into the harbor and tie up on the dock this afternoon. What you doin' in Brigands Key? Got business here?"

"Oh heavens no," Max said.

"We're tooling up the Gulf coast," Ernest said. "Up from Key West, fishing and sightseeing. We might make it to New Orleans, haven't quite decided yet."

Lou nodded towards the beer glasses. "Ain't you heard alcohol is illegal in this country?"

"We heard a rumor to that effect." He raised his glass in a toast. "To rumors."

"So you ain't a goody-goody. That's a start. Listen. You want to make fifty dollars each tonight?"

Max smirked. "Oh my. Fifty dollars. I don't think—"

"Shut up, Max," Ernest said. His eyes glinted. "That's a lot of money. What's a man have to do to make fifty bucks in one night?"

"Steal a boat back that's been stole from me."

"Why don't you just call the cops?"

"'Cause it's the cops that stole it. I'm gone to steal it back from them Coast Guard sons of bitches."

"Oh my," Max said. His smirk evaporated. "I don't think—"

"Shut up, Max," Ernest said. "This is becoming a good story. Why don't you go back to the room?"

Max pushed his chair away from the table and rose quickly. "Gladly. I need to arrange enough money cabled to pay your bail tomorrow. Or begin funeral arrangements." He dropped a dollar on the table and hurried away.

Lou watched him go. "He ain't gone to blow the whistle on us, is he?"

"Max? Hell no. I'm his meal ticket. He's not particularly fond of adventure."

"Adventure? This ain't no game, mister. Like the fancy boy said, you might get shot before the night's through."

Ernest leaned back, and seemed to consider that. "Tell me the story so I can see if this is worth sticking my neck out."

"What story? You drink booze, and that's against the law. I reckon damn near everybody is a lawbreaker now. Anyway, you drink it, and I haul it in, mostly from Cuba. I didn't have no trouble with the old Coast Guard Six-Bitters. They was too slow. Now they got them CG-400s, and them sons of bitches haul ass. So my boat, the *Pilar*, got caught this morning out on the Gulf. I wasn't on her this trip, but my first mate was."

"*Pilar*. I like that. Your first mate, what's his name?"

"Anna."

Ernest nodded. "Your first mate, you say?"

"It ain't like that. She's my dimwitted sister. Anyhow, they was gone skipper or tow *Pilar* all the way to Mobile. I know what happens next; they either sell her, re-commission her into one of their own, or scuttle her. I aim to not let any of them things happen. It's my goddamn boat."

"I assume you had contraband aboard."

"Don't get fancy. She ran full-loaded with whiskey and rum. There ain't nothing can be done about that now. That's a loss, and a big one. I aim to get on board and get my sister out. She ain't going to prison on account of me. You uncomfortable with that?"

"Not unreasonably so. In fact, it almost smacks of chivalry."

"After they hijacked *Pilar* and arrested Anna, they'd a gone straight off to Mobile. They figured *Pilar* was based here out of Brigands Key, and the last thing they wanted was to have to bring her in here, amongst the riffraff. But I had a bit of luck today, first time ever. The CG gunboat had engine trouble, and the *Pilar* wouldn't have held up towing something that big all the way to Alabama. Their mechanic up and got too sick to stand, much less fix an engine. So they was stuck puttin' in here for the night. They rustled up a new mechanic, Bobby Watson, to fix her come morning. So I got until daybreak. I been watching. They still got Anna down in the hold of *Pilar*, and one guy keeping an eye on her, and God knows what else. The rest of their crew is on the gunboat. I count six, all told."

"Lou, this has disaster written all over it. I'm in."

* * *

Lou held back in the shadows, watching first the *Pilar* and then Ernest. The *Pilar* nestled snugly moored to the dock, tied fore and aft with heavy lines. The Coast Guard boat, a seventy-eight footer, rocked gently alongside *Pilar's* starboard, lashed to her and the dock, pinning her into place. She was going nowhere until that Coast Guard boat cleared out.

From the north, the beacon of Hammond Lighthouse swung its arm of light across the island, each pass brightening the waterfront for an instant.

The day had been overcast, but that cover had blown away and a full moon hung high in the east. Damn the bad luck; need good weather, you get a mess. Need bad weather, you get a clear beautiful night with moonlight on the water. Too late to worry about that, though.

He'd studied Ernest when the guy had first pulled up the channel. The guy oozed college boy, but had nails and broken glass in his gut, and pain, too, and knew his way around a boat. Now the guy showed just the opposite, just like they'd planned, like a rich man with too much boat not enough sense.

Ernest sauntered down the dock, whistling like a goddamn playboy, and stepped onto the *Pauline*. Lou had taken note when she first berthed in Brigands Key. Nice looking craft, a sportsman's boat, polished wood and brass and all that rich-man stuff, maybe twenty-eight feet long.

The main dock jutted a hundred yards from the inland side of the island, pointed like a middle finger at the mainland. Smaller docks teed out from the main dock, about half occupied by the commercial trawlers. In better times, ever last one would be occupied, but the

Depression wiped out a slew of them and drove them off to other places. The ones that stayed in business, like Lou, did a little moonlighting.

Kerosene lanterns washed a good bit of the dock in a dim orange. A couple of CG sentries, carbines slung over their shoulders, stood fore and aft on the deck of their gunboat, the meanest-looking vessel on the waterfront. The aft sentry seemed jittery, like he was watching Ernest too. The one on the bow sat cross-legged on the deck with a deck of cards, playing solitaire. Lazy son of a bitch.

Ernest fiddled about on the *Pauline* for a few minutes, trying to look busy, rustling about in a locker, and withdrawing a can. Lou knew what he was up to. Ernest glanced at the cutter, and moved aft with the can and a paint brush. He dipped the brush into the paint and leaned out over the transom as if to inspect something, and slopped paint over the name of his boat. He'd already yammered on about not getting caught up in Lou's felony. Smart. A college boy.

The paint job done, Ernest stowed the brush and can, and unhitched his mooring lines. He went into the pilot house and a moment later, his engines purred and churned up the water behind the boat, and he eased it away from the dock.

Lou looked at his watch. It turned four A.M., not an unreasonable time to get seaward for daybreak fishing. The seaman aft kept an eye on *Pauline* as she drew nearer.

Pauline's engines throttled up a bit, and the boat gained speed, maybe to six knots. Not what fishermen like to see in a too cozy harbor around the boats that put food on their tables, but exactly what you'd expect from a rich playboy.

The *Pauline's* engines suddenly died, and Ernest glanced about, looking puzzled and concerned. The boat plowed ahead with momentum now.

Lou pumped his fist. This stupid idea just might work.

The *Pauline* closed toward the CG now, and Ernest made a show of frantically trying to restart the engines.

The alert seaman leaned closer. "Ahoy," he shouted. "Control your vessel. You're coming too close, too fast." The lazy one glanced up, and slowly got to his feet.

"I can't," Ernest called back. "The engines died, just like that. Can't get 'em up again."

"Damn, man," the seaman called, "you don't need power, just turn the wheel and rudder her away."

Ernest, looking panicky, faked a hard twist of the wheel, and fake-twisted it back again. "I can't get a response!"

The *Pauline* closed in on the CG.

"Shit!" the seaman cried. "Sound the alarm!"

The lazy bastard aft sprang to a mounted bell and rang it furiously.

"I can't turn," Ernest wailed.

Lou slipped out of the shadows and hurried to the dock. The two seamen on the CG deck stared at the *Pauline*. It looked to plow straight into them.

At the last second, the *Pauline* edged out of the straight-on collision course and struck a glancing blow. There came a sound of splintering wood. The CG-400 lurched. Men shouted, curses flew through the air.

The sailor on the *Pilar* bolted up and stared at the commotion.

Come on, Lou thought. Get off my livelihood and go help your pals.

The man stayed with his post.

Lou had no choice. He sprinted down the dock.

In the corner of his eye, he saw Ernest glance at him. The *Pauline*'s engines roared, and the craft drove into the side of the CG, pushing it around. More shouting.

"I can't stop," Ernest cried. "Now it's stuck!"

Lou reached his boat and leapt aboard, hurling himself full into the Guardsman. The man went down with a thud, and Lou slugged him in the mouth. The man slumped and rolled, stunned. Lou snatched his revolver and threw it overboard.

The sailor was just a kid. A damn big one. Lou had gotten the drop on him, but when the kid came to, he'd manhandle him, and at any moment the other sailors were going to see that trouble had commenced aboard their rum war prize. Ernest waved and shouted, a crazy man now, and hurled oaths and threatened each and every sailor who ever wore the Coast Guard uniform with lawsuits that would bankrupt them.

No time to lose.

Lou tried the door on the wheelhouse. Locked. He grasped a fire axe from underneath the gunwale and smashed the lock and pushed the door in.

Anna bounded out, grinning. "I knew you'd come!"

"Shut up, girl." He took her hand and pulled her along. He whispered instructions and pushed her out onto the dock. She knelt in the shadows.

He reentered the wheelhouse, reached underneath his jacket, and pulled out a taped bundle of three sticks of dynamite. He wedged it into a locker against the lower hull, took out a match, and lit the fuse.

He ran.

On deck, the sailor stirred and looked dazedly about. Lou punched him again and heaved him up onto the dock. He looked at the commotion on the other boats. Five crewmen swarmed about, screaming at Ernest, who waved and stabbed a finger at them, shouting back. Ernest saw him, turned back to his wheel, and spun it starboard.

A crewman turned and saw Lou, who scrambled onto the dock. The crewman shouted and drew a sidearm. The revolver roared, and Lou felt something sting his foot with fire. Another gunshot, and splinters of wood flew from the dock.

Lou took two steps and collapsed to his knees, the damage to his wrecked foot too great. Pain blossomed with each step, and he marveled at how goddamn important a foot was. And how goddamn much it could hurt.

The shooter took three swift strides closer, until he loomed close over Lou. He steadied himself, and drew aim at Lou's face. He'd lost any interest in taking a prisoner. And at that range, he couldn't miss.

"Hey, you son of a bitch," Ernest shouted. He twisted the wheel hard and shoved the throttle.

The shooter hesitated, glanced at Ernest. Lou rolled sideways. The gun roared and a hole appeared in the deck of the *Pilar*. The crewman swore, shook his head, and leveled his weapon again.

The *Pauline* pulled free of the CG-400 with a lurch and a groan. The crewmen stumbled. The *Pauline* spun back to port and banged against the end of the dock.

"Now, Anna!" Lou shouted.

They ran toward the *Pauline*.

The explosion roared behind them. Chunks of fiery debris sprayed about.

They leapt on board the passing boat, and Ernest heeled it hard to starboard and opened the growling engines wide. *Pauline* shot away into the channel.

Lou turned to watch. The sailors scrambled about, one of them firing wildly at them with his revolver. The captain directed this and that, demanding the chase begin.

Pilar rolled onto her side and settled lower. Flames crept up the side of the wheelhouse. Air escaped her with a sigh and she sank still lower. And then she slipped under.

The lines linking her to the CG-400 drew tight, and the boat heeled over as the sinking boat pulled it downward. The captain yelled and pointed everyone to the new threat and the crewmen scrambled to unhitch or sever the lines. Too late. The bow of the vessel went low and wedged under the dock with a shriek of metal and a splintering of wood.

The gunboat ground to a stop.

Gunshots chased the *Pauline* in eruptions of white foam as the bullets struck water.

* * *

Pauline sped into the blackness of the open Gulf, bouncing along on waves, its running lights dark.

"Where to?" Ernest shouted.

"Hell, I don't know. Veer south, drop us at Cedar Key. We'll hitch a ride out of Florida from there." He peered down at his foot. Slippery wetness filled his shoe, and blood seeped from it. "Son of a bitch plugged me in the foot! I'm gone have to buy new shoes now."

"Christ, man, you need a doctor."

"I reckon that's so."

"And you scuttled your own vessel! I thought this was a rescue only."

"Hell, what did you think, I could keep out of reach of those Revenuers? They knew the *Pilar* now, and they got bigger, faster, meaner boats of their own."

"But why . . . ?"

"Principle, son. I put a lot of sweat into that boat, but it weren't no living human being. I got my little sister out, but I'll be damned if I let them sons of bitches commandeer my boat and make it a Revenuer boat. It ain't right. I don't expect you to full understand, but some folks got it made and most folks ain't. Haves and have-nots. I reckon I'm one of them have-nots, and it don't look to ever change." He thought for a moment. "Besides, it weren't a total loss. By now, all them hundreds of bottles of whiskey and rum will be bobbing on the surface of the channel, being picked up by the good folk of the island. That'll be my late Christmas present to 'em, 'cause I sure didn't get them nothing else."

Ernest nodded, scratching his whiskers. "This will make one hell of a story."

"It might, son. But me and Anna's got to start over somewhere else, so don't go using my name in your goddamn book."

"What book?"

"Listen, you ain't as anonymous as you think and I ain't as illiterate as I sound."

Anna spoke up, grinning. Her red hair caught the fire of the sun as dawn broke. "And you ain't as lucky as you think, Lou. You thought it was a lucky bit of engine trouble that brought *Pilar* into Brigands Key? Ha! Coast Guard's got top-drawer mechanics."

"So?"

"So, their engines don't run so good when they got a bag or two of sugar in the carburetors. And their mechanic don't feel so good when he's got half a bottle of castor oil in his food."

"I'll be damned. How'd you manage that?"

"Sailors will do anything to impress a pretty girl. Now you think I'm smart?"

"I think you might turn out to be a pretty fair Denton after all."

"One hell of a story," Ernest said. He opened a small locker in the side of the wheelhouse and withdrew a bottle of rum. "By my reckoning, we just passed the twelve-mile limit. Drink up."

"Well," Lou said, taking the bottle. "Long as it's legal."

Notes

Demon Rum. My father once told me of my grandfather's investment in a "fishing boat" outfit in Depression-era Daytona Beach. In reality, it was a bootlegging boat. Don't get the wrong idea; it's not like Granddaddy—a bricklayer by trade—was Al Capone or something. Times were tough, and he moved the family around trying to find enough work to feed them. Bootlegging was a valued trade, because, frankly, no one quit drinking just because it was illegal. Stupid law.

"The Rum War" delves into the waning days of the Prohibition in the bare-knuckled island town of Brigands Key, never a place to shy away from doing the dirty work the rest of society demands.

Nothing like a good scratch to fix an itch. Sometimes, even that's not enough.

Itchy

It began seven, eight months ago; I've lost track. I *think* I know why it started.

My left arm was in a plaster cast at the time, one that went from hand to elbow. I had earned it while cleaning leaves out of the roof gutter. I reached too far, just a little too far, stretching with the rake, tipping my ladder, ending up giving myself a nasty break of the forearm.

Doctor Wicks encased my arm in a heavy, ponderous cast that, I'd heard, was largely obsolete these days. Aren't they using much lighter casts now? They should be. A nurse with clenched hair laughed and said, yes, they are, but Doctor Wicks, bless his heart, is Old School, and love him some bulk and plaster, tons of it, in his casts. The cast soon bore the signatures and well-wishes of friends, and wasn't too much of a bother. Being right-handed, I didn't consider it a hindrance. For a couple of weeks anyway.

Then it started itching.

I first noticed it while at the office. A minor irritation, a mere notion of an itch, way down under the cast. So I ignored it, and like most itches it disappeared in a couple of minutes. Mind over matter.

It returned the next day to aggravate me enough to take my mind off work. I poked a pencil underneath the cast to scratch the offending flesh. I managed to reach the itch and relieve it. I recalled the cast I wore as a little boy and the itch it had also caused. That's the thing about casts. Knitting bones and decaying skin decay like lawn grass under a board. They always itch.

And so it went for a couple of days.

I awoke suddenly in the third night, clawing at my broken arm. The flesh tickled maddeningly, as if the epidermis had sprouted spider legs and wanted to crawl away. I turned on the light, peered underneath the cast, scratched with a finger as far under the plaster as I could reach. Blessed relief! But only for a second. I scratched with a pencil; that felt better, but the whole area beneath the cast itched, and I couldn't reach it all, and what I could reach, I couldn't scratch all at the same time. I got out of bed, hurried to the closet, found a wire coat-hanger, straightened it, bent it to my tool-making will, and scratched like there's no tomorrow. That brought some relief; I probed the length and breadth of the cast. Salvation was mine.

But I still couldn't scratch all the itchy skin at once.

It itched everywhere, as if someone tickled it with a down feather. Scratching only served to incite it. If I stopped, it itched even more.

That long, damned night stretched into an eternity of torture.

I called Wicks's office first thing in the morning but couldn't get an appointment with him until the day after. The son-of-a-bitch's receptionist said his schedule was full, but she agreed to squeeze me in. I could hear her rustling papers for my benefit, making a reasonable sound of business. As for the absent Wicks, I suspect he was golfing.

When I finally got to see the good doctor, he seemed to think the itch was funny. Comedy gold. A grin lit his jowly red face. "Come now, Mr. Jenkins. It's a good sign. Shows there's some good mending going on. Tissue recombining, and all that."

"I haven't slept in three nights."

"Oh, you're just paying too much attention to it. It'll pass. Napoleon had the same thing you know, on his stomach. Haw!" Wicks had this annoying habit of snorting—*Haw!*—whenever he tried to make a joke.

"I want the cast to come off," I said.

"Don't be silly. It's much too early for that."

"I want it off anyway."

"Mr. Jenkins, malpractice costs too much for me to even consider it. Relax. It'll go away. You'll see."

I finally got to sleep that night, with the aid of pills.

At the office, the itch was relentless. I fell behind in my work, attracting the attention of my boss, Robertson. I tried to ignore it when I saw him coming, and leaned into my desk with a determined look, only to be distracted as soon as I was alone again. I could look busy, but damned if I could get any work done. Robertson, looking quite grim, growled at me to get on the ball.

I began taking greater numbers of sleeping pills at night, and I hid a bottle of whiskey—and a lot of breath mints—in my desk drawer at the office. Alcoholic numbness proved a minor savior. It helped for a while; I could keep my mind on work for greater lengths, proportionate to the number of drinks I sneaked. I had to keep tweaking the dosage—upward, of course—in order to maintain that balance. That was in the third week of my torture.

By the fourth week, the itch had crept from the dark confines of the cast and spread to my shoulder. It produced no visible difference of the skin, by itself. Yet incessant scratching reddened and angered my flesh. No scars, no sores, no welts. Just an angry, creeping, driving itch.

I made another appointment with Doctor Wicks. He furrowed his brow, feigning concern about the "rash," and recommended some wonder goop. Again he refused to remove the cast. The time wasn't right. Knitting bones and all that shit.

The goop was a waste of time. I applied it in dabs at first, and great gobs after. Whiskey and pills offered fleeting and fading relief.

I lost my job in the fifth week. Robertson gave me until five o'clock to clean out my desk. He used alcoholism and lack of productivity as the excuse to screw me out of my severance. I bent the antenna on his Cadillac on my way out.

In the sixth week the cast came off.

Wicks was pleased with his handiwork, said the bone had mended beautifully. Suggested a specialist for the rash, which had spread to my chest and back. "And go easy on the scratching," he advised, grinning his fat toothy grin. "I once had a cat that scratched itself to death. Damnedest thing you ever saw. Can't have you in the same mess, can we? Haw!"

I looked up the specialist and made an appointment. He stood tall and angular, and liked to overdo the earnest, concerned act, I assume to compensate for his rampant youth. He sported a dark hipster suggestion of a beard, and hipster blue jeans. For me, it was hate at first sight.

He examined my skin, poking it, scraping it, pulling at it, and listened to my story of pill eating and alcohol guzzling, and of empty sleepless nights. He did something rare to his profession, and admitted he had no idea what in hell was making me itch, had never seen anything like it. He promised to call in other specialists from Omaha. Maybe they would recognize the malady. In a few days, they would all arrive to examine me. Meanwhile, I would just have to bear the unbearable.

My money was running out, but I still had insurance and I started collecting a meager unemployment check. The job outlook was bleak; that bastard Robertson had branded me in the industry as a careless drunk, so I couldn't even get a decent job interview.

One afternoon at my neighborhood liquor store, *Lou's Booze, Cigs, and Vape*, purely on impulse, I sneaked a pint of whiskey under my jacket while the clerk studiously arranged a display of beef jerky treats. Back home, I gulped it down and hated myself. I fell into the sweet fat arms of sleep.

The specialists came and poked at me. They ran tests by the dozens, studied skin and blood samples, prodded, tweezed, squeezed, and referred to many volumes.

Still no answer.

At last, they summoned me and gave me opinions. Must be genetic, they surmised, something locked within my DNA, something that had reared its ugly head well into my life. Damn the crapshoot of the genes, they said, tugging stylishly short whiskers. They couldn't prescribe a cure, but speculated that it might run its course and eventually disappear. But why did it attack me now, I demanded. Well, they said, we think it was dormant, possibly never to awaken, but the cast on your arm irritated the skin and caused some decay. Must have triggered it. Funny, they said, that type of cast seems unwarranted and a bit overdone for the type of fracture sustained.

That was six months ago.

The itch has not run its course. It has spread to my face, my legs, my right arm. Even to my balls. My life is a clogged toilet full of shit; I have no job, no money, no health. Relief comes only after drinking myself into a stupor. But the bad thing about a drunken stupor is, it eventually passes.

As I write this with one hand, scratching myself with the other, the itch is prickling even my scalp and the soles of my feet. Cripes, even my eyeballs itch. I can't stand it. I have to avoid the bottle until I finish this, though. Must be clear. I refuse to endure another six months of this skin-crawling hell, nor even another six minutes.

The pistol in my desk drawer will see to that.

One other thing. The worthless specialists discovered that a solution of my blood caused a furious scratching in lab rats. The little vermin literally scratched themselves to death. Odd, the specialists thought, and they went back to more lucrative patients.

Odd indeed.

Just like Doc Wicks's damned cat. I think Wicks carries something from that cat and gave it to me, activating it with his Paleolithic cast technique. That's what I think.

A few nights ago, I broke into Wicks's dark house. I eased like shadow into his bedroom, and came alongside his bed. I could hear his long, slow breathing, and the mildest of a contented snore. I held my breath, and cracked the sleeping doctor's forearm with a hammer. He shot bolt upright and screamed. I ran from the room, listening to him howl in pain, and sped off into the night.

I checked on the good doctor this morning. He had directed the placement of one of his ponderous casts, from his hand to his elbow.

He scratched and gouged beneath it with a pencil.

Haw!

Notes

When I was a third-grader, I one day wisely rode my bicycle along the top of a sandy ditch in the woods behind our house. The loose sand performed like loose sand will, and shifted, and so did the bike, and I was airborne for a fraction of a second, and executed a landing in the bottom of the ditch. My arm was broken and I spent an eternity in a great heavy cast. Itched like crazy.

With the brush we merely tint, while the imagination alone produces color.

—*Théodore Géricault*

The *Medusa* Jump

Part I
The Louvre, Present Day

Corinne DuChamp, pragmatic and skeptical, was never one for silly chatter about premonitions. Still, the feeling that she'd reached her own crossroads between past and future electrified her today.

Easy, girl, she told herself. *Be ready.*

She moved through the galleries of the Louvre, drinking in the sights, her life shifting with each moment. She belonged here. Here, in her cathedral of art.

Today made Corinne's fourth visit in four days, and she'd already been here six hours today. She would immerse herself, know every painting, every nick in their frames, every play of light and shadow on the marble statues. Her job interview loomed, thrilling and terrifying. It would be Friday. *Tomorrow.* She was one of just eleven to be interviewed, a select few pared down from hundreds of applicants. The other finalists boasted more experience than her. Three already sat on staff. Daunting odds, but she would nudge them in the right direction by knowing the museum like an old friend.

It was a chilly offseason day, midweek, the best time to visit the great museum, away from the thronging mobs of summer. She could negotiate the galleries without negotiating hordes of grumbling tourists. She mentally ran through notes on the great paintings all about her, stopping to scroll through her tablet to check this or that, to uncover obscure gems about them. It would be interview suicide to bungle facts about the greatest of the artworks. They must be second nature, recitable as if in casual conversation.

Corinne's feet ached, and she glanced at her watch. The hours had caught up with her. Today she'd limited herself to the Denon Wing, having plowed through Sully and Richelieu the two previous days. But Denon in itself comprised a vast collection. Just one more hour. Or two. The job meant too much to ease up now, but a bit of a rest would help her rally. She entered the Mollien Room, and the blessed, broad, cushioned benches in the center beckoned. She sank onto the end of the empty bench, and exhaled. Mollien's openness, with its blonde parquet floor, its towering rose walls, its vast skylight high above, calmed her. Artists and art lovers would sit in the middle of the bench, the better to appreciate and sketch. Bored teens would sit at the end communing with phones, scarcely noticing the paintings. Her own motive was simple. If she sat at the end of the bench, she cut in half the chances of engaging with someone.

And there was always someone. Usually a middle-aged man who'd eased away from his wife to sit by the young, pretty brunette. Impress her with his worldly knowledge, self-importance, and fake sensuality.

Corinne looked down at her tablet, scrolled through notes, typedin a few more, and returned her attention to the Mollien Room's glorious French Romanticist paintings, mentally ticking off the artist and title of each. As always when she settled in this gallery, she finished her appraisal with the gigantic Théodore Géricault canvas, *The Raft of the Medusa*.

She studied its careful composition, the arrangement of volume and mass, the sweep of the eye from element to element, crafted for drama and emotion. The vision of death and despair and hope on a tossing ocean dared you not to look. She pitied the paintings near it.

Corinne stirred from her reverie when someone sat upon the other end of the bench. A sideward glance revealed an elderly man.

Corrine continued to admire the Géricault.

After a moment, the man sighed. "Stunning, isn't it?"

Don't engage. "Mm," Corinne said, not turning. She felt a small sharp stab of guilt. Years of self-suppression warred with her compulsion to accommodate, so often to her own detriment. After a moment, she said, "Yes." Perhaps he would take the hint. But they never do.

And he didn't. "What do you suppose Monsieur Géricault missed?"

The question surprised and annoyed her. She glanced at him. He seemed harmless enough; an older man, well-dressed and groomed, wavy gray hair, dark brown eyes. His French was fluent yet tinged with an accent she couldn't place. She looked back to the painting. She knew its details as well as—or better—than anyone she knew. "It's not a photograph, you know. It's an interpretation."

"The men all look a little too robust, don't you think? They're adrift and starving. Sea life in that time was hard enough, and deprivation the norm, even when all is going well."

He made sense; the survivors exuded strength and power, some thin, but all muscular. None emaciated. "Géricault expressed an ideal of the common man," she said defensively, realizing the answer sounded rehearsed. "And besides, they'd only been adrift thirteen days before being rescued."

"Thirteen days starving on a raft. Everyone should try it."

Corinne withdrew pad and pencil from her satchel and began sketching, a detail of the survivor waving a cloth, hoping the man could take a hint. Several minutes of silence followed, but he remained seated. At last, he turned to her again. "I need to tell you something, Mademoiselle DuChamp."

She spun to him as he spoke her name, fear stabbing her thoughts, her skin tingling. She looked about, searching for a security guard, spotting one standing resolutely in the corner.

"Don't be afraid, Corinne."

"You're spying on me?"

"Only today."

She stuffed her pad and pencil back into the satchel. "Keep away from me, old man."

"I met Théodore Géricault," he said. "Such an intense, engaging young fellow."

At first, she'd imagined herself the object of some elderly man's misguided sexual fantasies. Then the attentions of a stalker. Now it was worse; the man was out of touch with reality.

"You've done your homework, Corinne. You will do well in your interview tomorrow."

She hesitated, her thoughts racing. How could he know about the job? Was he in the employ of the museum? How else could he know of her job interview?

"I no longer want the job," she snapped, gathering her belongings and stuffing them into her bag. "I'd rather sketch caricatures for tourists in the Tuileries."

"I'm not with the Louvre in any capacity."

She stood and took a step towards the security guard, but stopped. The guard glanced at her, his eyebrows arching with concern and questions.

"My son studied you at great length," the old man said. "It's because of you that he could study Géricault and all these others. And the reason I'm here."

"I'm going now."

"This is your cathedral, is it not?"

She stopped.

"Your cathedral of art."

She tensed. She had never shared her secret name for the Louvre. With anyone. Not her father, who cared little for art, nor her mother, a talented, shy watercolorist who had succumbed to breast cancer when Corinne was eleven. Not her little brother. Not to friends. She had never even committed the phrase to her notes or diary, fearing she may sound sentimental.

"How . . . why do you say that? Guess that?"

"It's in my son's book. Please, Corinne, sit a moment. Hear my story. My son's story. It will help you tomorrow."

Against her better judgment, she sat. "Two minutes," she said. He smiled gently. "Thank you for your moment's trust and I—"

"Your name?"

The man hesitated, as if debating the wisdom of divulging. "Ah, well. It's the least of my worries at this point. My name is Henri Komarov-Banks."

"Sounds made up."

"May I begin? My two minutes will be up soon."

"Speak."

"My son, Marcel, has made a name for himself as an art historian. Not to be too boastful a father, I daresay he has become one of the four or five best in the world. He did so by focusing his expertise. Like the best, he concentrated and specialized." The man gestured toward *The Raft of the Medusa,* and swept his arm around the room. "French Romanticism. Your favorite as well."

"Hm."

"Marcel has made the Romantic movement his life's work, immersing himself in it, experiencing the art first hand, not just brooding over moldy treatises."

"So he visits museums and private collections. Good for him."

"More than that. He's dived headfirst into inspiration, environment, and context. What fuels the artist's passion? What makes a painting *live*?"

Something buzzed in Corinne's mind. She'd often felt the same desire to know.

"Are my two minutes up?"

She studied the man. Something so familiar about him. "Do I know you?"

"We've never met."

She wasn't so sure. Something bothered her, coiled below the surface. Alarms had gone off in her mind, but his calmness dulled them. "I don't know any art historians named Marcel, top ones or otherwise."

"He isn't well known yet."

"But you said—"

"He'll be world-renowned in three hundred years."

"Ah, a misunderstood genius, years ahead of his time. Marcel keeps good company."

Komarov-Banks nodded toward *The Raft of the Medusa.* "You understand, of course, why this subject became the fevered project of a Romantic idealist?"

"Out of frustration with the restored monarchy."

"Corinne, stop. Stop reciting history, and *feel* it. When the loss of the *Medusa* struck, it tore at the French conscience. You can see from Géricault's sketches how he struggled to find the exact moment to capture, to tell the story as if he'd witnessed it himself. Most casual viewers today see an exciting shipwreck and survival, but without context. Géricault knew his fellow citizens and the feelings burning in them. This was his clarion call to them. Centuries later, the painting survives. It survived even the second world war, spirited away from this museum disguised as theatrical scenery to keep it out of Nazi hands. And here it is, the passion still bursting off the canvas, even though most viewers have no idea of its context. My son has been writing a book about it. He wanted to experience its origins firsthand."

"Rather impossible," she said reflexively.

"From your perspective. Listen. My son has written and published seven books on Romanticist art and the Louvre's collection."

"I would know of such books, but I don't. What's your game?"

"Ah! I use the wrong tense, a frequent mistake. I said Marcel has written and published these books. What I meant is that he *will*."

"You seem pretty sure. You must be the one who'll publish Junior's books."

"He was writing the new book."

"Was? Changing tense again?"

"It's a matter of perspective. He both *will* write these books and he *has* written them. I have a story to tell you."

Part II
New Stockholm, 2367 AD

I leaned forward in my apartment, staring at my son in disbelief. My boy—Marcel was thirty-two, but still a boy to me—had that earnest, passionate look on his face that told me all I needed to know. "Marcel, listen to me. It's still a bad idea. A terrible idea."

"Dad, I need to see the *Medusa* to understand it. To experience it. I need you to make it happen. No one else can."

"And I won't."

"This book will be my crowning achievement. I can feel it. It just needs authenticity. Truth."

"Time travel seduces us, Marcel, but things can go wrong and they do."

"Dad! Five decades of temporal expeditions have not once changed the world. Not in the slightest. In spite of accidents, in spite of overshoots, our world is unchanging. What difference does it make if an expedition flops?" He threw up his hands. "You and I will still be here in this moment having this same damned conversation."

"That's what we think, not what we know. So we try to manufacture a little insurance. Temp jumpers are carefully screened and trained, and then we monitor and regulate the hell out of them."

"So regulate the hell out of me. But send me. Please, Dad, I'm begging you."

I sighed and leaned back. I could make it happen. I'd clawed my way up the stifling ranks of the Temporal Manipulation Congress to earn a seat on the Expeditionary Council, one of only seven persons in the five worlds that could authorize a temporal jump. Once there, I earned a reputation for uncompromising adherence to protocol and safety. I simply refused to let anyone bend jump rules. Only ninety applicants had ever been approved for a jump, each strictly monitored and accompanied by a Council member.

"Marcel," I said at last. "It's not as simple as you think. There are politics and this will certainly be cast as nepotism."

"Fine. Put family aside. You've studied my proposal. You know my credentials. Do they come up short or not? Be honest, Dad."

I wanted to lie, to put an end to this nonsense. But when he was a little boy, I promised him I would never lie to him. "No," I said. "In fact, I've already taken it to Council. Your credentials are the best we've seen. Ever."

Marcel's eyes widened and he leaned closer. "And?"

"The vote was four to three to approve the jump."

He gasped, and struggled for words. "By one vote? Dad—thank you! With all my heart, thank you. You don't know how much this means to me."

I nodded, my eyes moistening. "Council requires me to accompany you. Nguyen-Ramos led that charge; she hates my guts, you know."

Marcel hugged me, squeezing tightly.

He didn't need the whole truth. That's not a lie, is it? I voted against approval, in a loud, fist-pounding dissent. But once the vote was made and the *Medusa* jump approved, I demanded that I be the Council member to accompany him.

* * *

Jump calibrations went smoothly, the working out of an exact 4D point in space-time so that we would not materialize within the void of space, within a hill, a wall, underwater, or in a tree. As it was, the open countryside near Rochefort, France in 1816 offered simple negotiation. We materialized a meter above a wheat field, and tumbled in a heap onto the ground, laughing. Marcel turned an ankle, and bruised and scraped my palms. They train you for spills but I'm too damned unathletic to learn. But we held up, more or less intact.

The engineers pinpointed that exact same location for our temporal exit and return. We would need to be back in the wheat field at noon in three years and ninety-five days, with organic temp marker implants intact, to be whisked back to 2367, back to the New Stockholm jump chamber, exactly ten seconds after we'd left.

We made our way to Rochefort, three kilometers west, and caught a ferry to Ile-d'Aix, in the mouth of the River Charente, where we found lodging in a weathered inn. *Medusa* rested at anchor in the snug harbor, a fine, trim ship, its gleaming hull freshly painted white and black. Our plan had been worked out in minute detail, following the strictest protocols. *Medusa* was a warship, a frigate, under the command of Captain Chaumareys. The French Revolution had been undone by the defeat of Napoleon in the War of the Sixth Coalition in 1814 and the monarchy restored. The Bourbons raced to solidify power, appointing old royalists to positions of rank in the military, a hedge against new revolts. They gift-wrapped and handed

Chaumareys command of the *Medusa* even though he'd barely been to sea in twenty years.

Medusa would take on passengers and leave for France's colony in Senegal. Important passengers. The voyage would deliver the new governor, Colonel Julien-Desire Schmaltz, and his wife and daughter, along with two-hundred and fifty soldiers to restore French rule over Senegal.

Over the next few days, Marcel and I wandered the town, bantering with shopkeepers and fishermen and maids; chatting up whores and the sailors and drunks they clung to; and arguing politics and the price of ale with bureaucrats and gadflies alike. Marcel even wrangled a laugh or two over a beer with Governor Schmaltz.

We knew *Medusa*'s departure would be delayed two days by blustering headwinds, and once it left would never reach Senegal. The Council had approved expeditionary time before and after the tragedy, but had laid down strict prohibitions against boarding the doomed ship. Any positions taken by ourselves aboard ship affects things. The plan allowed us to observe the workings, the loading, and the staffing of the ship and her companion vessels, and to get to know the temperaments and talents of those to sail upon them. After the ship's disembarkation, we would make our way to Lisbon, book passage to the Portuguese colony in the Cape Verde islands, bribe our way to Saint-Louis in Senegal, and interview survivors as we could. Then we would buy passage back to France, where Marcel would observe Géricault at work and interview those near him, but never approach him. We would attend the unveiling of his masterpiece at the Paris Salon on August 25, 1819. At noon on the fifth of September, from the field outside Rochefort, we would be jumped back to 2367. It was a good plan, a meticulous, robust plan.

But Marcel had other ideas.

June 17th arrived, and *Medusa* would sail at seven that morning. We would be at the dock two hours prior to witness the final preparations and boarding. But when I awakened at four-thirty,

Marcel was nowhere to be seen. I dressed and searched our neighborhood, thinking him out on one of his restless walks, or a breakfast. Again, there was no sign of him. On a sudden, uneasy feeling, I returned to the inn and sorted through his belongings. Most were there, but a change of clothes and a few essentials were missing. I counted out our money; most remained but a sizable amount—more than enough to secure passage on a ship—was missing.

My pulse quickening, I stuffed the remaining money into my pocket and hurried down to the dock.

* * *

Marcel stood on the aftercastle deck of *Medusa*. He saw me but pretended not to, and drifted away from the railing. "My son," I called. "What are you doing? Come down at once!"

He glared at me and shook his head. "Dad, stop. Please. I won't miss this opportunity and. I'll see you in Saint-Louis." He dismissed me with a wave and disappeared below the aftercastle.

I shouted again, earning scowls and suspicious looks from the crew. I ignored them and approached the foot of the gangway. Three officers, seated at a small table, stared at me. One raised an abrupt, cautionary hand. "Name?"

We used false names, of course. "Jean-Luc Rousseau," I said. "I wish to come aboard."

He scanned a list of names, and then a second list. "You are among neither crew nor passengers, Monsieur Rousseau."

"I could have told you that. My son has boarded and I wish to remove him."

"And does he have a name? That might prove useful."

"Algernon Rousseau."

"He is listed. A late addition."

"Let me speak to him."

"He appears disinclined to listen."

"I need to talk him off this ship. We have…urgent family business that needs attending."

"If I had a centime for every young man that went to sea to escape urgent family business, I would buy the damned ship and sail to Martinique. Now if you will please be on your way, Monsieur, we have a schedule and more pressing matters that need attending."

"Ten minutes is all I ask."

He shook his head. "All passengers have boarded."

A sudden, chilling thought occurred to me. I already knew how many that would sail aboard *Medusa*. Four-hundred, precisely. "How many are sailing today? Total number?"

"Why?"

I slipped the three men each a silver franc, a considerable value in 1816. "Simply a request from a superstitious old man."

The officer's eyes widened. He studied me for a moment, glanced about, and stealthily pocketed the coin. His compatriots followed his cue. "Louis, give him the number of passengers."

"No!" I slapped the table. "Tell me the total, passengers and crew."

"Three hundred and ninety-nine."

I felt the blood drain from my face, and a cold shiver raced through me. Unbending, unalterable history—the fact of the four-hundred—held me in its grasp. With trembling hand, I withdrew my billfold. "Name your price. I wish to book passage aboard *Medusa*."

* * *

Marcel leaned with his hands upon the railing, gazing down at the placid brown harbor water.

"Marcel," I said softly.

He startled, and surprise colored his face. "Dad! What are you doing? Get off the ship."

"It's done. The future doesn't change. Fifty years of expeditions have proved that. I was last in the queue to board and the gangway was hauled right after me. *Medusa* carried four-hundred on this voyage. With my boarding, I complete the four-hundred. The officers confirmed it. It seems that joining you on this doomed ship is not a violation of space-time, but in fact a requirement."

"You don't know that! Someone may buy a passage at the last moment, or there may be a stowaway. Or a simple miscount."

"If that were the case, I, or someone else, will be removed from the ship."

He struggled for words. "I—I'll speak with the Captain."

"You're tilting at windmills. I'm here. But damn it, why did you do this?"

"You've never really gotten me, Dad. Half-measures don't bring understanding. This will be my greatest work, and just interviewing sailors and survivors won't capture the entire scene. If I'm going to write it honestly, I need to experience it, to live it."

"You know I can't protect you when we return. I can't even protect myself. This is the severest breach ever of the protocols and the Council will demand full accounting. I'll lose my job and we'll both go to prison. You get *that*?"

"Dad—I'm prepared to suffer consequences for my life's work. But not to harm you. We can stop, get you off—"

"No! I'm here with you."

The *Medusa* shifted gently underfoot. Sailors and longshoremen cast off lines and the frigate edged from the mooring. Men shouted and scurried; men in tender boats leaned into their oars, their lines to the ship tightening and creaking. *Medusa*, accompanied by our companion ships, the slow, clumsy *Argus* and *Loire*, and the sleek, speedy *Echo*, eased out of the unworried waters of the harbor and entered the restless, flexing Atlantic.

* * *

What a feast for the senses is a grand sailing ship of old! *Medusa*, less than ten years in age, breathed power and grace, and heeled sharply in a brisk beam wind, groaning with the swells of the ocean, its great clouds of sails flapping and thundering as they unfurled. Men clambered like monkeys high into the rigging and onto the yardarms. We plowed the sea southward at a good nine knots, foam arcing from the bow, glowing white in the sunshine.

Marcel made friends with many of the crew and passengers, recording every moment with the multiple, organic nano-computers hidden on him. Nano, designed to dissolve in four years, is the only future tech allowed to be carried into the past. Leave only footprints, we say.

While preparing for the journey in our home-time, Marcel had pored over the details of the *Medusa*, and even designed a holo of the vessel at full size. The dimensions of *Medusa* made it sound like a large ship, one-hundred fifty-four feet in length, thirty-nine in the beam. In reality, it shocked me to see the cramped conditions of such a vessel with four-hundred aboard.

On June 22nd, we lost sight of the sluggish *Argus* and *Loire*, making haste at the insistence of the Governor. All went well, the officers, crew, and passengers brimming with good spirits. But shouts of alarm raised when a lad of only fifteen fell overboard. Crewmen reacted as one and brought the ship about. But even with haste and skill, such a maneuver devours precious minutes. The boy screamed and flailed, and it became obvious that he could not swim. We watched, helpless, horrified, as he disappeared under the waves before we drew within fifty yards. Marcel impressed me with his resolve not to prevent the tragedy, but his silence the rest of the day told me it had struck him in the face. And the incident stabbed me inside; like Marcel, that boy was someone's son. The trip changed in a heartbeat from an engrossing academic exercise to a reality of pain and tears. A pall hung over the ship, an ominous note of sidelong glances and reddened eyes.

Marcel befriended another boy, Léon, a twelve-year-old. Léon shied from others, friendless, bullied by a few bored soldiers. He seemed alone on the voyage, drifting away from attention, making himself invisible. Fitting in with neither his own class nor the aristocratic class. He needed relief from his wrenching unhappiness, and Marcel convinced a kind young officer, Midshipman Coudein, to take the boy under his wing and teach him ship life.

We both knew Léon would be dead within three weeks.

As for myself, I sought out the acquaintances of Monsieurs Henri Savigny, the ship's surgeon, and Alexandre Corréard, a rather excitable engineer and explorer, both fine gentlemen, well-spoken and thoughtful. I ascertained they deftly straddled the chasm between the republicans and the loyalists. But I knew the incendiary nature of their coming account of the voyage, a tome that would inflame anti-royalist rage in the aftermath of the tragedy, blistering the monarchy and the system that allowed such a thing to happen.

Their gentlemanly demeanors made me wonder what agendas they harbored.

We passed Madeira, far off Morocco, on June 27th, and crossed the Tropic of Cancer on July 1st. We enjoyed a day of celebration, a mock ceremony with a sailor playing the Lord of the Tropic, who granted us passage into his realm.

Though we made good time, the Governor grew impatient, and cajoled Captain Chaumareys into speed and haste, a shortening of the route. Chaumareys dithered but finally acquiesced and sailed us southeast, defying orders and common sense, close in to Africa, into the treacherous Arguin Banks off Mauritania, which had earned a reputation as a graveyard of ships. The *Argus* and *Loire* refused to follow and stayed far out to sea. The *Echo* stayed with us for a while, with lanterns hung from the rigging for us to see in the dark, before giving up and moving out. We lost contact with all.

Discontent among the sailors brewed. These may have largely been uneducated men, but they knew the sea and sailing. They knew the murderous reputation of the Arguin Banks.

Chaumareys knew too but ordered his men to bother him only if soundings read less than eighteen fathoms, at which point he would calmly guide the ship into deeper water.

I watched Ensign Maudet, whom I'd befriended, at the bow casting the sounding lead out and hurriedly hauling it back in, time after time. I eased near. He shot me an angry glance, huffed, shook his head, and cast the line again.

"Maudet," I said. "Are we in good shape?"

He swept his arm all about. "The color of the sea changes."

"It's beautiful, the color."

"One man's beauty is another's horror. And see, the fish swarm all about. Any fool, even a landsman, can read the signs of shallow water."

I stayed with him for some time, chatting. His demeanor became one of increasing worry. At last, with one cast, he drew eighteen fathoms. "God damn him," he growled. He shoved me aside and shouted for the captain. Chaumareys strolled to him.

"Eighteen fathoms, Captain!" Maudet cried. A hundred men stopped work and turned. "We're upon the Arguin!"

Chaumareys nodded calmly. "Take care, Maudet. Take care." He ordered the lowering of the studding sails on the port side, and the bringing of the ship about one-quarter to starboard and into the wind. It was the afternoon of July 2nd.

Maudet cast his line, drew it in. The sounding came back with a reading of ten fathoms.

Chaumareys paled. He stammered a moment and shrieked for two quarters more to starboard.

More hurried soundings.

Six fathoms. A mere thirty-six feet.

The sailors knew what this meant but said nothing. *Medusa* itself had a draft of just thirty feet. Silence and terror filled their faces.

A crunching scrape. A shudder ran through the deck below our feet. *Medusa* heeled and lurched to a stop, sending men and women stumbling to the deck. I fell hard, and Marcel crashed into a mast. A cut opened in his scalp, and blood streamed down his face. Cold fear ran through me, knowing the fate of so many aboard. The ship seemed to feel a bit more life and moved again, but twice more ground to a stop.

I examined Marcel. His wound was superficial, and we stanched the bleeding with a bit of cloth torn from my sleeve. Still, in the age before antibiotics, any wound could be life-ending, and I bathed his cut with rum, much to the discontented grumblings of a few sailors.

The sails were quickly lowered. But bad decisions have a bad habit of piling one onto another. At high tide, we were at that very moment in the best opportunity we would get to refloat off the reef. But Chaumareys shouted down his officers' pleas to jettison the fourteen valuable three-ton cannons, and *Medusa* settled deeper into the sands of the bank.

The crew worked furiously, the long hours of afternoon stretching into evening. As darkness descended, fear and anxiety simmered, reflected in the eyes of crew and passengers alike. The fate of the *Medusa* rested with the power of the tides and the unpredictable, shifting winds.

The next day, the officers attempted one measure after another to lighten and refloat the ship. Top-masts and spars were taken down and thrown overboard. Water butts were pumped empty. Anchors were hauled and sunk in deeper water to drag the *Medusa* free. Nothing worked. The *Medusa* would never leave.

We had just six small boats. For four hundred people.

After heated debate, Schmaltz and Chaumareys decided to ferry groups in turns to the coast, some fifty miles east. The important people would be first to leave. There was never any consideration for something as simple and just as who was most fit or suited.

France being a divided, broken nation, its tensions had sailed aboard the *Medusa* from the moment it had put to sea. Among our number, there mingled uneasily many royalists and many

Bonapartists, revolutionaries. Marcel had spent the voyage engaging both sides, as best he could. But the Captain and Governor saw only his fraternization with the Bonapartists.

Governor Schmaltz, largely responsible for the calamity, earned some small redemption by drawing up plans for an enormous raft, onto which a great deal of the cargo could be loaded. The men fell to feverish work on its construction, stripping the *Medusa* of spars and planks, lashing them together, and soon had built the thing, which stretched sixty-six feet in length and twenty-three in width. A great, groaning beast, in sheer size almost a ship in itself. The seamen dubbed it "*la Machine.*" A small makeshift mast and sail were tacked on, not a worthless gesture but pitifully inadequate for steering.

The plan was to have the raft towed by the boats, but human nature and the elements soon destroyed that plan. The next night, heavy drinking swept through the soldiers and discipline broke down. A gale whipped up the sea's fury as midnight approached on the 4th, pounding the stranded ship with wave after wave, threatening to tear it apart. A ship stuck in one place has no defense against storms. With a loud splintering creak and a crack, the keel broke in two. Waves crashed over the deck, tearing loose the helm and whipping it about like a toy. Water poured into the aft cabins. Panic gripped the ship. Chaumareys abandoned the ferrying plan and decreed that the longboats would tow the raft, with people rather than cargo, to shore. Accompanied by two officers brandishing clubs, he hurried through the four-hundred, singling out those chosen to board the boats by tapping them on their chests and motioning them towards the craft. He paused at me, scowled, and moved on.

Sailors and soldiers, officers who'd fallen out of Chaumareys' favor, and suspicious Bonapartists were consigned to the raft.

I grabbed his sleeve, unable to take it any longer. "Captain! We are gentlemen, our passage paid in full."

He shook me loose, glaring. "*Je m'en fou*! Gentlemen you may be, but also revolutionaries and not even true Frenchmen. You'll not cut my legs out from under me. Onto the raft with you."

"But, Captain—"

Chaumareys nodded to his officers, jerked a thumb at me. One of the men struck me with his club, knocking me to the deck. "Get on the raft!"

I struggled to my feet and took a step toward the officer, who raised his club for a second blow. An arm encircled me, restraining me.

Marcel.

"Dad, stop. You can't win this fight but you can get yourself beaten senseless. We have to get on the raft."

"That raft will be the gate to hell," I whispered.

"But we will survive it. You know the numbers better than anyone else in the world. In hundreds of temporal jumps, not one jumper has died or even been seriously injured. A few scrapes and scratches. And the future was not changed one iota. Nothing can happen to us because the future is set. The statistics prove it."

"Statistics prove *probabilities*. Not *possibilities*."

"Dad, we have no choice! We will survive, and as men not even of this time, we cannot—I will not—take the place of any other who might enter the boats."

I knew he was right, although the horror of what lay ahead tempted my refusal. My son was a better man than me.

We boarded the raft.

* * *

The Governor's boat, a fourteen-oared vessel, took on thirty-five persons. It could have carried more, but his belongings were judged more valuable than people, and took up space in three massive trunks.

Overloaded with men and a single woman, our raft settled low into the water, its deck below the surface. One hundred and forty-seven souls had been crowded aboard it.

We hitched *la Machine* by ropes to three of the boats, and all six boats began to pull east for the desert coast of Africa.

Seventeen men chose to stay with the *Medusa*, some too frightened to set foot on the overcrowded boats, some too drunk to care.

We made slow progress that first day, six or seven kilometers, our officers estimated. At that rate, we would make the coast within a couple of days.

I knew better.

Strange, how stress and danger twist manageable situations inward upon themselves. Frictions soon erupted aboard the boats. Shouting, arguing, shoving. One boat, its helmsman glaring, veered sharply toward one of our tow boats. Perhaps fearing he was to be rammed and capsized, the tow boat's officer drew his saber and with three blows severed our line. The other towing boats followed suit, hacking their lines and leaning into their oars. One circled back, its young officer pleading with the other boats to help us to shore. His own crewmen spat curses and threats at him. One sprang to his feet and took a wild swing at him, missing. On the brink of mutiny, the officer sank into his seat and gave up, weeping, his eyes fixed upon us.

The men of our raft shouted pleas at the boats. A gray-haired sergeant shoved me aside and stared at them. "Heartless bastards, pigs all," he growled, and leapt into the sea and swam after them. A wave rolled over him and shoved him under. He surfaced, sputtering, and returned to the raft. Our pleading boiled into shaking of fists and hurling of obscene curses and threats of revenge, anguished begging and tears and, at last, stunned silence, the only sounds remaining being the splash of sea and the whispering of the wind.

The boats receded into the distance and vanished below the horizon.

La Machine drifted, abandoned and alone.

* * *

That first day on *la Machine* slid into a morass of minutes and hours as we drifted between endless sky and ocean. The sun beat down, and our hunger and thirst grew. In the confusion of the panicked abandonment of the *Medusa*, the promised stocking of our raft with provisions had gone undone, other than a woefully inadequate store of water, biscuit paste, and wine. The officers portioned and passed a bit of each to each of us.

Anger at our abandonment simmered and grew, hostile glances and whispers becoming ever more frequent. Men in authority had left us to die. And now new men in authority commanded the raft.

With the night came growing wind and waves.

We strung a rope in haste about the perimeter of the raft, a desperate and pitiful excuse for a railing. The seas rose and pitched us about as twilight gathered. Terror gripped us and the officers aboard commanded the center of the raft, the safest spot, away from the dangerous edge. Already partially submerged, waves swept into us and over us in the darkness, hour after hour.

A raft of such size, built of timber and masts hewn from mighty tree trunks, might make you think such a craft is sturdy. But the massiveness of the timbers created a new menace. Bound together by rope, and flexing and moving with the sea, they were as nothing against the power of surging mountains of water. Men slipped between the gaps in the shifting timbers and were mangled and crushed, or fell through them into the sea. Screams of agony, cries for help, and the sharp crack and dull crunch of breaking bones punctuated the long night.

Pitch blackness and blind terror engulfed us. I clung to Marcel and he to me, entwining ropes about our arms and hanging on with fists clenched. Midshipman Coudein, next to us, held Léon tightly, knowing the boy could not swim. With each wave, I believed I would be torn and swept into the pitching ocean. I told myself that Marcel was right, that we could not die in that time, that the future was written and unchangeable. But fear smothers reason.

The gray of morning came at last and the sea eased its assault. The raft rode a few inches higher, and I knew the reason; in the night, twenty of us were dead or gone. One hundred twenty-seven remained.

On the second day, the seas and temperaments calmed. Those about us mustered a hopeful dialogue of reaching the coast in short order, many convinced the boats would return that day and deliver us to salvation. Marcel and I said nothing about this, and just as we knew it would, the ferocious waves returned and slammed into us that second night.

Despite the pummeling of the Atlantic, the night sky remained clear and moonlight glittered like diamonds on the waves. Fear and discontent drove the soldiers to drinking, whispers became grumbles, and grumbles became shouts of rage at the officers and passengers. And at us. A soldier grabbed an officer by the lapels and shook him, and the officer landed a blow in the man's face. A melee exploded. Mutiny and fighting raged throughout the night. Screams pealed in the dark. Fists thrown, eyes gouged, men hurled overboard. We held our own amidst the melee until dawn, exhausted, bleeding, and battered. My son and I were no longer enlightened men from a gentle future; we fought as cornered animals bent on survival, and the rules of temporal expedition, of non-engagement, meant nothing now.

Sixty-five men died in the blood and violence of that long second night. Sixty-two of us still lived.

I examined my bruises and cuts and found nothing serious. Marcel had a broken finger, an eye swollen shut, and a cut across his chest that dripped red into the sea. I tore a bit of cloth from my shirt and pressed it against his wound, managing to stop the bleeding.

There were no medical supplies amongst us.

Worse, our only cask of water had been lost overboard.

A semblance of order returned, the fury of the night subdued by the stark realities of survival. No boats or ships appeared. Only an empty horizon of ocean stretched in all directions. Pushed about by current and wind, we made scant progress east toward Africa. Sharks now circled and haunted us. We tried catching the smaller of them for food, without success. A few of us ate belt leather or linen. Without food now, the realization dawned that we had but one resource in ample supply. Human flesh.

That third day, some gave in to hunger. The nightmare faced us. They drew knives and cut flesh from the dead—the meat coming away in brownish, purple chunks—and ate it raw. Some cut the flesh into strips and hung it from the little mast to dry.

Marcel and I, and the majority of the survivors, turned away in revulsion, unable to watch. My stomach heaved, but nothing remained inside me to vomit.

On the morning of the fourth day, we found ten more dead, and let all but one slip into the sea. That poor man would be saved for food.

Blisters and ulcers scarred our bodies. Our lips cracked, our tongues grew swollen. Our feet and lower legs, immersed in salt water, deteriorated into masses of red sloughing skin, the pain making it impossible to stand and rest out of the water. Saltwater stung our wounds without cease.

Suspicion and delirium swam through me, and I suppose, through everyone. We had reduced to a crawling, numbed, weak mass of humanity. Despite that, anger at the officers welled up once more, and fighting erupted yet again, an animal snarl of clawing and wrestling. By dawn, there remained only thirty alive on *la Machine*, down from the hundred and forty-seven that had boarded it. The lone woman amongst us had twice been thrown overboard by mutineers, but rescued both times.

On the sixth day, trembling and mad with hunger, I took a dried strip of human flesh, tore a bit free with my teeth, and ate it. I handed a strip to Marcel. He took it without a word. Neither of us spoke or looked at each other.

Though most of the wine had been lost in the fighting, we still possessed some, and some tiny flying fish that had been caught in the timbers of the raft. We agreed, after sullen stares and a few thrown fists, to strict rationing. But on the seventh day, we caught two men stealing wine, passed a quick judgement, and threw them overboard. I smiled as the thieves died.

Léon, who had gone to sea on his life's first great adventure, fell ill, and sank into a fevered delirium. He drifted for hours, by turns whimpering or crying out for his mother, at last quietly dying in the arms of Coudein. Marcel and Coudein wept tearlessly for the lad, while starving soldiers watched in sullen silence. One soldier glanced at his compatriots, and crept closer. Marcel kicked him, knocking him back, and nodded to Coudein. Together they committed the boy to the depths of the uncaring Atlantic.

Just twenty-seven of us still lived.

Marcel's certainty that we could not die in that time seemed to be holding true.

You read the accounts of such disasters. You think you understand. You are bigger, stronger, than the victims. You aren't. You fail to understand how the human mind works, or doesn't work. I found myself confusing faces, hallucinating. I strolled with my dead wife among the towering redwoods of California, dreaming of our unborn child. Under such extreme deprivation and terror, the mind tries to construct a safer reality. It wants to stave off its own gathering whispers and darkness.

A dozen of our number lingered near death, too weak and sick to move, and drew ragged breaths, their eyes glazed. And yet they clung to life, and we faced a desperate decision. Should the doomed live and endanger the whole of us? By our calculation or wishful thinking, their absence granted the remaining of us an additional six days of life. The debate raged, in the presence of those whose fates we were deciding.

I had journeyed to that wrenching moment and place from my pampered 24th century existence, with strict orders not to affect outcomes. I wish I could tell you I followed that rule, a rule I myself had crafted. But thirst, hunger, and fear ruled my every thought, and I cast my vote. We sent the twelve overboard to their deaths, convincing ourselves we acted out of need and mercy.

The lone woman, her thigh having been snapped in the shifting timbers, and whom had twice been saved after being thrown into the water during the riots, was among those we now sacrificed, along with her husband. The terror, the pleading in her eyes, will haunt me the rest of my life.

Marcel's condition deteriorated, his face turning pale and gaunt. What sleep he could get was wracked by cries of terror, and in his waking moments he shivered and moaned, suffering through spells of hallucination. He grew weaker by the hour.

I could stand it no longer. Coudein and I loudly demanded a conference, and in one of the few moments of reason aboard the raft, it was agreed the violence must end. We threw all sidearms and weapons into the ocean, with the exception of one saber and a few tools.

Yet the next day, one soldier eyed Marcel, and claimed he'd fought alongside Napoleon at Waterloo and knew a dying man when he saw one, and he saw one in Marcel. My son should be tossed, he growled. Or killed and eaten.

I shouted him down. Marcel remained healthy, I argued, his wounds superficial, and he would recover. Savigny, the surgeon, examined him and agreed, giving me a concerned, unconvinced look. But his opinion carried the moment.

The blistering sun of the tropics worsened our condition by the day, by the hour. On the tenth day, the sodden timbers of the raft drifted into swarms of giant jellyfish and Portuguese men-of-war, and we endured painful, debilitating stings.

Every man on *la Machine* lingered near that fragile boundary between life and death, inching closer by the minute.

* * *

Marcel worsened, and fell into delirium on the morning of July 17th, our thirteenth day aboard *la Machine*, the raft of death. He awakened sporadically, lucid and fearful. I cradled and rocked him in my arms, lest he be swept overboard by the waves. Upon his third awakening that morning, he gripped my forearm, weakly.

"Dad. What day?" His voice cracked, barely more than a whisper. "What day is this? The 17th? It's today, isn't it?"

I shushed him. "Yes, son," I whispered. "And there are fifteen of us. We've made it. The *Argus* will save us today. We've survived!"

He coughed and smiled. "The future is set, Dad. It's set. We would always survive." He paused, drew a deep, dry breath. "Fifteen survivors. There would always be fifteen. That couldn't change."

And he was right. The fifteen survivors comprised an unchangeable fact. Fifteen of us *would* be rescued by the *Argus*.

And to comfort him in his last hours, I lied to my only son.

Sixteen still lived. One of us would die before the *Argus* saved us.

"Yes, Marcel, beautiful boy." I drew him close against me and stroked his hair. "We've come through hell. We will be off this raft in a few hours, fed and clothed, and taken to luxurious homes to recuperate. We'll see Paris, the City of Light. We'll meet Monsieur Géricault and drink coffee and wine, and talk of tragedy and art, and witness the creation of one of the greatest paintings the world has known. Your book will be completed, and the 24th century will read it in awe. Be still now, and rest, and know it's coming to pass." My eyes clouded and I swiped at them with my arm. "Rest now. Rest."

Marcel smiled and closed his eyes. His breath came long and slow and labored for some time, and minutes stretched into hours.

He shuddered in my arms. His grip tightened on my arm, then relaxed.

His breathing stopped, and his body sagged.

I had lost him. My whole body shook with anguish and sobs.

A shout. One of the men pointed, his hand trembling, at the northern horizon. "Sail," he cried in a voice like wind through brittle, dead leaves, and louder, "A sail!"

Men scrambled and shoved and clawed to see.

A tip of white sail peeked above the edge of ocean far away, its hull hidden below the curvature of the earth. Men waved rags, screamed, begged the ship to come nearer.

And yet it receded and disappeared from sight. The men collapsed in despair, weeping.

But within a few hours more, the shout went up again. Nearer, much nearer, the *Argus*, with its sails full, bore down upon us.

We were saved. The fifteen were saved.

I eased Marcel to the edge of the raft and released him to the sea.

Part III
The Louvre, Present Day

Corinne stared at Komarov-Banks, her mind reeling.

He sat silent now, looking down at his folded hands. His eyes glistened, and he shook with sobs.

He had told his story in barely more than a whisper, sometimes looking deep into her eyes, sometimes at the great painting, sometimes staring at some unseen world.

The tale was too fantastic to be believed, yet told with such depth and anguish it had to be true, at least to this poor old man. Delusion is truth to the mentally ill. Whole worlds and realities can be constructed within the mind and believed with certainty. Her apprehension of this man had morphed into pity during his tale, and she felt it her duty, the right thing for any person of compassion, to hear him out and to comfort him.

"So you see, Corinne," he began again, looking up at her, "I survived what few of those that boarded the raft did. Nothing of my world varied from when I had left, except that I now had no son. I languished in a quiet, shaded hospital, recuperating, regaining my strength. Or what of it I could; I've never returned to my old self. But I got better and traveled to Paris. I met young Monsieur Géricault in a café and told him my story. Everything except my journey across time. He watched me with wide eyes, questioning often, capturing every detail. And he drew me, dashing off sketch after sketch. Never have I seen such magic, such genius, at work. Look at his greatest work, Corinne. *The Raft of the Medusa.* Look closely. Tell me what you see."

Corinne turned to the painting. Géricault had captured the moment of hope, the swirl and movement of the living, the stillness of the dead, the moment the sail of the *Argus* appeared on the horizon.

And a pale old man in the painting, turning away from the joy, the hope; uncaring, as if he knew what would happen. An old man clutching the body of a young man. A pale man, bearded.

The man, now clean-shaven, sat next to her.

The blood drained from her face, and she shivered.

She touched his arm. "You're the old man on the raft."

His eyes shone with tears. "I lost my son and my soul on that expedition. Géricault captured that. He captured me and the entire nightmare in a single canvas, and with it, shook France to its core. The Bourbons never recovered from the fallout. France righted and set itself again on a course towards democracy."

The museum guard gave them a phony cough and arched his eyebrows in both a frown and a question. Corinne glanced about to see the gallery had emptied. Down the corridor, the remaining few headed for the exit.

Komarov-Banks touched her arm. "We've overstayed. Apologies." They stood and he gave a slight bow. "And I've broken a half-dozen laws by telling you what I have. I trust you'll never mention a word of your talk with the crazy old man, ever? Not in confidence, and certainly not in writing?"

She nodded.

"Adieu then, Corinne. I'm completing Marcel's book for him. His way. He'd have loved to meet you because you have a hand in the future of this painting. But meeting you meant more than I thought. This has been cathartic. Healing."

"Mr. Komarov-Banks."

"Call me Henri."

"Will I—my interview is tomorrow. Will I get the job?"

He smiled. "Corinne, you know the answer. This is much too political a hire for such a young, unconnected person, even one of brilliance. No, the job will be awarded to an elderly gentleman on staff, who has put in years of work and obsequiousness. That's the way of the world. Hasn't changed, even in the 24th century."

She sagged. Why then even bother?

"A minor setback, dear. You will interview, be passed over. But in eleven days, you'll get a call from the retiring director, offering a lesser job, that of an entry-level curator. You'll be working here within the month, and in seven years you will be the new director of the Louvre. The youngest ever. The greatest ever. You'll design the plan that will preserve the world's greatest art from the destruction of the next great war, twenty-three years from now."

Corinne gasped. Her skin prickled, and her legs grew weak. She sat down, trembling.

Henri smiled sadly. "Go now, Corinne. Rest. As I said, you will assume a great responsibility for this painting." He swept his hand across the gallery. "For all these paintings. You have a world to save."

He took her hand, kissed it, bowed, and strode away.

Corinne drew a deep breath, and stared at *The Raft of the Medusa*, and Henri clinging to the body of his beloved Marcel. Her eye moved to the nameless dead, and to the saved men, and found the last gathering of will within them, focused on the moment of hope, on salvation, on the ship on the horizon.

Salvation.

All these works of brilliance, the world's treasures. Humanity's legacy. The world's art would soon need a hero. A savior. The seeds of a plan to save them took root.

Marcel knew his life's work, his purpose.

She now knew her own.

It stretched before her, a great unfinished canvas, defined yet unbounded, a canvas of strife and struggle, but also one of hope and promise, like a sail beckoning from a far horizon.

Notes

Théodore Géricault created his masterpiece after reading *The Shipwreck of the Medusa*, by Corréard and Savigny, the only account written by survivors of the raft. Other accounts were written by survivors of the wreck and of the march across the desert to Senegal. Not all accounts matched on all points; experiences and agendas differed, and biases and lies arose, as they always do. A great source that sorts it out is *The Wreck of the Medusa: The Most Famous Sea Disaster of the Nineteenth Century* (2007), by Jonathan Miles.

The tragedy marked a turning point for France. The Revolution had come apart, the monarchy returning to power in the Restoration. But France simmered, embracing anything but unity. When the Crown began appointing favorites to positions of power more for loyalty than competence, something was bound to explode. And then *Medusa* ran aground, inflaming an already angry public. The details of bad decisions and gross incompetence are too many to corral within a short story, but they were all too real.

The notion of Corinne saving the great works of art from a future war is rooted in the reality of World War II. In August of 1939, with conflict with Germany just days away, the Louvre suddenly shut its doors for three days of "repairs," during which the great pieces were secured and secreted away to other locations. *The Raft of the Medusa* was trucked to Versailles, and later to Chateau de Chambord. In 1940, the French army collapsed under the onslaught of German blitzkrieg, but dedicated saviors of art, led by Jacques Joujard, risked their lives in a shell game with the Nazis, who looted cultural treasures wherever they went. Shifting the art around, stalling with endless letters and red tape, and pitting German officers and bureaucrats against each other, Joujard and others managed to delay surrendering the art. An engrossing look at the rescue of the world's cultural treasures from Hitler's plunderers is Robert M. Edsel's *The Monuments Men* (2009).

Can unlike people find common ground and purpose? Of course, and quality kitchen equipment always helps.

Great Minds Think Alike

By the time Luanne had finished with him, no part of Eddie was bigger than a breadbox. She took a step back, smiled, wiped her hands. It—or rather, *he*—was nice and tidy, her usual standards of cleanliness upheld.

"Well now, Mr. Bossy-Bossy," she said. "Let's just get snippy about the chili *now*."

Eddie's glazed eyes stared at nothing.

"No smarty-pants remarks? Gee, Eddie, you're slipping. It might be nice to hear you come up with a nasty one now. Not half as nice as knowing you won't, though."

Luanne glanced around the diner's kitchen. It looked pretty good, considering. No sign of struggle. No sign of Manager and Husband

Eddie, except for fourteen little cellophane bundles behind the counter. She removed her apron and tossed it in the washer. She dialed the machine to a chugging start, and donned a fresh apron.

She hadn't planned this when she got to work for the graveyard shift. Not exactly. It just happened. Eddie started complaining the second she arrived. The counter is greasy. The forks are dirty. Stop licking your fingers while you're cooking. On and on, lots worse than most nights.

The sneeze was the last straw.

That came just after one o'clock. Nobody had come in for over an hour, typical for a Tuesday. Luanne sniffled her way through a cold, a small, inoffensive one. Was that her fault? She was being hygienic about it, wiping her nose on her arm so as not to drip into the hamburger, and stepping out every twenty minutes or so to clear her nostrils onto the sidewalk with a vigorous honk. But that wasn't good enough for Mister Smarty-Pants, no. She sneezed over the grill, just once, no big deal, right? Eddie launched into one of his profane *fer-chrissakes-Luanne* tirades, sputtering, spitting, and shouting. Luanne calmly listened to him rant, and when he turned away, still shouting, she brained him with the laminated cypress wall clock from Florida. The clock stopped. Just like in the movies.

Long ago, Luanne had cooked up a plan against the likelihood of this day. Freeze for a while, maybe a couple months, and a run through the meat grinder. She'd invested in a good one. Now he lay neatly wrapped and stacked behind the counter, ready for the freezer. Luanne unlocked it and picked up a few bundles of Eddie.

The little bell on the front door jangled happily.

Luanne froze. She thought, sure, it's an all-night diner, but this is *Tuesday*. It's not fair.

Bobby L. Truman swaggered in, grinning. Still in uniform. Luanne had always figured Bobby was the breed of cop who wore his shoes a little too tight and puffed up like a blowfish while bullying jaywalkers.

Luanne dropped Eddie and punted him back under the counter. She cracked a stiff smile. "Bobby, what a surprise. What're you doing here so late?"

"Hi, sweets. This is an all-night diner, isn't it? My cop contract requires me to stop and grab a bite at joints like this every other night." He winked and took a seat at the counter.

Wonderful. Never a cop around when you need one, always a horny one around when you don't. "What can I get you?"

"Chocolate shake and cheeseburger'd be nice."

"Coming right up." She forced a smile and headed for the freezer.

"Cow meat only in that burger, please."

Luanne stiffened. Did he know? Course not, it was only a feeble joke. She opened the freezer.

"No ground-up manager for me," Bobby said. "No ma'am, just plain old hamburger."

Luanne slammed the freezer door and turned. "You taking me in, Truman?"

"Take in a sweet thing like you? Naw."

She watched him. The silence swelled between them. "What then?"

He smiled. "I wouldn't mind taking *on* a nice thing like you."

Chrissakes, thought Luanne.

"Eddie was a crud anyway," Bobby continued. "Into all kinds of shit. Nobody's going to miss him. You married the guy, and you'll manage the place just fine. I figure you did the world a favor. Trouble is, the D.A. don't give a shit about that. He loves to lock up pretty little hash-slingers with a thing for murder. He's running for office and he'd love to get some face time on cable, which this would guarantee. Tough on crime, and all that."

"You've got a wife," she reminded him.

"Which is why this should be fun."

"How long you going to do this to me?"

"Long as it takes. For a couple years, at least. After that, I'll get tired of you and only want it once in a while. See? It ain't so bad."

You won't last that long, chump, Luanne thought.

Bobby held up a pair of handcuffs. "I've always wanted to try these."

* * *

The diner went on as always. Luck held and Bobby was right; no one missed Eddie, no one at all. Because no one liked him. His only family consisted of his worthless brother Phil out in Wyoming, who called once, and Luanne told him Eddie's gambling debt had gotten out of hand and Eddie'd lit out late one night on "vacation" after a couple of bruisers paid him a visit. Didn't say where he was going or when he'd be back. Luanne asked Phil if she should put him in touch with the bruisers. No, he said quickly, that wouldn't be necessary. Phil had placed more than a few bets now and then through Eddie, and knew firsthand about debt bruisers. Next time Luanne called, his girlfriend said he packed a toothbrush and moved to Ecuador to bet on cockfights.

Bobby came by twice a week to collect, on the nights of the late shift.

One night in the eighth month, he was followed.

After collecting his dues, Bobby yanked up his pants and stood, sweating shiny beads from his reddened face. "Put a little life into it next time, Luanne," he said. "I got no use for a limp dishrag."

Luanne lay still for a moment on the linoleum, and reached into the bottom counter drawer and found the heavy smooth stone from Rock City she had hidden there. "And I got no use for a smarty-pants."

Bobby smirked and began to speak. The doorbell tinkled quietly, with the effect of a gunshot. Bobby spun and faced it, tugging his shirt on. His redness paled to yellow and his lips moved, searching for words. Luanne heard footsteps.

"Get home, Jill," Bobby managed. "Now."

"'Get home, Jill'," came the mocking reply.

Luanne adjusted her skirt and peered over the counter. A petite redhead, eyes like steel, mouth drawn into a hard line, approached. So this was the little woman. "Why, Bobby," Luanne said. "Looks like domestic strife."

"Shut up, whore," Jill said.

Bobby's face oozed sincerity. "Listen, honey, this here ain't how it looks. I got a call and was back here helping this young lady out with some breaking and entering issues. Kind of tripped and fell." He turned to Luanne. "Right, Miss—I'm sorry, I forgot your name."

"Right! Bobby's been helping out back here on the floor a couple times a week. Helping out and helping himself."

Bobby swung and backhanded her. Sparks flashed and glittered behind her eyes. The glitter faded and she lunged and clopped him between the eyes with the Rock City souvenir. He screamed and stumbled backward, clutching his face. Blood seeped from beneath his fingers. "Shit, you crazy thing! You assault a peace officer?"

Luanne caught a flash of movement and jumped aside as Jill smacked Bobby's skull from behind with the cypress clock that still registered the moment Eddie had gone on vacation. It started running again.

Luanne and Jill stared at the mess that had been Bobby the cop-husband. Their gazes met. A silence, tomb-like. Jill glanced toward the door. "Maybe you should lock up now."

Luanne held up the clock. "You fixed it."

"He thought he could fool me. Thought I was a little red-haired dummy. He was such a . . . a . . . "

"Smarty-pants?"

"I was going to say 'prick,' but whatever."

Luanne brightened. "Say, Miz Truman, how about helping manage this dump with me while Bobby is running from the Mob?"

"He *is* on the lam, isn't he? Sure. By the way, do you have a meat-grinder?"

Notes

This story first appeared in a punk rock magazine, *No Idea*, in 1988. I'm still not sure why they wanted it. I had great hopes that it would win the Nobel Prize for Literature, but the deeply-ingrained politics and prejudices of the judges worked against me. That needs to be addressed.

Motivations to evil are often primal, lustful, and powerful, and have changed little over the centuries. William Shakespeare understood this, and his work resonates with such unpleasant truths even today.

When the Hurly Burly's Done

Brigands Key, Florida, 1934

Sunlight like slanted gold peeked through the wooden blinds, alighting Sam Hawke's face, nudging him awake. He squinted, picked up his pocket watch, swore softly. The sun climbed already and here he lay, still in bed. *Her bed.*

His fitful sleep ended, not by morning sun but by a dream of gathering darkness, and three pairs of glowing white pinpoints—eyes—circling him, studying him. Judging him. He sensed something expected of him.

Good thing dreams and nightmares were ghosts and not real.

Mary MacGregor stirred next to him. He leaned in and kissed her on the cheek, and patted her shoulder. She opened her eyes, the fog of sound sleep evaporating from them, and smiled.

He kissed her again, this time on the mouth.

In the soft yellow light, he appraised her again and congratulated himself. She knocked you out with her looks, the most beautiful on the whole damned island of Brigands Key.

He drew a strand of blond hair back from her face and tucked it behind her ear. "I got to go, Darlin.' Fred will be back up from Tampa soon."

Mary stretched and rolled toward him, slow and sinuous. "Oh, he won't be back for a couple hours. We've got time for more."

"Time ain't the point. It's Saturday morning, and even if most of the fleet's sleepin' off a drunk, there're always a few busybodies up and about. I can't have them seeing me sneaking out of your house while your husband's away. Bad for business."

"My husband. Your boss. It doesn't matter, sweetie. We're going to make it official and respectable someday. Right?"

"Someday. It takes a long time to climb that ladder, even in good times. Maybe you ain't heard the news; the whole damn country's out of work."

She giggled. "Work. Yes, I heard of that somewhere, Baby."

He studied her for a moment, refusing to smile back. At times, he wondered what he saw in her. Lines around the block at Relief Offices and soup kitchens all over the country, but she could still buy anything and everything. Worst part was, she came from as meager a background as anyone else on Brigands Key, her daddy a fisherman like all the rest. A bad heart killed him young. She was way too young then too, maybe seven, left with a drunk mother. Hardscrabble, like most in town.

But her *looks*. Damn, was she pretty. Movie star pretty. She'd turned heads from the moment she got to high school, and soon as she got out, the springtime after the stock market crashed and sent millionaires jumping off buildings in New York, she'd turned the head of the richest man on the island. Hell, the *only* rich man.

But he was three times her age.

Sam flipped the covers and swung his legs off the bed. He stood, stretched, and wrangled a satisfying pop from his back. He reached for the bottle of rum on the nightstand, good Cuban stuff from the smuggling days, and took a pull. Wouldn't burn a hole through your stomach like the domestic shine.

Mary said, "You don't have to go, Baby."

Sam grunted. "Yeah, I do. You wouldn't be able to live like the Queen of England if Fred ever caught wind of his wife and his foreman."

"Maybe I could."

He turned to look at her. "Ha! Just how's that, Darlin'?"

"Oh, I don't know. I just can't live with someone that old forever."

"Well, stick around. Fred's sixty-two and drinks like a fish. Can't live forever. Time comes, and you'll come out like a rose. A rich, beautiful rose."

"His daddy's eighty-eight and fit as a fiddle." Her face drew into a perfect little frown.

Sam shrugged. "You picked this life of the waiting game yourself. Might take a bit longer than you'd like."

She hesitated. "It doesn't have to."

He studied her for a moment. "What do you mean?"

"I think you know."

"You're going for a divorce?"

She giggled, the sound of her voice like honey. "Divorce! If I filed, you think I'd come away with *anything*?"

"I don't know why not."

"Then you don't know a thing about money and how it works. How the courts work when you sew 'em up with money."

Sam snorted. "You got money."

"I *live* on money. Fred's money. It ain't my money."

Sam watched her, struggling through things he might say. None seemed to fit.

"Sam?"

"Yeah?"

"I'm not going to wait out my life."

He held up his palms in exasperation. "Run away with me then."

"And be poor? I love you, Baby, but not that much."

He wouldn't put words to what she was saying. That would be stupid. "Guess you're out of luck then."

"I don't know. Like you said, Fred drinks like a fish. Who knows, maybe he'll fall off one of his damn boats and drown. Accidents happen all the time." She rolled onto her stomach, laced her fingers together and propped her chin upon them, her eyes bright. "Then I'll be rich! And still young, and needing an upstanding husband that knows Fred's business. Think of it, Sam!"

Accidents happen all the time.

Silence hung in the space between them. At last Sam turned and pulled on his clothes. "I got to go."

"Wait, Honey. You going to that thing at the high school Fred's all excited about?"

"What, that Shakespeare play?"

"Yeah. I'm going with Fred."

"I don't know."

"Go. It'll do you good. You got to start looking smart if you want to be my husband."

"Smart? Like Fred?" He snorted. "Fred's only going 'cause it'll make *him* look smart."

"No, that ain't it. He is smart. Real smart."

"He finished high school like the rest of us. Nothing special."

"He couldn't afford college. He worked to get where he is. Promise me you'll go see that show."

"Don't know why."

"God, you are a dummy. I want it to look like you and Fred are pals. Like he wants you to succeed." She opened the bedside drawer, rummaged a bit, and tossed a yellow card flyer to him. He picked it up.

"*Macbeth*," he said. "I heard of it."

"It's got witches and ghosts and sword fights. Freddie said it's real good. Course, he's never been to a play his whole life. It's a big deal it's even coming to Brigands Key, and folks are even coming over from Cedar Key and Chiefland to see it. Folks with money."

"Puttin' on airs, ever last one of 'em." He shook his head, headed for the door. "Eight o'clock tonight, huh? I guess I better go."

"You *will* go. For me." She paused. "For us."

"Us?" He half-turned toward her, not wanting to hear what was coming.

"Sam. I want *you*, Darlin.' I love you. Not that hateful old man. And the only way we are together is if he's dead. You understand? I want him dead!"

Sam stood still, the words caroming through his mind. He began to speak, thought better of it, and opened the door and stepped out into the heat of a Gulf of Mexico morning.

* * *

Sam stopped at the biggest boat on the dock, admiring it resentfully. Gleaming white hull, and the faint aroma of richly oiled and polished wood, the scent of a rich man's boat. A beauty. *Ellenore*, the painted name on the transom announced. *Ellenore*. Fred never even bothered to rename the boat after his first wife died and he managed to wed and bed Mary.

Fred hired him back when he got home from Texas and oil rigs and a little jail time for drinking and fighting. Needed a guy with a little wildcat in him, he'd said. A guy with a little good in him and a little bad. And that's what Fred got; a loyal guy who knew how to work hard and how to keep his mouth shut. Better yet, a guy agreeable to do a little extra if a job needed to be out of sight. And Fred rewarded Sam and made him his right-hand man, which came as close to a friend as Fred was likely to get.

Folks around town lumped Sam in with Fred. They liked him or hated him, or didn't care one way or the other, pretty much based on how they felt about Fred. That suited Sam just fine, just as long as he got a little of the same respect Fred got.

Fred came around the cabin and spotted him, beamed, and waved him closer with a whiskey bottle. "Sam!" he bellowed. "Come aboard. I'll name you first mate. Bet you never figured you'd be mate on a boat like this." When Fred wasn't bragging about his giant power boat, a 29-foot Richardson, he would brag about his giant damned car or his giant damned house. Always showing off. Rambled about his trip to Paris the last year, about London and King George. Like he was one of them.

Sam pulled his pocket watch out and flipped it open. Seven o'clock. Fred had insisted on a little something before the show, just like they do in Tampa. Like he needed an excuse to drink.

Fred fetched a highball glass, grabbed a handful of ice from a box with his greasy fat hand, shoved it into the glass, smothered it with whiskey, and shoved it at Sam.

Sam forced gratitude and a smile and took the glass. He'd never turned down a drink before, not a free one at least.

"You ready to go get you some culture, son?" Fred roared. He clapped Sam on the back.

"You bet, boss. I heard this will be good."

Mary emerged from the cabin, her own drink in hand. Sexy as ever. Dressed to the nines. She looked a little wobbly.

"I heard of this one, *Macbeth*," Fred continued. "Sword fights and stuff. It ain't no Roosevelt WPA touring number either. Nothing communist about it."

"Now, Fred," Mary piped in. "The WPA kept my daddy employed when there wasn't no work for him. They built this dock, remember?"

"The old one was just fine."

The old one was about to crash into the water on its own, Sam thought. But he kept his mouth shut and just nodded his support. He took a sip of whiskey, raised his glass in acknowledgment. "This stuff is sure better than what we used to haul, boss."

"Better tasting. Ain't better for us, though!" Fred snorted and held the glass up and peered into it. "Probably send me to an early grave."

"Prohibition had its good points and bad points, didn't it?"

"Made me a rich son of a bitch."

Mary laughed. "I'll drink to that." She took a quick sip. "Fishing has made you respectable though, Honey. Kind of."

"Respectable *and* famous." Fred added.

"Fame ain't a good thing for a smuggler," Sam said. "That night Capone dropped in to check up on you on his way to Miami, I thought I was gonna die."

"You and me both. But he liked your hillbilly jokes." Fred raised a toast. "To Samuel Ross Hawke. My right-hand man and best hillbilly foreman!"

Sam took another drink. "Bootlegging's done with, though, and fishing just ain't as lucrative as liquor. Course, nothing else is, either. Ever thought about lumber, Fred?"

Fred looked at him with watery eyes. "That's a whole different game, son. I ain't changing my game this late."

"But it's money that just grows on trees. Fine. Oranges. How about oranges?"

"It'd take me years to get a cash crop. Nope."

"We'll spend his money 'til it's gone, Sam," Mary said with a giggle. He looked at her. The giggle hid a lie. No laughter in her face, just a what-about-it look.

Twilight and stars gathered above. Venus hung low and silver over the sea. Sam stared at it. "Goddess of Love," he said. "Pretty, ain't she?" He glanced at Mary.

Fred grunted, and pointed into the sky opposite. "And there's Mars. God of War. A better planet for watching *Macbeth*."

"Guess we ought to get over to the high school, boss. That show'll be up directly."

Fred turned narrowed eyes to him. Sam hated that look. Knew it came with a scolding. "We'll go when I finish my drink." He brought the glass up slowly, making sure Sam and Mary knew full-well they'd leave when Fred felt good and ready.

Sam couldn't wait to knock that smug grin off his face one of these days.

* * *

The high school boys were still dragging oak chairs noisily across the gym floor and lining them up in rows when they arrived. Brigands Key High didn't even have an auditorium yet, but rumor had it they'd start building one in another year. Or two. Or never. In the meantime, the school had a makeshift stage they'd drag out and set up for events and graduations and such, and it never looked better than tonight, decked out with a heavy curtain the color of red wine.

Fred had brought a fifth along with him for good measure and kept hitting it. Though with the way he smelled, he didn't need anymore.

Chief Toomey drifted over, his bulk and attitude filling space. He nodded and gripped Fred's hand. "Knew you'd be here, Fred. Course, ever'body in town is here." His usually gloomy face almost looked to carry a little pride and excitement. He lifted his chin in a ghost of a nod to Sam. And turned his eyes on Mary, looking her up and down.

Being the richest man in the county, Fred sauntered to the front row and took a seat. Sam and Mary sat on either side of him.

The kerosene lamps dimmed and footlights flickered and glowed. A murmur of anticipation pulsed through the crowd. Some slick Midwesterner—already in costume of a medieval warrior—came out and announced in a loud voice, and with a sweep of his slender arms, that he was Jerry Kowalski or something, of the Minneapolis Players or something. He blubbered about how happy he was to be here in Briggins's Key. Sam knew it wasn't lost on the crowd that the guy couldn't be bothered to get the name right. Blathered on a minute or two about Shakespeare and how he wrote this stuff three hundred years ago. Talked about the blood-soaked Scotland of Macbeth's day. His flat, nasal accent didn't fit the costume. Sam hoped it got better than this. The man strutted, almost pranced, off the stage and disappeared.

Silence filled the gym, and the curtains rustled and parted. A wisp of white mist drifted out and around, hugging the floorboards and curling around fake rocks. Light flickered and flashed from somewhere and a sound of thunder pealed and rolled and lingered and faded. Sam glanced about, startled. It sounded like the real thing. Maybe there was something to this live stage stuff. *Oohs* and *ahs* peppered the crowd. More lights lit the stage.

Three gaunt, hunched figures, each carrying a glowing lantern, moved from the shadows in the rear of the stage and crept closer, almost gliding with a sinuous movement to the front of the stage, not more than twenty feet from Sam. Women, of indeterminate age, dressed in torn, filthy rags.

Fred leaned toward him. "Them's the witches," he whispered. "Macbeth's witches." Like Sam was too stupid to figure that out.

The gym grew silent as a windless night on the water. The witches became still and glowered at the audience. Their heads swiveled slowly, side to side, as if searching each person in turn. Their eyes seemed to glow, points of white, in the lantern light. Three pairs of white pinpoints.

Just like Sam's dream.

He found himself leaning closer.

Seconds passed in utter, profound silence. One of the witches locked her eyes upon his and held them for a moment. Her face, though filled with menace, held a certain seductive beauty, her features flawless and smooth. Her eyes came alive, glowing with bottomless depths of white. She whirled upon her companions and spoke at last. "When shall we meet again, in thunder, lightning, or rain?" Her voice rang clear and sweet and strong.

A second witch, the tallest, answered, her voice like the rustle of cracked and brittle leaves. "When the hurly-burly's done. When the battle's lost and won." She drew a slow circle in the air with a thin outstretched finger. The circle glowed, a thin, drifting wreath of white fire. It hung in the air, and dissolved. A murmur stirred the crowd.

"How'd she *do* that?" Mary whispered.

The third witch, an ancient being, leaned against her staff, and looked to an imagined horizon. "That will be ere the set of sun."

The first witch spoke with a sudden menacing grin, "Where the place?"

"Upon the heath," the second witch answered.

The third witch nodded. "There to meet with…Macbeth." Her head swung suddenly and her eyes fixed, glaring, upon Sam's. A bony, trembling finger pointed at him.

All three witches glared with white, pupil-less eyes at Sam, and spoke in unison. "Paddock calls, anon! Fair is foul, and foul is fair; hover through the fog and filthy air."

The mist boiled higher and the lights dimmed and brightened again.

The witches evaporated.

The audience, shaken from silence, clapped furiously.

Sam felt swept into the story. The scenes of the play rolled and surged with grim urgency. King Duncan received the news of Macbeth's rousing victory with Banquo over the rebel army of the traitor MacDonald's. The field of battle lay littered with the bloody and dismembered dead. Macbeth and Banquo, exhausted, bloodied, triumphant.

And the witches. The witches drifting among them, planting the dark idea into Macbeth's mind:

All hail Macbeth! Hail to thee, Thane of Glamis! Hail to thee, Thane of Cawdor! All hail, Macbeth! That shalt be king forever.

The witches again locked their eyes on Sam.

He felt his heart racing, his forehead slickening with sweat. He sensed both Fred and Mary looking at him, but he couldn't turn away from the players on the stage.

The tale grew darker. Evil compounded evil, and ambition and deceit and murder took their tolls, the spoils of evil raising Macbeth to the throne, and dashing the new tyrant and his queen into ruin. The mists and stones and trees and banquet halls and moors of the set became real; the cold windswept Scottish moor and highland, and the blood-soaked stones, and the clash of metal upon metal, and metal upon flesh and bone, and the oaths and fury of pitched battle to the death of Macbeth and MacDuff, sparks flying from striking blades, sweat flying, threats, shouts, blood, death, and over it all the glowing, greedy eyes of the witches, the Weird Sisters, those leering puppeteers of lust and hate and murder.

And Macbeth, realizing at last the great lie of prophesy, of his invincibility, of the gifts imbued by the witches, casts aside doubt and crying, "Lay on, Macduff, and damned be him that first cries, Hold, enough!" And Macbeth sinking, sinking, falling, redness welling and splashing onto the cold earth, dying at last, his evil undone, the victim of his own ambition.

And with the final curtain, the shouts and roars and thunderous clapping, Sam shaken as if from a dream. He found himself on his feet with the hundreds of friends and enemies, the islanders, clapping as never before.

The players assembled afterwards in a line on the stage, clasped hands, took their bows, basking in the rapturous applause.

The Weird Sisters were not among them.

* * *

The crowd filed out from the little high school, buzzing with excitement, and into the dark streets headed for home.

Sam watched silently as his boss lingered on the broad steps of the school, collaring and jabbering at anyone and everyone about what they'd just witnessed. Fred withdrew a bottle from his jacket, took a long swig, and passed the bottle to Sam. Sam obliged, cast a furtive glance about, and took a sip. Mary too. Propriety and sobriety be damned, Prohibition got sunk forever and even though it had made him a pile of money that would someday run out, Fred could drink in public as much and as loud as he wanted.

"Toomey!" Fred yelled, as he grabbed the Police Chief's sleeve and pulled him closer. "Did you see that? Hell, that was something. Best thing ever to hit Brigands Key, don't you think? Here, have a drink, pal." He shoved the bottle at Toomey.

Toomey shook his head. He gave Mary a quick anxious glance. "Fred, much appreciated, but I still got some inspections before I get home. Mary, you see him safe to bed now, you hear?" He returned his focus to Fred.

Sam watched closely. Mary glanced his way, her eyes penetrating, with that look again, that look of expectation, of demand. She kept her eyes on him, the urgency and heat in them growing. And she swung back to Toomey and her husband, all smiles and youthful happiness.

The images and words of the play swirled through Sam's mind. The spiral of lust and greed had dragged the characters to their ends. But the retribution and repaid debts for misdeeds made no impression on Sam. He had seen himself in Macbeth, had seen the witches ordain him for greatness and set him upon its path, murdering his beloved king.

Fate. There was no such thing, Shakespeare was saying. But destiny lay out there, only it had to be made. It had to be *taken*. And for the first time in his hard, bruised life, Sam saw his destiny, saw himself sweeping aside the most powerful man in Brigands Key. Brokering deals, controlling the high-and-mighty, maybe becoming even the most powerful in all of Florida. The witches made him see when they turned their bright shining eyes upon him, even as they schemed and ordained the faraway Macbeth's future.

Macbeth listened, acted, and made his own destiny happen once told it truly was his destiny. He had no choice.

But wasn't there always a choice?

The idea consumed Sam. Unlike Macbeth, he didn't have a driven outsider like Lady Macbeth pushing him into action. But he had an insider. The ultimate insider.

He had Mary MacGregor.

He had the king's own queen on his side and in his bed.

All he needed was the backbone to see the thing through.

Toomey continued to listen to Fred. He had to, the poor sap. He earned his pay by listening when the town's richest man opened his mouth.

"Damn, that was good," Fred shouted. "We need to celebrate."

"Beautiful weather tonight, Darlin'," Mary said. "Perfect for celebrating under the stars!"

"Honey, you're beautiful and smart! It is a perfect night! Let's take *Ellenore* out on the water."

Sam shot a glance at Mary. She ignored him and sipped her drink. "Are you sure, Honey? We can sit on the dock with all our friends and listen to the current." She slurred a few words. "We don't need to go out on the water. Sheriff Toomey can join us!" She giggled.

"I'm not a sheriff," Toomey said drily. His eyes drank her up and down. If Fred noticed, he didn't care. "And besides," Toomey continued, "I still got inspections, and to see folks home all right. Got to make sure this bunch of Gypsy actors gets squared away too. For their own good."

Fred hoisted his bottle. "To the Gypsies!" He took another drink, spilled some, and wiped his mouth on his sleeve. "And you make sure and tell 'em to come back around next year. Let's get to the boat. I think there's a case or two aboard."

* * *

The engines of *Ellenore* grumbled and smoked. Sam lit fore and aft kerosene lamps, and cast off the lines, and Fred eased the boat away from the dock. The tide raised up enough they should be able to get out okay, if Fred didn't manage to run them aground in his drunken stupor. A channel dug into the waterway would sure be a handy thing for a town that relied on fishing, Sam thought. Someday they might get one dug, but it might take another world war before anybody draglined the first bit of bottom out.

Fred negotiated the passage well enough for a drunk and they rounded the corner on the north end of the island. Overhead, the Hammond Lighthouse swept its lantern across the island and sea. The shadowed form of Old Man McConklin perched like a buzzard on the lighthouse catwalk high above them, presumably glaring down at the nighttime fools in the boat. Old Man McConklin glared at everyone.

Wispy clouds cleared away, revealing a glorious night sky, glittering with stars like diamonds. A cool breeze brought on a shiver. Fred cleared the island and turned *Ellenore* out to sea and cruised slowly west. Minutes passed. Sam searched the sea for other boats. No running lights, but that didn't guarantee there were no boats out. Some fools clung to the old Prohibition habit of lights-out to avoid the Coast Guard, and some few still smuggled illegal hooch anyway. Some were just fools. Sam looked aft to study the dim points of light that marked Brigands Key. No one followed, as much as he could tell. The sea rolled low and long and slow, the gentle waves lapping the bow as *Ellenore* eased through them.

Five miles out on the Gulf, Fred cut the engine and the boat drifted forward. Silence embraced them. "Hell of a night," Fred bellowed. He had not for a moment let the whiskey bottle wander more than an arm's length away. He waved it, drank, and passed it to Sam.

Sam obliged, mumbled his thanks, and took a sip. He passed the bottle to Mary.

Her eyes glinted in the dim flicker of the boat's lamps. She gave him the tight-lipped look again. The look that said *now or never.*

Sam felt his resolve fading. Murder, he thought. *Murder.* Had he come to this? Fred MacGregor was an ass, but who wasn't?

Fred was drinking himself into an early grave anyway. How many more years could he have? Would it be such a loss? The guy had no children that would grieve for him. His two brothers both died of heart attacks, like the one Fred seemed bound for. The only family he had left wanted him dead.

Tonight.

Fred headed aft, stumbling. "Look way down yonder," he said, pointing south along the black line of coast. "Cedar Key. They got the right idea, y' see? They got the trees and that means they got the lumber, and are making it pay off."

A fine idea, Sam thought. When he'd pitched it not three hours ago, the idea stank. Now Fred laid claim to it, making it a damned fine idea. Just fine. Just like every other idea Fred had stolen.

"Lumber," Fred continued. "That's what I need to get into. Lumber. Don't you think, Mary?"

"Sure, Honey. There's a lot of money in lumber. That is, 'til you cut all them trees down. Then what? Cedar Key cut down all the cedars a long time ago and the pencil company up and left. Now they stumble along like all the rest of us."

"You got no vision, Mary, so just sit back and look pretty. Let the thinking to me."

"Lumber." She took another drink.

Sam shook his head slightly. She glared at him. He wondered if she were becoming a problem herself. At least Fred could recognize a good idea, once he'd taken credit for it.

Mary went to Fred and squeezed his arm, brushed against him, whispered into his ear, giggled, kissed his cheek. She topped off her drink and took another sip. He turned to her, soft-eyed, with a widening grin. He reached down and pinched her ass. She giggled again and swatted his hand away. But her own hand traced lightly down his shoulder, his chest, his stomach, and lingered there, and moved lower. He pawed her and she skipped away from him, giggling again, so light and sweet, and headed forward, to the bow.

She winked at Sam as she passed. "Freddy, come on up and let's enjoy the bow. Sam, you go down to the transom and turn your back and sulk, why don't you? Me and my honey got some things to do."

Fred, clutching his bottle tight, lurched after her. Determination and lust lit his dull eyes. He ignored Sam, shoved past him, his eyes locked on his wife.

It dawned on Sam; it had arrived. The moment. They had been aft, at the transom. The gunwale there rose high, not at all good for falling overboard. Now she lured him fore, to the bow, where nothing but a low rail atop the low gunwale separated the deck from the sea. A little water on the deck, a little slip, and over you go. She led him like a dance partner to his own death.

They reached the bow and Mary drew Fred close and kissed him hard, savagely. His hands roamed clumsily over her body. She twisted, maneuvered him closer to the side of the boat. But he outweighed her by double. No way she was ever going to shove him anywhere he didn't want to go. She angled her head, still kissing him, and looked straight at Sam. That demanding look again.

The witches of Macbeth whispered in Sam's mind.

> *For a charm of powerful trouble,*
> *Like a hell-broth boil and bubble*

He drew a breath, and another, and crept toward Fred and Mary. He measured his steps, planted his feet as softly as he could. An old sea dog like Fred would feel the boat shift with each step.

Closer, he came. Closer. Ten feet away. Eight.

Mary pushed herself free from Fred's hands and stepped back. He glared at her and moved in again. Sam had his instant, his opening.

He hesitated.

"Do it!" Mary hissed, her eyes still on her husband's.

Fred stared dully at her.

By the pricking of my thumbs
Something wicked this way comes

Sam rushed forward and threw himself at Fred, striking him high in the back, between the shoulders, like throwing a block on the field with his arms tucked tightly in. The last thing he wanted was an open-armed entanglement, one that might end with his going overboard along with his victim.

It felt like running into a wall of muscle. Fred grunted and staggered and began to twist about, and Sam struck him again. Fred's heel caught on the rail. The big man teetered, seemed about to right and catch himself. The slight swell of a wave rolled past the boat, nudging it, adding imbalance. Fred clawed at the air, swayed, disappeared over the side, and plunged into the Gulf of Mexico with a splash.

Sam leaned over the side, his hands clenched on the gunwale. Bubbles stirred the water, but Fred had vanished. Mary darted forward and fell to her hands and knees, staring down at the black water. Fred could swim like a fish. It came with the job for a rumrunner. But he was drunk and waterlogged in full clothing. He had to sink. He had to. In silence, they waited.

Show his eyes and grieve his heart
Come like shadows, so depart!

"It's done," Mary whispered. "Done!"

A splash. Fred's hand broke the surface and flailed, followed by his face. He sputtered and coughed.

"No!" Mary cried.

Fred thrashed about and clawed at the hull. He reached upward for the gunwale, but *Ellenore* was built to ride high in the water and her sides slanted steeply out over the surface.

"Help me," Fred cried. "Mary! Sam, pull me up!"

Sam shook his head. "Don't think we will, boss."

A flash of terror, and a slow turn to anger transformed Fred's face. "You son of a bitch! You whore. This is what it's about then."

Mary shrugged.

They watched him struggle. He regained his composure, steadied himself. Sam knew Fred could swim like a fish and could stay afloat for an unknown time, maybe even hours. This made a new wrinkle. But Fred was fully clothed, boots and all, and even the strongest swimmer couldn't last weighted down in drowned clothes.

Fred pushed himself away from the boat and peeled off his jacket.

Sam pounded the gunwale. So it would be a waiting game now. Fine, time was on his side. No. They couldn't wait and hope. If a boat chanced by, Fred would call out.

"Mary," Sam said, "fetch me an oar." He would beat the man until he sank, and pray that the battered body never drifted ashore. No. He would beat him to death and wrap the body in chain so it would never come to the surface.

How did simplicity just become so complicated?

Mary continued to stare down at Fred.

"Mary, get me an oar! Now!"

She started, shot him an angry glance, and scampered toward the rear of the boat.

Sam continued to watch. Fred appeared to be removing a boot.

A movement, a short distance out in the water, maybe sixty feet, caught Sam's eye. He glanced in the direction and saw nothing. He returned his attention to Fred.

The movement, again. He was sure of it. Something in the water, closer than before. Had the commotion gotten the attention of a shark? Maybe, but it was nighttime. He'd not see a shark under the water if it swam around two feet away, much less sixty.

He saw it. The faintest hint of pale light under the water, coming swiftly toward them. Like a ghost.

No. Like *three* ghosts. Three apparitions of glowing whiteness.

They drew near, and within each apparition there appeared two glowing points of white.

The witches of *Macbeth*.

They encircled Fred, mere feet away and not more than two feet below the surface. Their faces turned upward, their long hair fanning and drifting about, and their pale, burning eyes fixed upon Fred, and malevolent hungry grins formed. One of the witches looked up at Sam. A claw of a hand broke the surface, glistening and dripping, and pointed at him. She mouthed a word. *Macbeth*. And withdrew her hand.

Behind him came the clatter of an oar onto the deck, a small curse, and Mary's footsteps returning.

Fred stared, terror-stricken, into the water about him.

The witches closed upon him.

Soundlessly, he disappeared under the water.

Not a sign of any of them remained.

Mary reached his side and dropped the oar onto the deck. She stared into the water, this way and that. "Sam! Where'd he go?"

Sam continued to peer into the deep, wanting to see, hoping that he would not.

"Sam!"

"He sank, Mary. He got tired and just . . . sank."

She gasped. He stood and backed from the gunwale, still watching the water, trembling, and drew her into his arms. "He's gone. Fred's gone. It's just us now." He at last looked at her and drew her close and kissed her.

* * *

Sam piloted the *Ellenore* back into channel, dropping speed as he rounded the north point, under Hammond Lighthouse. They worked it all out, having gone over it again and again. The thing would raise an eyebrow or two—everything that happened on this coast did—but tear-choked grief would sell it. On account of money.

Fred MacGregor lorded over the island as its richest man and sometime benefactor. *Ellenore* was the first boat in five counties to get a wireless. Even the yachts down in Tampa didn't have wireless. What's more, Fred bought Chief Toomey's office a wireless radio and mechanically recharging batteries, when the island didn't even have electric power yet. Made quite a grand show of his gift to Brigands Key.

Sam had wired Toomey on the way in, the bearer of awful news that drunken Fred stumbled and fell overboard and sank to his death. Once Sam discovered his best friend and boss missing, he'd dived in to search in futility. He shivered now in believably drenched clothes.

The story would work.

He neared the dock and eased *Ellenore* into her slip. Toomey waited on the dock, watching, his thumbs hooked into his belt. Two cops, Jenkins and Merriwether, stood to his left and right, each carrying a bright kerosene lamp. Sam throttled down and the boat bumped gently into place. He killed the engine, moved fore, and tossed a line to Deputy Jenkins.

"Hell of a thing, Sam," Toomey said.

Sam stepped onto the dock and took Toomey's hand. "He went up to the bow, up there alone." Sam's voiced cracked. He looked at his feet, then back into Toomey's face with carefully applied tears. It was important now that he retold the story like he'd done over the wireless. Mary had tearfully corroborated his story on the radio. They were in lockstep. Quite a pair. A year and a half from now, after dutifully comforting the grieving widow and helping her out with the business, they would get engaged and no one would bat an eye. A woman needed a man, after all. "I was aft, shining a light on the prop. I heard a splash, thinking a fish jumped. Mary was in the cabin; she screamed. And then I looked. He was gone." He shook with nice sob, inspired maybe by the glories of theatre. "Just . . . gone."

A movement, a pale light under the dark water, caught the edge of his vision. He turned to see, but the light had vanished. He stared into the darkness.

Toomey followed Sam's line of sight for a moment, and turned back to him. "Hell of a thing," he said. "I appreciate you looking for him. But I could see he weren't in no shape to be out on the Gulf at night." Toomey glanced up and down the boat. "How's Mary taking it?"

"She's all tore up. Down below in the cabin, bawling her heart out. Can't believe what's happened. All tore up."

Toomey nodded, and patted Sam on the shoulder. "Jenkins, go fetch her and be real gentle about it."

Jenkins eased onto the boat. The *Ellenore* shifted, as if unsure of the stranger. He went to the cabin door and knocked softly.

A moment later, the door flew open and Mary emerged, wide-eyed, gripping and brandishing a fish gaff, its wicked barbed hook glinting in the light. "Stay away," she cried.

Jenkins took a step back. Mary seemed surprised to see him, her eyes wide and darting about.

She'd steered off-script. Way off.

"Back away," she screamed.

Jenkins held his lamp high, casting her in a pool of shaky yellow light.

Her lip was swollen and cut, her eye blackening and nearly shut. She spotted Toomey, then Sam. She screamed again, and swung the gaff in the air. "Keep him away from me!"

Sam took a step and said, "Mary, what . . ."

She swung again. "Keep him away from me! It was him! Toomey, it was Sam! I saw him. I saw it all." She shook and trembled. "He lied about it to me but I saw it all. He shoved Fred over and watched, just watched, and kicked him down. And Fred was drunk and clothed and sank. He killed my Freddie!"

Sam overcame his sudden shock. "No! That ain't true at all! She saw it all right, she stood right there watching him go over."

"A second ago she was in the cabin," Toomey said. "You changing your story that quick?"

"He said he'd kill me if I told what I saw," Mary sobbed. "He choked me to make it clear. Look!" He pulled her high collar down, revealing bruises on her neck. "I was so scared!"

"No," Sam cried. "I didn't touch her! She did that to herself."

"Beat herself up. Choked herself," Toomey said. He slugged Sam in the stomach, doubling him over. "Merriwether, draw your gun and haul this son of a bitch in."

* * *

Mary watched the filling courtroom, fidgeting with a set of rosary beads her weasel lawyer said would look good. The date had been ramrodded up the calendar, and the trial would be speedy and sure. You just don't kill the town's biggest employer and throttle his pretty young wife and get away with it. Sam's word against hers, and his word wasn't worth a thing. He'd lost this case before it even got to court.

Judge Carter of the circuit court strolled in, stern and angry, and settled in as if he were the show, not her. Fine. A little chest-thumping always made a man feel big. There would be a hanging soon.

Mary studied the two major players. Sam wasn't one of them. He was cooked. No, the judge and the sheriff were the two biggest fish now. She needed a man, not for the sex, but for the expectations of the world. She had worked them both during the trial, a shy smile here, a gentle laugh there. They were eating it up.

Toomey lumbered about, old and fat. She could control him without breaking a sweat. But he had little future, other than maybe getting elected a small-county sheriff someday. Judge Carter, on the other hand, had a slick way about him, a way of climbing. And a background in getting elected. Maybe he could win a governor's mansion someday.

Judge Carter earned the prize, then. She cast him a sweet smile. He returned it with that look all men got around her.

She saw her future unfold before her. Lavish banquets, mansions, movie stars. And theatre. She had gotten the same vision that night at the gym, when the witches of Macbeth glared at her, and named her the future queen. They as much as crowned her that night.

And the night before, in her dream.

All she had had to do was make the vision come true.

She smirked at Judge Carter. He wasn't going to run the show. That too had been ordained.

> *No man that's born of woman*
> *Shall e'er have power upon thee.*

Notes

At a stage production of *Macbeth* a couple decades ago, I sneaked into an unused front row seat. It was worth it; the clash and clang and spark of steel upon steel, the bellowed curses, the flying sweat . . . this production came alive and I felt part of the action. But the thing that stood out above all was when one of the witches, one of the Weird Sisters, fixed her baleful stare upon me and let me know that I existed only at the merest whim of the mysteries of darkness.

Wow.

There's a reason the witches of *Macbeth* set the gold standard for supernatural evil.

Most critics rate *Macbeth* among Shakespeare's best. The story is a simple one of ambition, greed, and murder, with questionable prophecy driving man and wife to acts they would once have never contemplated. At its heart are the elements of horror, all set into motion by the prescient visions and machinations of the witches.

"When the Hurly Burly's Done" was written for *The Masters Reimagined*, an anthology of speculative stories based on classics of literature, and won a silver award in the Royal Palm Literary Awards.

Changes in technology always come with growing pains. Some more painful than others, as in this story. Rural electrification was a miracle for folks outside the cities and towns, but would not necessarily have been welcomed by everyone.

The Light Keeper

Brigands Key, September, 1938

McConklin the light keeper sat up reading all night on the porch of his house, same as every night, poring over a grease-smudged copy of *The Sea Wolf.* He puffed contentedly on a corncob pipe, and had just refilled and relit it when the lights went off all over Brigands Key, everywhere but his porch. His porch stayed lit, bathed in the bright reliable glow of kerosene.

He looked out over the town. Blackness everywhere. He drew his pocket watch. Four AM. Most folks wouldn't even notice, being still in bed. He ran out to the yard, looked up at the dark spire of the lighthouse, and swore a blue streak when he looked up and saw that the lantern room was dark.

He ran his fingers through his hair, and shook his head. Only a couple hours until dawn. Maybe it could wait until then.

No. Even a couple hours without a beacon would put men in mortal danger.

He emptied his pipe on the ground, stamped out the ash, and hurried back to the porch. He grabbed the lit lantern and two more unlit ones.

He ran down the driveway to the rotting picket fence, aiming for the new power pole. The electric lines came across the channel along the old wood bridge on stinking creosote poles that dotted the town. The nearest pole stood just inside his fence, near the shed that housed the transformer. The other transformers around town all hung on poles, but the town bosses reckoned the lighthouse important enough to warrant protection for its transformer.

He rattled open the tin door of the shed, spooking Mary Shelley, the broke-down gray cat, from atop a crate of equipment parts. Stupid cat, didn't know how dangerous living inside a transformer house might be. Mary Shelley rewarded him with a hiss and a swipe. He retaliated with a kick and knocked the wide-eyed thing aside. "Git, you worthless animal!"

He hung the lantern on a hook and tweaked it brighter, sweeping aside the darkness of the little shack. The transformer itself gleamed metallically, like the silver the electric boys said it was.

He stared at the goddamn thing, his pulse quickening, his face flushing with a sudden hot resentment. Thirty-two years he'd tended the light on kerosene, and never a stop in service. Seven months on electric, and down she goes. A perfect record, shot all to hell.

"That's progress," the electric boys had claimed, a thousand times. Maybe they were right. Electric didn't stink and smoke like kerosene, and didn't have to be refilled daily.

Better most nights, but not tonight. Tonight the electric boys had failed miserably and the Hammond Lighthouse had lost its beacon for the first time since it went on in 1872. The first time that ships out in that shallow uncertain sea would search the horizon without success for the old Hammond beacon, relying on it to keep them from running aground or sinking.

McConklin swore out loud. He'd warned them.

The thing about electricity was, its fanciness fooled everyone with convenience. Sure, it was convenient. But you held a clawing tiger by the tail.

Kerosene had done a workman's job, but them new boys argued that kerosene made the danger, not electric. Kerosene would burn the place down one day. That was laughable; there weren't nothing in Hammond Lighthouse that could catch fire. It was all concrete and steel.

Get on with it, he told himself. Don't think about how they ruined it and how they're going to somehow hang your ass for it.

He thought back to the one lousy day of training they'd shoved him through as they'd strung the wires and hung the contraptions. His son Roy had gone through the same training with him. It seemed like the only time the kid had ever gotten truly worked up by anything.

Roy.

He hadn't seen his son for six months, but that wasn't his fault. McConklin had always figured Roy would inherit the light keeper's job once McConklin retired, but the kid left for Galveston and said he'd never be back.

McConklin had gotten his hopes up. Penny Merriwether claimed she'd seen Roy at an inn in Perry just two days ago. She must have been mistaken; if Roy had come that close, he'd have come all the way home. Wouldn't he?

He and Roy didn't see eye to eye. The boy had once been the quiet one but turned since his older brother, Tom, had died nine years ago. Tom ran around, drinking and chasing girls, even married ones, and McConklin had tried to put a stop to it, clamping down on both boys. The boys' mother had run off and left him to raise them alone. He wouldn't spoil them the way she did.

Tom had stayed out late one night too many. Not a word, just came home late and went straight upstairs. He should've apologized. Everything would have been fine if he had. McConklin shook his head, remembering the blows at the top of the stairs, the long slow tumble, and Tom motionless at the bottom, his face turned an impossible direction, and little Roy coming out of his room to see Tom's broken twisted body, and blinking through tears at his father.

It was an accident, McConklin reassured himself. It was. Chief Toomey agreed, so it must have been.

But Roy blamed his old man, and grew into a sulkier, more venomous hellion than Tom had been, sniping, ignoring, resisting at every turn. But never fighting, not like Tom. Roy's way was worse, and he got worse, and McConklin had to rein him in. And as with Tom, the demon come over him and in an alcoholic haze he had beaten the unresisting boy bloody and senseless, somehow stopping short of killing him.

The closeness to murder shocked even himself and he swore off the bottle for a time.

The boy said nothing to nobody. Just an explanation that he'd fallen in the lighthouse. But the whispers began about town. Chief Toomey gave him a hard look and watched him closely after that.

Then came the rural electrification. Roosevelt bought a lot of votes with that, and folks in Brigands Key weren't no different than folks in the Tennessee Valley. A boon to the economy, the local Babbitts claimed. Course, their jobs weren't threatened by it. McConklin's was. He'd gone from pillar of the community to unnecessary relic almost overnight.

At least he could prove his importance tonight.

After his one day of training Roy got full of ideas and said that electrification was the best thing that ever happened, and went off to study it for six more weeks in Charlotte and came back with a fancy certificate. Not enough to call himself an engineer or anything, but enough to make a dollar or two. He even got some WPA work, stringing wires, hanging transformers, charging lines. Got the hometown hero treatment the day they threw the switch and the lights came on all over Brigands Key. They bought him steak dinners and drinks. Everybody fell for the convenience. And when Tallahassee said the lighthouse kerosene lamp was coming out and an electric lamp going in, McConklin could read the writing on the wall.

It wasn't over yet. Roosevelt kept banging his war drum, scaring people into thinking that Hitler was up to no good and Nanking showed the things to come, and insiders whispered that FDR planned to nationalize all the lighthouses and turn 'em over to the goddamn Coast Guard.

What then? McConklin saw no way them military boys would let him keep his job.

He eyed the transformer housing. Where was Roy and all his training now?

Mary Shelley meowed and watched him curiously.

"Shut up." McConklin said.

For his six weeks of training, Roy knew bunches of diagrams and whatnot. McConklin had gotten the six-hour training, and that seemed like plenty. He knew the shutoffs, the shunts, the routine maintenance, which said basically, "call an expert." That slung a goddamn insult into a man who'd kept the beacon on without fail for three decades.

The transformer hunkered in the dark, a steel barrel bolted to a concrete floor. McConklin held up his light, inspecting it. From his training, he knew that the whole point of this thing was to ratchet the high power in the lines down to a manageable power for buildings. They'd showed him the power by hauling out one that had blown, a blackened, smelly wreck. This one here, on the other hand, was as slick as the day it was installed. Not a whiff of burned wires and insulation. He looked at the row of arrestors, three glass mushrooms attached to a beam alongside the transformer. Pretty little things, kind of like the Fresnel lens. They were supposed to protect from power surges, like if lightning struck the lines somewhere. They'd explode if that happened, but they were intact and shiny.

So the town lights glowed, the arrestors looked good, and the transformer, too. That meant the problem hid in the line between the transformer and the lantern room.

This electric stuff weren't so danged hard.

He checked the conduit out from the transformer, and went outside the shed. He followed the conduit to the base of the lighthouse, where it disappeared into a hole that'd been drilled just for this purpose. Chest-high above it hung another steel housing box, the shutoff for the lighthouse. He opened the door with a squeak, checked it quickly, and shoved the heavy switch lever to the off position. If the power came back, he'd be safe.

He went to the lighthouse door, unlocked it, pulled it open with a metal groan. He held up his lantern and located the conduit again on the inside. He began ascending the spiral ladder, holding aloft the lamp and checking the conduit as best he could.

Minutes later, huffing just a bit, he reached the lantern room. The conduit and cable running up the lighthouse shaft had been intact the whole way, as far as he could tell.

The beautiful old Fresnel lens, the finest in all the Southeast, sat there motionless, useless. Since the upgrade, he couldn't even manually add a lamp to it.

He opened the outer glass door to the encircling catwalk and stepped through. He hung his lighted kerosene lamp on the railing and fixed it there with a few twists of baling wire. He lit the two remaining lamps and attached them similarly to the railing, spaced equidistantly around the catwalk. He turned the wicks bright as they would go, and studied them for a moment. They made pitiful excuses for a beacon, but they'd have to do until power came back on.

He leaned gently against the glass panes and stared out to sea, watching for boats. He figured that was all he could do. If there weren't no electricity, there weren't nothing else for it.

His thoughts returned to Roy, and that damn girl that lured him away. What was her name? Melissa? Little pie-faced Melissa. A life wrecker, that one, like his own wife, Georgette, had been. Georgette had left them all, left the boys when they were little, on account of the fights and the discipline.

You couldn't warn a boy about a girl when his pecker did all the thinking. When Melissa tried to talk Roy into leaving, McConklin got after her and told the little conniver to stay away, to mind her own business, to sink her claws into someone as trashy as herself. She left in tears, and told Roy all about it, tarting up the facts. She left town, like he hoped, but with an unplanned side effect; Roy left a week later.

McConklin reentered the lantern room and studied the cable to the beacon lamp. It occurred to him that the wiring from the distribution line to the transformer to here were all fine. So the problem lay in here.

The rain that had come tonight came in with a little bit of touchiness. There had been lightning strikes off over the Gulf. So most likely lightning had struck the lighthouse and knocked out the equipment.

But the tower bristled with lightning rods to take care of that, and there had been no thunderclap. One that close to his house would have made him jump out of his skin.

Something else was wrong.

He spotted it.

At the junction of the cable to the electric motor, a second wire had been spliced in, skillfully hidden under the main cable. It ran just a few inches over the steel floor and was attached in a dark corner.

Awareness dawned in him.

The whole room was steel, and glinting slick with rain. If the power came back on . . . but it couldn't. He'd thrown the shutoff to be safe.

Unless . . .

He heard a hiss and a crackle. His hand, gripping the rail, burned like fire, and the muscles in it squeezed tight. A shot of electricity blasted him, and his heart clenched like a fist. He couldn't release his grip.

His mind fought for consciousness as the current surged through him.

He shook violently. Vaguely, he smelled flesh and hair burning.

A last thought flickered. Roy had wired the lighthouse. Roy . . . kid wasn't so hopeless after all . . .

* * *

Chief Toomey thumbed a notepad and poked around and asked questions, hoping to sound like he understood the technical jargon. Two or three locals tried to convince him the light keeper's death wasn't no accident. Stupid island hicks. He knew better, even if he didn't know how electricity got stuffed into wires and what made it move. He knew people and motives. Killers don't go around killing with wires when bullets are so much more reliable.

Oswald Denton, the town drunk—one of them, anyway—stuck to his own foggy delusions on the matter. He lived in a wine bottle, but swore a blue streak that he'd seen a man that night fiddling around with the switch at the base of the lighthouse. Goddamn silly Oswald. Who'd be out in the rain fiddling with wires? Nah, it had to have been a lightning strike. Besides, Toomey pointed out, who in the whole county even had the smarts to rewire a whole building to kill? Electricity was new, and a lot like magic. You'd need a goddamn magician.

A week later, an electric boy moseyed over to the island to investigate the wiring and render his professional opinion. He said it was all up to snuff. Nobody had tampered with anything.

Oswald Denton then claimed he'd seen the mystery man again, fiddling around in the dark, messing with the switch, and climbing the lighthouse to the lantern room. "Changing things back the way they was," Denton claimed. "Don't you see, it's the perfect murder. You kill a man with something nobody understands. Folks understand guns and knives, but they got no idea what electricity is and how it gets pushed inside their house." Denton grumbled and belched and wandered off to Bill's Tavern.

Stupid old drunk.

Toomey closed the case. Mary Shelley purred and rubbed his leg. He ignored her but she followed him home anyway and basked in the electric warmth of his house. That was progress.

Notes

"The Light Keeper" represents a second chance at life for a story I wrote some years before. In that earlier version, it wasn't a light house that needed fixing. It was a broken washing machine. Not a bad story, but it lacked something—interest—and languished in a drawer for some years. Until I dusted it off and rewrote it as a Brigands Key story. The changes breathed life into the manuscript.

We take electric power for granted now, but it wasn't so long ago that much of rural America had no power. Electrification was a big deal for country folk, and in 1936, Franklin Roosevelt signed the Rural Electrification Act, launching a determined push to get power into the homes of farmers, 90 percent of whom had none. The lights came on and banished the darkness, the radios delivered the baseball game with breathless excitement, and the kids read *Weird Tales* late into the night.

Ireland is a small country of great beauty and rich, ages-deep history. Outsiders may see opportunity in the island nation's green hills, maybe even easy pickings. But plunder often comes at a price.

The Queen Beneath the Earth

Charles Bonham started out in construction, quit that to go into accounting, quit that to become an actor, and quit that to rob graves.

Most grave robbers followed crap business models and ended up shot or jailed, or both. Not Bonham; he knew the answer. You needed a scam, a carefully designed one, and he'd designed the best. It worked like a charm in Guatemala and would work here in the northwest of Ireland. Different hemispheres, different cultures, different climates. Didn't matter. Bonham had discovered that one great thing that everyone, everywhere, held in common.

They wanted to be on TV.

Charles Bonham wasn't his real name but it oozed that highborn British self-satisfaction the Irish hated, and fit perfectly for a Cambridge-educated documentary filmmaker. It opened doors out here in the sticks. To pull off a scam, to open doors, you become the character, you believe in it. His father never believed in anything, and had refused to pay for acting classes, swearing that they promised a ticket to a life of poverty, but dear old dad never understood art.

Bonham pulled over onto the non-existent shoulder of a skinny Irish road at the foot of Knocknarea, shoved open the creaky car door, climbed out, and slammed it shut behind him. An early March wind knifed off the North Atlantic, whipping over stony hills and stinging his eyes. He'd been in Ireland two weeks, just long enough to get geared up and educated, not nearly long enough to get used to the cold and wind, but a bright and blue and heatless sky buoyed his spirits. Ribbons of snow lay here and there, unwilling to give up the winter.

Central America had suited him better. Hot, buggy, and wet. But with Santiago's disappearance and a lot of uncomfortable questions from the Federales about the missing Colonel's dealings in El Petén, that lucrative region had been cut off for him. So miles and continents seemed a good refuge.

The summer hordes of Americans lurked still months away, with their demanding, entitled ways. What constituted a horde required relative judgment though; up here, past Connemara, way past Galway, the tourists swarmed in far fewer numbers. The area lay too far outside their hurried ways, and they had to check the Cliffs of Moher off the list, snap a few shots, pile back into their snarling tour buses and hustle back to Killarney.

Bonham started the hike uphill on the less-traveled of two trails. Ahead, a young couple picked their ways downward, measuring careful steps around the mud and snow. Americans, he guessed. You could spot them a mile away, in their heavy coats and gloves and scarves like they were on an Arctic expedition. Just something about them, and this pair of twenty-somethings wore American smugness like a badge. The chick even had blue hair. Not your nice, demure Sligo country girl type.

They stopped when they reached him, nodded. The guy said, "Hey, how's it going?" Sure enough, in an American accent. A northeastern accent.

Aussie time. Bonham smiled and said, "G'day, mate." Americans loved Australian accents, however poorly done. This pair didn't need to know he was American, from Idaho Falls. No one did. If questioned by the constabulary, they would report with conviction that they'd met an Aussie on Knocknarea. Bonham's Irish accent still came off kind of phony, and even Americans would say it sounded fishy without knowing why. But any clown could fake Australian, flattening out vowels and grinning. "Anything to see up there, mate?"

"Great view," the guy said. Nice. A talker. He wore a leather jacket that looked like it came from a second-hand store.

Blue Hair nodded toward a streak of slate clouds and distant but closing rain. "Pretty cool place. We'd stay longer, but a rain's coming."

Bonham glanced at the sky and quickly scanned the horizon. No one in sight. "How'd you hear about this place? Not really in many guidebooks, is it?"

"No, it's not. A guy in a pub in Sligo told us about it, said we could just walk up to it."

"Unreal, ain't it?" Bonham said. "Nothing and nobody to keep it protected. Crikey! Back home, we'd post armed guards on it."

"Maybe," Leather Jacket said. "It's a different outlook here, I guess."

"Did you get to visit with the queen?"

Blue Hair grinned. "She's there all right. We think. Mostly there are rocks. Lots of rocks."

"Lots of rocks," Bonham said. "That's Ireland. Headed down so soon?"

"The place gives me the creeps," Leather Jacket said.

"Graveyards always give you the creeps," Blue Hair said.

* * *

Lots of rocks. Rocks that would defy Bonham's efforts.

He plodded up Knocknarea, breathing hard. The view stretched out all around, affording a sweep of the Irish countryside and shimmering blue of Ballisodare Bay, but aesthetic appreciation occupied a low level in his business. Sightseeing belonged to tourists. His idea of sightseeing involved sitting in a sunny café in Beverly Hills or a piazza in Tuscany, sipping wine and ogling the girls, after he'd made a ton of money on this venture. That's how you could enjoy it. Climbing a steep hill in an Irish jerkwater kicked the fun out sightseeing.

But you do what you must.

He paused to rest and take a sip of water, and pushed on toward the summit. He at last reached the top, relieved to get to the flatter, easier part. He took a nervous look about, turned and scanned the trail below and the valley beyond. Not a soul in sight. The American hipsters had gotten into their cheap little rental car and puttered off into the distance, back in the direction of Sligo. Good riddance.

He returned his attention to the cairn.

The mound rose above him, some forty feet high, and stretched nearly two hundred feet across at the base. A big-assed pile of uncut white and gray limestone rocks, no joints, no mortar. Just rocks, the voids between packed with the dirt of centuries.

So here lay Queen Maeve.

He'd seen enough, read enough, to know that Maeve's Cairn held many secrets.

He strolled the perimeter of the cairn, inspecting it with an affected casualness, looking to see if anyone else happened to be about. Nope, no one. He took out his cell phone and snapped a number of shots, high, low, offset, straight on, silhouetted from all sides. Trying his best to get something vaguely artful out of it. If he took enough shots, some were bound to come out slightly better than pure shit, and one or two might be really good. Law of averages.

He really should take a course in photography someday or, better yet, a course in the art of film. These might prove valuable skills in keeping the scam afloat. So far, he'd muddled through by having to fool only provincial types. They fell for it willingly as long as he tossed out references to obscure movies from his well-thumbed paperback copy of *1,000 Greatest Movies*. He bandied about the names of Hitchcock and Scorsese and Kubrick and Kurosawa, and the hicks' eyes lit up. Follow that up by expounding on the light and dark in film noir, the great empty canvas of the desert in *Lawrence of Arabia*, and the quick spare cuts of *To Kill a Mockingbird*, and they would make him mayor of their stupid little town and buy him Guinness. And when he pulled out the little eyepiece he'd stolen off a telescope in a hobby shop, and that now dangled from a chain about his neck like a diamond, and peered through it at his surroundings and murmured about the light and authenticity, the hicks would shit their pants.

Someday, though, someone would call him out as a con man upon discovering that he had no actual skills. It behooved him to pick up a skill or two.

He sat and ate a chocolate bar and some God-awful Irish potato chips and washed them down with a Coke. He unzipped his massive hiker's backpack and eased out his latest prized possession, a pro-grade ground-penetrating radar mapper. He admired the black steel frame, the twelve-inch spoked wheels, the heavy-duty electronics. Had to be worth close to forty thousand dollars brand new, yet he'd procured it in Dublin in a fantastic deal—free—from the back of a geotechnical engineering firm's unlocked panel van. The two engineers had slipped into a pub for a pint or two. He watched them and simply opened the van and pushed the GPR like a baby carriage down the street. Served them right for not being more careful with company gear.

He switched on the GPR, listened to the tiny high whine of the electronics warming to the task, and ran it around the base of the cairn, watching the LED readout of squiggles give away the secrets of the past. He turned off the recording function. Whatever he saw, he would see in real time and then it would be gone. He knew what to look for, and if it lay buried there he'd remember the spot. Recording it just invited trouble, and records worked for academics, not lawless tomb raiders.

He understood science and shit. Cairns showed an unusual type of matrix and made great targets for GPR. He had already dug a few test pits in cairns across Ireland and calibrated his equipment against them. Maeve's Cairn looked similar to those.

He studied the depths the monitor graphed. Forty-one feet, as predicted. The radar penetrated to the very bottom of the cairn, down to the natural earth of Knocknarea hill, where the radar drew a different map, different densities, the signature of the glaciated landscape that stretched to the horizon all around.

He studied it, holding the GPR stationary, and moved on, continuing his upward spiral around the structure. If he guessed correctly, once he got halfway up the slope he would be pointing the GPR at the rough geographic center of the cairn.

What he "saw" in the GPR screen looked nothing like anything. GPR never gave a true picture. It rendered stuff worse than sonograms, and those things made babies look like squids. All ghostly blobs and jagged lines. You had to understand what they meant, so he'd educated himself. He had run a dozen expeditions into the Connemara Mountains and her hidden farmlands, scoping out what a buried foundation looked like, what an empty culvert looked like, what an old mine shaft looked like.

He needed a hit that looked like the blobs and lines of a mine shaft. Get that, and he'd have the mark of an ancient burial chamber or passage tomb.

And that spelled big money.

He ran a few passes over the cairn, his pulse quickening when he reached the magical midpoint of the slope. Sure enough, a jagged arc appeared in the GPR readout, marking a horizontal void there, deep down under his feet. He'd found the passage tomb. A big one, too.

Cairns and dolmens and stone circles dotted the region. Maeve's Cairn dwarfed the others and commanded a spectacular view all around. Would a peasant be buried at such a place? Nope. Whoever lay beneath his feet had wielded power and wealth in a distant past. *That's* where you dig.

But not just yet.

He needed to wait for the right time, and it wasn't today. A successful operation needed its own pace.

He studied the void in the radar image, and ran a slow pass over it again. It stretched eight or ten feet wide. Six feet high. He pushed the GPR up the slope, following the outline of the void from above. He traced it about fifty feet and saw that it continued, roughly with the same dimensions, a little higher here, a little narrower there. At its closest, it came to within twenty feet of the slope. Perfect.

He retraced his path back to the point at which he'd first found the void. He glanced about. Solitude, luxurious and expansive, enveloped him; Maeve's Cairn remained devoid of interlopers. Almost. A hiker in the distance headed his way, from the little parking lot. No problem; he had found what he needed, but he wanted one last peek at his find. He settled the GPR once more over the start of the void below.

Something had changed.

Was the void now smaller? No, it couldn't be unless part of the chamber had caved in, and the odds of that occurring during his brief visit came close to nil. There appeared to be a mass of something—

rock, dirt, pottery—in the floor of the void. Funny, it had escaped him before. But then, radar fluctuated in all that great mass of earth and stone. Most likely, he stood a couple of feet off from where he took his first reading, and that threw it off, redrew it a bit. He cleared the screen and moved the machine over about two paces and got another reading.

The mass within the chamber was still there. He studied it closely. Had it moved a couple of feet?

He shook his head. Radar never had been an exact science. You bring the best equipment, and you still get shit readings. Ah well, the day's exploration had yielded good news. Maybe a pile of treasure did in fact lay buried there.

He switched off the machine, folded it and stashed it into his pack, and started back down the trail of Knocknarea, humming a little tune. Just another nature lover on a day hike.

* * *

Five days later, Bonham sat in a dark little pub in Sligo, nursing a Guinness and gobbling down a bone-warming Irish stew.

The bartender, Sean, had taken an interest in Bonham over the week, perhaps too close an interest, with lingering glances and smiles and whatnot. Sometimes that kind of thing could be played to an advantage but this time hadn't gotten to a point yet at which it warranted a play.

He checked his phone for the time. Just past noon. Outside, the day had grown gloomy after a dispiriting couple of beautiful sunshine days. Count on Irish weather to screw things up.

Nevertheless, things now worsened and brightened his outlook. The wind whipped and a charcoal and iron sky blew in off the North Atlantic. Flurries of snow now and again. He scrolled his finger up and down his phone, checking the weather. The forecast and radar confirmed what he saw brewing through the thick windows.

Looked like a shit day with a low ceiling of clouds and constant hard rain, and that promised a fine night for grave robbing. Better still, there would be a new moon, darkening the night even more.

"You the filmmaker, love?"

Bonham glanced up. The pretty red-haired girl he'd seen about town had sat down four seats down the bar from him. "I beg your pardon, miss?" he said, slipping easily into upper class London accent mode.

"The filmmaker. I heard you was with the movies."

Bonham nodded. He didn't want to talk to anyone at this stage in the operation. Not much good could come of it. But damn, her eyes glittered in the light and her face possessed that country girl charm and innocence. It should be his duty to cure her of that innocence. "Why, yes, I have a few projects in the works."

"You got one here in Sligo, don't you?" She smiled like the sun. "We saw you head up Knocknarea."

Bonham gave a small sheepish smile, gestured a surrender with open palms. "You indeed have me, I suppose. I am researching and scouting locations. I like to know my subjects inside out before we bring the crew on location. The chaps don't work cheap, you know." He hoisted his beer. "Unions."

"Bet you can afford them," she said, with a coy flourish.

A rough, scowling young man, built like a small truck, sat a few more seats down, staring hard into his beer, unmoving. His eyes glanced toward the girl and back to his beer.

Bonham paid him no heed. Jealous local farm boy, no doubt. The girl held far more interest. "Perhaps you've seen my work," he said. "Bonham. Charles Bonham."

Bewilderment flitted across her eyes like a butterfly and vanished.

Bonham laughed. "Oh, that's all right! Actors and directors get all the publicity. Producers just get the projects paid for and made. In fact, I would be terribly shocked if you'd known my name."

"No, I think I heard of you. I know I have."

Precisely, he thought. That's the whole point. Getting people to think that. "You are extremely kind to say it," he said. "Your name is... Kate? I believe that is correct?"

"Why, yes sir, it is! How'd you know?"

"As I said, I'm scouting the area. Not just for locations, but for on-camera talent. You, Kate, were mentioned." Not exactly true, to be honest. He'd spotted her and made a discreet inquiry. He grasped the eyepiece dangling around his neck, with his best honest, sincere arching of eyebrows. "Do you mind?"

She blushed a hot pink. "Um, no, of course not. No." She brushed a strand of hair from her face. It fell back into her face and she worried it back behind her ear.

"Oh, leave that be," he said. "It's natural. Real. More real than I see in Dublin, London, and Prague. Let it fall." He leaned closer, reached out and gently moved the errant strands back across her forehead and cheek. He murmured, held the eyepiece to his eye, and studied her. A classic move, one he'd been perfecting since college. "Hm. Very nice. Could you raise your chin just a smidge? Oh, that's marvelous. Have you ever acted, Kate?"

"Oh no. Acted? No. I used to sing choir."

"You should consider it. And I mean that. You have an indefinable quality. An Audrey Hepburn quality, I should say."

She couldn't suppress her grin, though she tried. The girl looked nothing at all like Audrey Hepburn, beyond having two arms and two legs. But Audrey Hepburn he'd found through trial and error, invoked that magical, waif-like, ephemeral comparison that never failed to open a young woman's legs.

The beefy fellow downed his beer and shoved it at the bartender for a refill. "What a load of rubbish," he said.

Bonham regarded him for a moment. Beefy described him well. A few sloppy tattoos adorned his thick forearms. A worthy applicant for any goon squad. The guy couldn't have been older than twenty-five, although his close-cropped hair beat much too hasty a retreat for someone that age. Youthful righteousness and anger lined his face. Bonham forced the smallest of smiles. "I beg your pardon, young man?"

"I said, rubbish. You are rubbish. A fraud."

Bonham tensed. Had Goon Squad seen through him so easily? Maybe the kid had done a little investigating. No, that didn't fit him. Bonham's act had held up just fine. He gave a small, friendly laugh. "I have indeed received some rather harsh reviews before, but I don't believe I've ever been labeled a fraud."

"I been listening to you, mister. You don't know anything about Maeve, and nothing about Sligo and Knocknarea either."

Bonham eased up. So. Goon Squad didn't really know a damned thing about Bonham and his little science projects. Jealousy over a girl and animosity towards the smooth, witty outsider merged into one vague hatred in the kid. He'd transferred those emotions into misguided principles about defending local goodness and heritage from outside takers and greedheads.

Easy enough to handle.

"Well, sir. I plead guilty to that charge! As I was telling the lovely Miss Kate, I'm scouting sites. I am in fact both a filmmaker and an archaeologist; just not one that has specialized in Irish archaeology. I know Maeve was an heroic iron age queen of Ireland, buried atop Knocknarea. Perhaps you can help me with the local take on her."

"Good and buried she is. But she weren't no heroine. She were a bitch in her day."

"Ah, the big question. Bitch goddess or heroine? It's a raging debate, or so I've gathered." Bonham took a sip of beer. "I'd like to hear your thoughts."

Goon Squad's scowl flickered and extinguished, and returned. "Queen Maeve didn't give in to nobody," he said, stabbing the bar with his finger for punctuation. "Nobody, not even to husbands, and she had five of them. You heard about the rocks?"

Again with the rocks. Bonham shook his head.

"You visit Queen Maeve's tomb, you take a rock up the hill and add it to the pile. To keep her in place. Nobody wants her to get out."

The old gent at the end of the bar chuckled.

Goon Squad gave him a jagged look. "You gon' spout your own rubbish now, Finn?"

"Oh, not on me life, Ian. Far be it from me to rob our good town of lucrative nonsense."

"It ain't nonsense. Maeve ruled mean and hard. She once took her people to war just to steal a bull so her husband couldn't claim the best in the land."

"Oh, that much may be true. But she's not buried *here*. Not on Knocknarea, anyhow."

A sudden disappointment pricked Bonham's gut. Not here? He'd heard the arguments, sure, but his research convinced him *this* place promised pay dirt. But to hear a local, one obviously educated and knowledgeable, take the side against her local gravesite, well, that would be shit. But shit news dogged every job. You roll with the punches. "What do you mean, sir?"

"That story's more local myth than fact. Oh, she's buried somewhere in County Sligo or nearby. Just where exactly, that's the conundrum. I'd put me money on Rothcroghan, over in County Roscommon. That was her home, after all. Knocknarea seems to have gotten confused with another burial near the time of her death. This was, oh, the year 500 or so. Got to remember, there weren't much in the way of record-keeping then."

"I've heard that too," Kate said, looking a little crestfallen.

"I guess I'll be visiting Rothcroghan next," Bonham said, smiling.

"Maeve's *here*," Goon Squad said. "Buried standing up, facing east, facing her enemies back home."

Finn chuckled. "That bit may even be true." He took a sip of beer, grinned at Bonham. "Course, if you insist on poking about in the dirt, you must beware the Fomoire."

"And what might that be?"

"Fomoire. The Fomorians, of course."

Shit, Bonham thought. He needed more Internet time. "I'm unfamiliar, I daresay."

"The Fomorians were the ancient demons from under the Earth. Or from the sea, depending on your source. They supposedly dwelt up here, underground, long before people arrived in Ireland. Nasty, violent creatures, not much fun at all. Good for bedtime stories to scare your little ones, I suppose. All cultures need boogeymen, don't they?"

Kate glared at Finn and edged in between them, returning her attention to Bonham. Her eyes caught the dim light and softened. "Um. Are you staying somewhere yet? I don't know if you'll find a place this late. The couple decent places are booked. I think they're booked."

Outside a rain blew sideways. Thunder rumbled in the distance.

Bonham winced. The girl practically begged to be bedded. But he liked the looks of a shit night, blustering about right outside the pub window. "Pardon me a moment, if you please," he said, and scrolled to the weather on his phone. Sure enough, horrible night tonight, nothing but clear blue and light for the next few days. He sighed, looked back to the girl. "I'd like nothing more than to join you. But, sadly, I must be back in Dublin this evening. Damned production schedules! The grips and gaffs have coaxed others into striking for more money." He didn't even know what a grip and gaff did on a movie set, if they did anything, but he'd seen them in the final credits a hundred times and he guessed so had the girl.

But circumstances dictated the moment. The natives tended to restlessness once you hung around too long, with no movie crew in sight. No, he had to make his move and slip out of Sligo.

The Queen Beneath the Earth, and her tomb of treasures, awaited.

* * *

Time ran short, but tight, clean plans tended to make that a common denominator. Limit the excess time in which things could go wrong. Because something *always* went wrong.

Bonham made a fuss and show about leaving Sligo. Everyone would know he had left. He had no intention of going to Dublin and barreled south on the N17, made it to Galway in two hours, found his hotel, made another noisy fuss checking in as Hans Bohmer, complete with German accent, and threw some money around at a late lunch. He returned to his room, shaved his mustache and beard clean, and darkened his hair in the sink from sandy blonde to dark brown. He changed into work boots, heavy dirty linens, and jeans. He went outside, scooped a handful of dirt from the ground and rubbed it onto his hands, and hustled over to the truck rental dealer, signed for a flatbed truck under the name Ian McShea. He drove it off the lot, found a quiet street, changed his shirt and put on thick-rimmed glasses, and headed to the heavy equipment rental place another eleven kilometers away on the opposite side of the city. He flashed some fake ID, signed a few papers as Eddie Carter, dropped some grubby Euros on them, and helped load the excavator onto the truck bed and chained it in place.

He drove to a park across the street from a road construction site, parked, switched off the engine, and waited. Darkness fell and the promised storm loomed closer to the west. He started the truck and headed north.

Two hours later he pulled over onto a narrow lane some seven kilometers from Sligo and waited for the storm. By eleven it swept in, a black howler of wind and sideways rain. He started up again, took a back road around the edge of town and past the scant few homes of Primrose Grange, slowed, checked all directions, the wipers beating out a hypnotic syncopation. He pulled within a few hundred meters of the foot of Knocknarea. A car approached and slowed; he slowed. The driver, a man, strained to see him. Bonham casually raised his hand to his face as if to scratch his nose, partially obscuring his face. The car moved on, Bonham watching suspiciously.

He found a break in the stone wall hugging the narrow lane, switched off his headlights, and turned the truck into a thick bramble. He pulled on his rain gear, got out, extended the ramp from the bed, struggling to subdue the clatter it made, released the chains that had secured the ex, climbed into the seat, switched it on. The engine rumbled an initial protest then settled into a purr, and he eased the excavator down the ramp and into the mud.

He paused, looked all about. No one around. The nearest dwelling, its windows warmly aglow, huddled in the blackness perhaps six hundred meters away, silent and domestic, its inhabitants no doubt enjoying a nice hot tea by the hearth and a crackling fire. Only a fool—or a grave robber—would be abroad in such conditions. Leaving the lights off, he turned the excavator and steered it towards the walk path up Knocknarea.

He veered off the path, knowing it took a steep angle, a dangerous path to negotiate in the excavator. The slick grassy slope, with a veritable torrent sluicing down it, proved no problem for its half-track treads. He zigzagged to manage the slope, the engine growling, its sound dampened by the downpour. The rain, he knew, would continue unabated through the night.

At last he reached the crest of Knocknarea and pulled up to the base of the cairn. He glanced at his watch. Just past midnight. Shit. He'd hoped to have already gotten the pit halfway dug by now. There wouldn't be much room for error; he must be in and stealing treasure by 4 AM or the project would be a bust. He couldn't be found up here as day broke. Still, enough of the long winter night remained in which to finish his job. He climbed off, did a quick sweep in all directions with his binoculars. He lingered on the distant farmhouse. Its lights were now out; the hicks had gone to bed. Not a thing to worry about now.

He turned to the cairn and found the spot he'd identified days before, climbed back onto the excavator and maneuvered it into position. He worked the controls and swung the shovel toward the great pile of stone. The shovel bit deep, its steel teeth scraping against the limestone, and dragged a good cubic meter of earth and rock free, and he dumped it to one side. His momentary satisfaction faded; the stone of the cairn had put up a struggle.

Again and again, the shovel bit and dug. The hole became a trench, angled slightly downward. The rock resisted his advances, and slabs of mud and rock slipped from the trench walls and fell with each dig. His hands squeezed tighter on the control levers and sweat beaded on his forehead in spite of the cold. His calculations *should* bear fruit; the extended arm of the excavator stretched a good twenty feet, sufficient to break through to the end of the open chamber deep within.

Dig, scrape, dump. Repeat. The routine went on and on, frustratingly slow. Dig, scrape, dump. He glanced at his watch. 3 AM. Shit! Where had the time gone? He'd needed to be into the tomb by now and extracting its riches, but the zigzag ascent had taken much longer than he'd counted on. He worked the levers with a fury, but the stony ground refused his attempts at increasing the speed. It's all well, he told himself. Stay cool. Almost there. The darkness remained inky and protective, the sunrise still a long ways off. He glanced off to the east to reassure himself of that fact. Not a glimmer of the grayness of dawn.

A flash of lightning and a rifle-shot of thunder startled him. For an instant, a dull white illuminated the landscape far down the hillside and into the distance. Ghosts of trees, rock walls, hedgerows appeared and disappeared in the fleeting moment of light.

Something struck him as out of place in that flash of illumination. A shadowy something faraway had been silhouetted down the hill. What was it? Probably a piece of equipment, a pile of rubble, a shrub. Yes, the latter. But it looked about the size of a man. He had read that the mind seeks human faces and forms in all manner of things.

Familiarity. That made sense. The suggestion of a human form had slithered into his brain. Human nature. But of all the shapeless forms in a rainy night, why had this one arrested his attention?

He knew the answer already. It had moved.

He stared downslope. The rain came down hard and angled, born by the stiff wind off the Atlantic. If what he saw was a bush or small tree, of course it had moved. The wind whipped the branches of all trees and hedgerows down the slope.

He needed to get back to his work but couldn't look away. A half-minute later, another flash and boom of lightning rewarded him. He kept his eyes on the spot he'd thought he'd seen something.

A scattering of bushes and small trees lay in that direction, all waving in the wind. Nothing else. Nothing.

He released a pent-up breath. "Get ahold of yourself, idiot," he mumbled. "And get back to work."

He shifted the levers and stabbed the shovel into the trench once more. He worked the levers faster now; to hell with caution and quiet. He'd wasted time submitting to fears and needed to make it up. And he knew he inched nearer to the tomb.

Focus on the work. Focus and dig. Get the job done, bust into the tomb, collect whatever, and get the hell out. Eyes on the trench. Forget about moving shadows. They're just vegetation blowing about. Do not look back again.

He looked back.

Lightning flickered and bathed the scene.

Not more than a hundred meters downslope, off the trail and in the field to the right, a figure darted behind the stone wall and disappeared. Bonham caught the merest glimpse, but that told him enough. Someone had followed him, and stealthily.

His mind raced. He reached for the ignition, his fingers suddenly trembling. Switch it off, kill the engine, be silent. He stopped himself. What good would that do? His dig had been discovered. If he switched off, his pursuer would assume that Bonham had spotted him. Leave it running, then. That would sustain a bit of illusion.

And there was something else.

He drew a Glock from his satchel of tools. He didn't particularly like guns and violence, and securing a handgun in Ireland was damned hard. But he'd done prison once, years ago, and had determined he'd never do it again. Someone—himself or some other fool—would die before he returned.

The Glock was a smart and lethal little weapon and he had proficiency in its use. He checked it, set it aside, manipulated the shovel a couple of times, hoping to trick his pursuer into thinking the operation continued, picked up his flashlight, took the gun up again, and eased out of the seat and onto the ground on the side opposite the direction of his enemy. He crept away and ducked behind an outcrop of stone.

His mind raced. Goon Squad, the hulking, angry, hormonal kid from the pub, had gotten his back up and sneaked uphill, hell-bent on becoming a local hero. He'd spotted Bonham and followed him out here. Or maybe the kid planned to claim-jump him and steal what he could. Either way, the kid had stepped way outside his league and would not leave the hill alive.

The kid had screwed the job, had busted up a site. Time dwindled too short already and now he'd have to take care of the kid and get the hell out. All Bonham's time, his planning, wasted. He gritted his teeth, tightened his grip on the gun.

Another lightning flash, another instant of twilight. The figure edged closer now, much closer, and crept towards the rumbling excavator.

The thought of a tangle with Goon Squad evaporated. The figure was much too small and thin to be confused with that oaf. So. He'd misread his adversary. It had to be the old coot from the pub, Finn. It made sense. Finn, the provincial know-it-all, the professorial twit that drank his way out of academia, had tracked him. Finn, the worst kind of loser, for whom hell had reserved a special level.

This would be easier than imagined.

Bonham eased the gun up to a comfortable position. Finn crept closer, but still too far away for a reliable handgun shot. Bonham decided on the best method of attack. Finn would arrive at the excavator in twenty, maybe thirty seconds, find it unattended, and suffer a moment's panic. That moment would put him at his most vulnerable.

Despite the chill and rain, Bonham felt the heat of adrenaline in his flesh. Any second now, he'd hear Finn blundering about at the excavator, hear his cry of dismay. And Bonham would dart forward like a wolf in the night, flick on the powerful police torch, blind the stupid drunk for a few seconds, and blow his head off. He tensed, gathered himself for the assault.

A powerful hand clamped onto his shoulder from behind and yanked him backward. He crashed to ground and two hands seized him and lifted from his feet. He attempted to bring the gun to bear in his right hand, and his assailant hand seized that wrist and squeezed with a terrible pressure, tightening, tightening. He heard the snap of bone, and the gun was wrenched from his grip. He shrieked at the sudden pain.

Lightning strobed the scene in a white flicker. The girl from the pub, Kate, held him with both hands, fury in her eyes. "You stupid little man," she said. "Did you think you would be the first to rob Maeve's grave? Better than you have tried."

Bonham struggled in her grip and kicked out at her. His boot struck her hard, but she barely flinched. She muttered something and shook him like a rat in a cat's jaws. He felt his neck would snap, so violent and stunning was the shaking. He ceased struggling. "Please, let me go! Let go!" he cried.

"Oh, do be still, stupid man. Queen Maeve shouldn't be disturbed, but I'm not going to harm you, not more than I have already." She struck his face with an open palm. It felt like a sledgehammer, stunning, sending sparks behind his eyes. "I guess I lied," she said in a low tone.

White-hot agony burned in his wrist and face. He gripped her arm in his good hand but her grip only tightened. Nausea dizzied him and threatened his mind with shutting down. He released his grip, trying to gather his wits. A ruddy dawn of reason crept into his panicked thoughts. "You…" Bonham struggled to comprehend, and fear coursed through him in a torrent. "You're not human. It's…this is *your* grave. You're Maeve!"

Kate stared at him and laughed. "Don't be ridiculous! Look at me. Of course I'm human, same as you. Well, maybe not same as you. I've just been around a while. No, I'm not Maeve. I'm just a handmaid, here to keep an eye on trouble-makers like you." She squeezed broken wrist and the pain threatened to drown him in agony. "Maeve is *much* worse."

She dragged him to the excavator and held him fast in one arm, struggle though he did. She climbed into the seat and studied the controls for a moment, manipulating first one and then another, and the shovel responded. "Looks pretty simple," she said.

The shovel dug into the trench and dragged earth and stone free. A few more shovelfuls and the shovel punched through the last remaining material. Kate withdrew the shovel and dragged Bonham down, toward the trench.

"You just had to have treasure, didn't you?" Kate said. "There is no treasure, stupid man. You watch too many movies. This was an iron-age backwater in Maeve's time. Back then, even a queen of her stature scratched out an existence, dirt-poor by your standards. Treasure. Ha! A few bits of iron, a pot or two, maybe. Maybe you could make a few Euros selling her meager belongings."

"Then why the great tomb?"

Again she laughed. "Not to keep you out, stupid man. Like that dimwit Ian said, it's to keep her *in*."

She gripped him by the collar and slung him into the trench. He fell hard to the rocky floor, his knee striking a protruding stone. Pain shot through the knee, and blood seeped from a gash in it. The kneecap moved laterally under his touch. He shifted and rolled his weight away from the knee. He cradled his broken arm against his chest.

Dead, musty air filled his nostrils and mouth and he coughed. He lifted himself up onto his palms and turned to Kate. She stared back at him, an eager hate in her eyes. "Scared of the dark, stupid man?" She tossed the flashlight in after him. "No? You should be."

He heard a faint rasp, a scrabbling, behind him. He turned, peered into the inky darkness. He fumbled the flashlight switch on and pointed. The beam lit the interior of the chamber. It stretched on and on, into the depths beyond. Rubble littered the chamber, a few broken pots. A rusting iron sword.

And bones.

"Maeve hasn't been out in centuries," Kate said. "I suppose she's going to get her fun in for a couple of hours before the sun comes up. Then it's back inside the tomb for her, where she'll starve again for another few centuries. She'll have a hell of an appetite to satisfy before dawn though. You're just the appetizer."

Bonham pinned the flashlight between his arm and chest and kept it trained on the dark reaches down the tomb. The light beam jittered and danced and threw nervous shadows about. He felt about with his good hand, seized a rock the size of a fist, and raised it. He drew a deep breath, trying to steady himself.

The scrabble of sound came again, a clattering of pebbles, from deep inside. Another sound issued from the depths of the chamber, like the wind over the rocky hills. No. More like a sigh, almost one of ecstasy.

A dim movement. The Queen emerged from the far shadows, gray and ghostly in the white light, crawling, hand over hand, human yet inhuman, sinuous, crawling towards him, her face young and ancient at the same time, beautiful and hideous, smeared with dirt, her nose broken. She was naked, but for a few scraps of rotted cloth about her wrists as if fashioned there out of some forgotten memory of fashion. Her body was emaciated, skin stretched over bones, her flesh scratched and scarred and filthy, her pendulous breasts swaying beneath her. Long, jagged, pointed nails scraped and clicked on the stone floor. Her eyes shone in points of luminous green fire.

She grinned, an impossibly wide grin spanning the width of her face, and a ragged hiss issued. He saw the teeth. Teeth like needles, long and curved, broken and blackened, glistened with the hunger of a thousand years.

The Queen crawled to her new king.

Notes

Life in Ireland is ancient and storied, and in the northwest much of it remains off the beaten path of tourism. Queen Maeve was a real person and a heroine to her time and people, a fierce warrior-queen that makes those imaginary ones of fantasy fiction seem tame. The description of her tomb is accurate, as well as the local custom of placing stones on it to ensure that she never gets out.

"The Queen Beneath the Earth" first appeared in *Shadows and Teeth, Volume 2*, a truly frightening anthology of horror published by Darkwater Syndicate. The editor said my story reminded him of H.P. Lovecraft. I couldn't see it, but I'll enjoy the company.

The world of big business. Memos. Bottom lines. Mission statements. A place where being noticed, being seen, leads ever upward on that ladder of success. Sometimes, being unseen can help too.

Empty Suit

"I wish you'd keep your fingers out of my eye," said the aerial voice, in a tone of savage expostulation . . . "I'm invisible. It's a confounded nuisance, but I am. That's no reason why I should be poked to pieces by every stupid bumpkin in Iping, is it?"
—H.G. Wells, *The Time Machine*

Edison Glass paused outside the gilded doors of B. Hemuth Corporation, sagging under an overloaded satchel slung over his aching shoulder. He took a sip of confidence from Starbucks, fiddled with his tie with his free hand, and strode in, just as he'd done for seven years. With a little extra pumpkin spice that morning; the big presentation loomed, and a nice promotion along with it.

Heather Wu, embedded behind a vast, shiny, reception desk, pushed aside the tiny mic of her headset, and gave him a twinkly smile. "Good morning, Eddy. How was your weekend?"

Edison returned the smile. "Morning, Heather, it—"

"Glass Ceiling!" Tyler Carpenter swept into the lobby, lugging his industrial cup of coffee. "Maybe this is the week you break through, eh, Glass?" He stabbed his cup at Edison, sloshing coffee onto Heather and her desk. "Little help there, Heather."

Heather reached under the desk and withdrew a paper towel.

"Hm," Edison said. He tried forcing a smile that resisted cooperation.

"Eleventh time's the charm, eh?" Carpenter's toothy grin seemed wider than his head. The Veep of Public Relations sloshed more coffee.

Heather wiped up the spill and lasered in on Carpenter's listing cup. "Can I get you a saucer, Mr. Carpenter?"

"I'm good, sweet meat. Well, Glass, better get working on your pitch to Belinda. Can't let one slip away again, eh?" Without waiting for an answer, he swept out of the lobby, leaving a trail of coffee splatters on the tile floor. Heather tore off more paper towels and came around the desk.

She hadn't been on the job long, maybe four months. In that short time, Edison had seen how she read people, reacted to them, always in the most courteous fashion. Never an angry word. She deserved better.

"Let me help," Edison said.

"Thanks, Eddy." She smiled. "It'll go well today. I just know it will."

* * *

B. Hemuth loomed large in the world of sales and shipping, always looking to expand its darkness to new cities. Edison knew he was considered a functionary, at best. But he could functionary the shit out of a project. And no one put in hours like him. Nights. Weekends. Didn't matter. He'd held the same midlevel position at B. Hemuth since day one. Maybe that would change next week.

A coveted slot in the Uppers had opened up with the retirement of Thomas Granger. Retirement. You could put it that way. Granger got aged out. Outlived his shelf life at fifty-seven. Old Thomas, they called him. Ancient in the big tech universe. He was sharp as ever, but people talked like he was a withered old coot, cackling over his bits of string and pointing a bony, accusing finger at the full heads of hair and untucked shirts of the whipper-snappers.

It was sad. Still, Granger's exit opened an opportunity, and no one in the Granger replacement candidate pool had Edison's years of experience.

Which was exactly the problem.

Edison had tripped that age wire himself, though he still clung to his early forties. With seven years in the same company, the same job. That was outrageous, the kiss of death, a quaint notion from a Netflix period piece, stuffed with the archaic language but without the costumery or coupling on the stairwells that grabbed the viewers. Certainly not a series anyone would binge-watch.

Everything rode on his presentation today.

The conference room gleamed with chrome and wood. People-wise, half-empty. Or was it half-full? Nah, exactly half-empty, only eleven seats of twenty-two occupied. A couple of Manhattan types sort of listened in online. All were his youngers, all squirmy and impatient, even including CEO Belinda Hemuth, and her sycophant, Tyler Carpenter. Belinda, her dark hair clenched even tighter than usual, sat leaning sideward as always when someone besides herself was speaking. She watched her tablet, tapped on it occasionally, and smiled now and then. Tyler pecked at his phone as well. He'd peck something in. She'd suppress a smile, tap something in return. Peck tap, peck tap.

Edison packed numbers and exclamations into his presentation like a packhorse and plowed through it like a plow horse, mustering all the enthusiasm he could about Atlanta for the Southeast expansion. The roads. The airport. The soul o' the Southeast. The hub o' the heartland. Etcetera, etcetera. All that good stuff. He positively glittered, scrolling through census data and pie charts, raining buzzy words like manna from heaven. Metadata, he said. Human capital, he said. Stark Industries, he said. Fungibly cloudify mission-driven action items, he said, to make sure everyone listened. He was nailing this dog-and-pony show. The dog was eating the pony. And vice versa.

Edison wrapped up and waited. It took nine seconds of deathly silence before Belinda glanced about, looked up at him, pushed her tablet aside. "Thank you for that, um, Edison. Charlotte is an interesting take."

"Charlotte who?" Edison asked.

"Not a who, a what," Belinda said. "Charlotte, North Carolina."

"Atlanta, Georgia," Edison said.

She gave him a moment of arched eyebrows, then looked around the room. "Anyone?"

"Atlanta, yawn," Carpenter offered. "Charlotte, now that's a great idea, Belinda. Would make a logical step. Hip. Youthful. Vibrant. Me like."

Nods all around.

Belinda looked again at Edison, disappointment stamped on her face. "Why didn't you look at Charlotte?"

"You told me to look at Atlanta."

"We want independent thinkers. If there's nothing more, this meeting is over." She glanced at her watch. "A whole hour about freaking Atlanta. The Board will be thrilled."

The room emptied, leaving Edison to stare out the window at a blank sky.

* * *

He went to the bathroom, enclosed himself in a stall, took a seat, hoisted his feet onto the rim, and waited. This was the best place in the 27th floor for intelligence gathering.

He was soon rewarded. The sound of the door opening and closing. Footsteps. Voices. Tyler Carpenter and his toady, River Tanner. Murmurs. Sports banter. Chuckles. Peeing. Flushing. Minimalist handwashing. And finally, the subject he knew they'd get around to. And the hated nickname.

"So," Tanner said. "How'd old Glass do?"

If eye rolls could make a sound, Edison heard one. "Oh, informative. Exciting. Pure adrenaline rush. Glass plodded through it like a jellyfish with no legs. Belinda almost put her head on the table for a nap."

"Ha! He's your classic empty suit."

"He doesn't disappoint. Oh, by the way, gather everything you can on Charlotte. Start this afternoon. Get me the goods on Hicksville, by Thursday. Get the art department to pretty it up, put a ribbon on it. I'll stick it on the bitch's desk Friday morning. I'm also going to sidetrack the empty suit, have him sort paperclips the rest of the week."

Ten minutes later, Edison got an email from Carpenter directing him to put together a prospectus on Akron for a subregional distribution center. Edison typed a response: "Akron already has a subregional."

"Don't be insubordinate. You know I meant a sub-subregional center," Carpenter wrote.

"Insubordinate sub-sub. Got it," Edison replied, and began combing U.S. Department of Commerce info on Charlotte.

* * *

Edison worked until nine, powered down, and drove home in both literal and figurative fogs, the world blurry to him. He reached his apartment, let himself in. His little brother, Winston, sat on the couch, feet on the coffee table, amid a tasteful, geometric array of empty beer bottles, gaming away in front of a gigantic monitor. Winston glanced up, killed the sound, and set his control aside. "Hey, brother mine. A little late getting home tonight. There's spaghetti on the stove."

Edison helped himself to a plate of cold spaghetti and warm beer. He sat gloomily opposite his little brother. "Thanks, Wince."

"That's Doctor Wince to you." A pause. "Bad day, huh?"

"Oh, the presentation went great. The reception sucked, even more than usual." He related the entire humiliating fiasco, including the subsequent recon in the bathroom. He concluded with a defeated sigh and a long pull from his beer. "I stayed late to get started on Charlotte. Not sure why; I'll be slathered by Carpenter with garbage tasks all week."

"He called you an empty suit, eh?" Wince said. "That's funnier than 'Glass Ceiling.'"

"Your empathy, as always, is comforting."

Wince leaned back. "Empty suit," he repeated. "Empty suit." He closed his eyes and laced his fingers, lost in thought.

"I'm getting another beer."

Edison returned, sat. He shunned derailing Wince's train of thought. His brother was the smartest man he'd ever met and the least focused, so when Wince actually settled into a state of focus, you ran with it.

Wince also worked for B. Hemuth, in the small annex on the opposite end of the giant compound. Like other Google and Amazon wannabees, the company dabbled as well. Belinda wanted to be seen as a Bezos-Musk burrito, and she established small science labs to make it look that way. They were habitually understaffed and underfunded, but created the illusion of B. Hemuth as a citadel of cutting-edge techie stuff. She hired brilliant, unmotivated scientists to flesh it out. Wince fit the bill perfectly. PhD in physics from Cal-Tech, dedicated stoner and gamer on the side. The company made few demands on his lifestyle. He could dabble this way and that, and his lab could apply for an occasional patent for stuff on the same excitement scale as refrigerator magnets.

Wince at last opened his eyes and leaned forward. "Empty Suit. I like it. Sounds like a half-assed superhero. Listen. I want to give *you* the powers."

Edison waited.

"I do physics. I specialize in optics. Sciencey stuff. I've invented a new material, Winston's Optical Meta-Rag, one that will give B. Hemuth ads, labeling, and packaging a signature look. It dicks around with light. Bends it. Let me explain like I'm talking to a six-year-old." He held up his half-finished beer. "The bottle is glass. You see the glass and the beer inside. Look closer and you see through to my hand on the opposite side. The glass reflects less light and refracts more light than my hand. It's still visible, but it's *less* visible. To make it invisible, I need to bend light, make it go smoothly around it. That's been done on a molecular scale, but it's way beyond anything we can do at a bigger scale.

"The necessary interferometry defies us. But four months ago, I wrapped a sphere the size of a basketball with it."

"A sphere the size of a basketball?"

"Okay, a basketball. Alas, only a tiny fraction of the light hitting it swirled past, just fuzzying up the edges a bit. I tinkered, tweaking this, upping that. Nothing. Then I had an idea; I cut open the basketball and wrapped its insides with Meta-Rag as well. I mounted a light and a 360 degree camera inside it."

"And?"

"And nothing. Weeks of nothing. Then I had a breakthrough.

"You achieved the interferer—the intra-feralonomy—the bendy light thing?

"I spilled beer on it."

"You were *drinking*? On company time? In a fifty-million-dollar lab?"

"Beer barely qualifies as drinking, but you're missing the point. The beer reacted with the meta-paint, amplifying the bent-light stream inside and out. The basketball remained visible, unchanged. But the inside of the basketball was *gone*."

"Gone?"

"Well. Not gone. You just couldn't see it."

"Because you spilled your beer."

"All great inventions start with beer, and this was good beer, artisanal as hell." Wince held his bottle to the light, beaming like he'd discovered the food of the gods, and took a sip. He glanced at Edison. "You could use it, you know."

"I already have a beer."

"Forget the damn beer. The technology. Have you heard a word I'm saying? I manipulated light to the point where the inside of a basketball became invisible. Completely invisible, not even a dotted line or a blur. *Invisible*." He clapped his hands. "Eddy. Bro. I can make you a suit of this material. *You* can become invisible. You can become a superhero. You can be Empty Suit!"

Edison settled back into his chair, letting the possibilities sink in. Invisibility. The stuff of dreams. He could move through B. Hemuth Corp with impunity, sabotaging projects as he saw fit. His career path might be paved with potholes, but with his brother's magic cloak of invisibility he could step deftly around them.

A thought occurred. "If you're so sure of this thing, why don't *you* become the invisible man?"

"Whoa, Bro. This is cutting-edge tech, and cutting edge can cut you. I'm a contented, scared little baby. Not a desperate baby. But you are. And crazy too."

"Wait. You could still see the basketball from outside?"

"Yep."

"But not the inside."

"Yep."

"How does this invisibility suit work then?"

"Any part of you covered by the suit becomes invisible."

"While the suit remains visible?"

"Well, yeah."

"And face and hands remain visible?"

"Um. Yeah."

"The suit, visible. Face, head, and hands, visible. How is that different from any other suit?"

"Um."

"This is the stupidest invention in the history of stupid inventions!"

Wince looked hurt. "That's what they said to Alexander Graham Bell when he invented the cotton gin, but look where we are today."

* * *

Two weeks later, Wince burst into the apartment. "I got it!"

Edison didn't look up from the TV. "The clap?"

"Immortality, Bro. I've reduced the active compounds in Meta-Rag to a clear liquid, and made an aerosol spray from it. Each tiny droplet becomes a double-coated sphere the size of a tiny droplet, bending light like a drunk bends an elbow."

"And?"

Wince held up an empty palm. "Catch," he said, and made a tossing motion.

Something unseen bounced off Edison's head. "Ow."

"That was a VHS cassette. *Beverly Hills Cop III*. No one will miss it."

Edison's mind raced and his heart struggled to keep up. "I want it. I want to be Empty Suit."

* * *

First thing on Monday, Edison entered the lobby of B. Hemuth Corp. Heather Wu looked up, beaming. "Looking sharp today, Eddy," she said.

"For a while, let's hope." He paused. "Heather, want to get coffee sometime? We could, um, get coffee. Sometime, I mean." So smooth, Mr. Superhero.

"I'd love to." She seemed sincere.

"Good. Great." He grinned, trying to contain it. "I like coffee." He wanted to hang himself.

"Tomorrow morning, before work? Seven, at H.G. Barista's?"

"I like coffee." *Where was that noose?*

At 10 AM, after making his presence in the office widely known, he took the stairs down six floors to Accounting, which swarmed with short-sleeved trolls flecked with doughnut crumbs, if you could call what they did swarming. They stared, transfixed and unblinking, at r screens. They didn't know him and didn't want to. He let himself into the janitorial closet at the end of the hall, flicked on the light, and stripped naked.

Almost naked. He kept his Pink Floyd boxers on. He folded his clothes and hid them behind a tower of toilet tissue rolls.

A light tap-tap came from the door, and it swung open. Wince entered, dressed in fake custodian overalls, fake mustache, and fake glasses, carrying a tray of brand-name cleaners. He gave Edison a quick look-over. "Ready?"

"Ready."

"No, you're not. You have to be completely coated. Get them panties off, boy," he said.

"Oh, for—" Edison shook his head. "Fine." He took off his Pink Floyds, stuffed them away with the rest of his clothes. "Can we get this over with?"

"Trust me, right now, no one wants you invisible more than me. I see you shaved your pits and chins and balls, as instructed. Good boy. He's a good boy, yes he is." He picked an aerosol can out of his tray, gave it a vigorous shake. "Close your eyes and keep your mouth shut."

Edison did so, and heard the hiss of the spray and felt its coolness on his skin. Wince turned him slowly, spraying every corner, working the liquid into his hair, which fortunately was already almost invisible. After a few minutes, Wince said, "Blimey! 'E's all eaten away."

Edison opened his eyes. Wince handed him a small mirror. Edison stared, disbelieving. "I'm... *gone*. Invisible. Every square inch." Then he noticed the flaw. "I can see my eyes, and my mouth moving when I talk. A pair of eyes and a talking set of teeth, floating in space."

"Well yeah, get this stuff in your eyes and mouth, you'll be blind and sick for a week. I gotta get back to the lab. You're on your own, Bro."

* * *

A pair of eyes and a mouth floated up the stairwell. The stairwell door opened onto the 27th floor and the eyes and mouth drifted out and paused, hovering, turning this way and that. The open plan, cubicles as far as the eye could see, heads popping up now and then like prairie dogs. Murmurs and snatches of conversation. One head, Vanessa Bundt's bluish one, looked in his direction, and froze, staring.

Edison closed his eyes and clenched his mouth like a fist. He eased nine steps to the left and opened one eye to the narrowest of slits. The Bundt still stared at where he had stood, shook her head, and went back to work.

He wasn't invisible, he was an apparition. A floating mote. People would notice. They would notice a fly buzzing the office. Still, he'd made himself invisible to escape the Bundt. But if he kept his eyes closed, how could he avoid colliding with immovable or moveable objects like people wearing clothes?

He glanced at his fist and saw nothing. He opened it and saw the tiny flash drive. He closed his fist, and the flash drive disappeared.

He collected himself, resisting the urge to cover his crotch. He stood outside the window of Carpenter's office and watched. The guy would be pitching to Charlotte Mayor Martinez and his top staff in an hour, the whole herd of them in town to hear B. Hemuth's plans for their fair city.

Carpenter projected a shiny eagerness, coiffed, and slick in Armani. A lot riding on this one, a $200 million project stolen right from under Edison's feet. Carpenter glanced at his watch, took a sip of Pink Cow, the power drink of weenies, and headed for the bathroom on his usual schedule. The guy even scheduled peeing.

As always, he left his laptop open and on.

Edison stepped in. Sure enough, Carpenter had been last-minute tweaking his presentation, the program still open. Edison had to act fast, before the laptop's security demanded the password. He sat, inserted the flash drive, and tapped furiously on the keyboard.

An hour later, Mayor Martinez's jaw fell when Carpenter showed a PowerPoint slide of him photoshopped wearing a tutu with Fidel Castro at a tractor-pull.

Two hours later, Carpenter stuffed the last of his personal effects into a cardboard box, sealed it with a grimace, and got hustled out of the building.

Two weeks later, Edison still had not received his promotion. And thus began Empty Suit's reign of terror.

Not exactly terror. More like annoyance.

Movie buff Mason Brix's autographed portrait of broody Lawrence Olivier disappeared, replaced with a portrait of grinny Owen Wilson. No one saw who did it.

A half-eaten, bleeding burger and fries were piled high on Rainbow Sunshine's tofu sprouts. No one saw who did it.

Opera lover Hunter Gaithers' playlist of Puccini, Verdi, and Mozart morphed into an endless loop of an Ashlee Simpson and Michael Bolton duet of "MacArthur Park." No one saw who did it.

Canadian Bob Smith's poutine-and-moose double-decker sandwich was thrown in the garbage. No one cared. No one knew what Canadian Bob Smith did anyway, other than be Canadian and exude mysterious Canadian odors.

The Reign of Annoyance raged until an anonymous accounting troll named Jeeves Butler, who'd suffered the horror of his meticulous stacks of paper being unmeticulously unstacked, demanded action and surveillance cameras. Serious men in jumpsuits installed serious cameras, covering all areas of the open plan offices.

But the spooky weirdness continued. All caught on video.

A PR flack got up to go to the bathroom and her stapler sprang to life and stapled her collection of cruise ship vacation ads to a *Southern Living* story on "Gardening with Gonorrhea."

A cup of coffee drifted through the office, darting behind plants or cubicles whenever someone approached or looked, and spilled itself on the head of River Tanner, before dashing itself against the wall.

A red rose flew through the air to settle gently on Heather Wu's desk.

B. Hemuth's offices were haunted. All floors, but especially the 27th.

The brightest minds in the company threw themselves into solving the mystery. One morning, Belinda summoned Edison into her office. She sat scowling behind her desk, flanked by a pair of stone-faced lawyers. Every fiber of her being manifested in that scowl. Even her mouth scowled when she spoke. "In our surveillance video, Edison, no one ever sees you at your desk—or anywhere else—when the Ghost strikes. Why is that?"

"Wait. You think I'm the Ghost?"

"How do you pull it off?"

"I don't. But I'm both flattered and offended."

"My lawyers here figured it out. You're remote-controlling things somehow. Probably a swarm of nanobots."

"That's actually a marvelous idea, Belinda. But I'm in distribution data analysis. Paperwork. Reports. Do you think I'd be here if I had technology even the Pentagon doesn't have?"

A long, drawn-out pause. "I don't know how, but you're behind it." She leaned back. "I know it. I'm CEO because my hunches are always right, and the Board agrees. I'm letting you go. But I'll be big about it. Your last day is two weeks from today."

Edison swallowed. "I—"

"Decision made. Better start getting ready, updating your resume, sorting your paper clips. The usual important work you do."

* * *

Two days later, Edison watched and waited, gathered up a stack of papers, and caught Belinda off guard as she patrolled the office on a casual search-and-destroy mission for slackers. "Ten minutes," he said. "That's all. You're doing me wrong and I can prove it. Ten minutes."

"Damn it, Glass." Belinda glanced at her watch. "Fine. I'll give you five." She marched past him to her office. "Close the door behind you." Heather Wu glanced up from her monitor and down again.

Edison followed and clicked the door shut behind him.

"Sit," Belinda ordered.

"I'll stand, thanks. Belinda, how can you do this to me?" He shook papers at her like voodoo chicken bones. "I've got the numbers to show what I've meant to the company, from the very start."

"Four minutes," Belinda said.

Edison swallowed, and launched into a quiver of quarterlies over the years, scarcely drawing a breath. At last, he straightened the papers and set them neatly on her desk. "Well?"

"Well what? I still know you've been sabotaging us. Sneaky, you are. I—"

A gentle rap came at the door. Heather eased the door open. "Ms. Hemuth?"

"Not now, Heather."

"Ms. Hemuth, you asked me to report immediately if the Ghost struck again. It did."

Belinda snorted. "What a shock. When, this morning? When Glass had to go potty?"

"Two minutes ago."

Belinda stared at Heather.

A potted fern had suddenly become an unpotted fern, rising up from its expensive vase, which fell to the floor with a crash and a spray of dirt. Cubicle heads popped up and stared. Murmurs. The fern gave itself a good shake, scattering dirt, made a couple of loops in the air, wiggled some more dirt loose, executed a barrel-roll, a loop-de-loop, a floppy-shake-forward, and dashed itself against the shiny "We're Bigger than You" B. Hemuth logo.

* * *

Edison twisted his beer bottle open, raised it, and clinked it against Winston's bottle. "That was awesome, Wince. Eye-catching, undeniable, and not quite over-the-top. Salud, Little Ghost-Bro!"

Wince bowed. "I shoulda been an actor."

"Got the whole performance on video and audio. Five different surveillance cameras caught it. Twenty-seven eyewitnesses. And all while I'm with the CEO and her sharks, my hands empty, my eyes pleading, my brow furrowed. Belinda spent all day with tekkies and janitors sifting through the potted fern mystery, poking around my desk, rooting through my files. They kept me in the conference room with her goons, then sent me home." He took a long drink. "That should end it."

* * *

That should've ended it.

Belinda summoned Edison back to her office the following day. Five shiny lawyers, a veritable pod of them, flanked her, backed by two huge goons. River Tanner, newly ensconced in Carpenter's Veep of PR job, stood glued to her left arm.

"I've investigated yesterday's so-called Ghost incident," Belinda said without a hello. "Sit."

This time, Edison sat. He leaned back at a jaunty Errol Flynn angle and crossed his legs. "So. I'm still employed, I presume."

"It *was* a clever stunt, but I've seen it all before. Drone technology is simply staggering these days. You can program dozens of them to act in aerial sync with amazing precision. That's what you did. Tiny little drones, all performing a single routine, snatch a plant and move it around the room, then scatter. You're still fired."

Edison sprang from his chair, struggled for words. "That's… that's the most brilliant and stupidest thing I've ever heard. I was right here with you! I couldn't do that. No one could."

Tanner giggled. Belinda silenced him with a flick of her finger.

"Oh, I'm not saying *you* came up with it," she said. "You couldn't fly a three-dollar toy helicopter from Walmart without putting your eye out." She leaned back, tented her fingers. Like a spider would if it caught a fly in its web, and had fingers, and could tent them. "You needed an accomplice. Your brother, he's got way too much time on his hands, and no one could account for his whereabouts during yesterday's Ghost story. So he assembled and programmed your drone squadron and operated it remotely. I am impressed. Really, I am. He's being escorted from the building as we speak."

"Oh, come on, Belinda. You don't believe that yourself."

Tanner leaned in. "It's the only explanation," he said through his grin. "Like Sherlock Holmes said, once you eliminate the possum, whatever remains, however improbable, must be the rodent of truth."

"I don't know if you're the world's biggest idiot, Tanner, but you win a participation trophy." Edison bit down on the urge to tell all. "You're both pretty smug right now. I demand to see the evidence."

Belinda tapped a claw on the desk for a moment. "You used stolen military tech. Maybe collaborated with the Chinese. That would make for an interesting call to the Pentagon. Wanna go down that road?" She glanced at her goons. "Tank, Howitzer, please escort Mr. Glass from the premises."

The goons grinned. They liked their jobs.

A rap came at the door. Heather Wu popped her head in, like a beautiful sideways meerkat. "Ms. Hemuth? A word?"

"Oh, for . . . not now, Heather."

"Yes now." Heather pushed open the door, held it aside, and a phalanx of seven full business suits marched in.

Belinda stood. "What's this?"

"A delegation sent by the Board. They held a little meeting this morning. You're done, Hemuth. You have thirty minutes to clean out your desk."

Belinda laughed, then paled. "What are you talking about?"

"The Board wasn't thrilled with the Mayor Martinez debacle. And Atlanta is where the Directors want to go, at least after I sent them Edison's prospectus. Still, you'd have survived if you'd only made amends with Charlotte, except that word got out that you'd rather spend your time ferreting out ghosts. Ghost-busting is not really mentioned in the company's mission statement."

"The Board doesn't know about the Ghost."

"I took care of that," Heather said.

"You! Why are you doing anything without my permission?"

"I don't actually work for you. I work for the Board. I'm their spy."

"You're a receptionist!"

"Tinker, tailor, receptionist, spy. Oh, ease up, Belinda. You'll slither into early retirement a very rich woman." Heather paused. "Well, maybe. Might want to lawyer up."

"But that's my name on the building. It's *my* company."

"It was. And the Board is rethinking the name." Heather glanced at her watch. "Twenty-nine minutes. Then your stuff gets stuffed in a box and thrown into a dumpster. And set on fire."

Belinda sulked away to her office. River Tanner and the lawyers adopted submissive primate expressions and eased away in an unsuccessful attempt at invisibility, pointing out that change is good, don't you think? Yes, change is good.

Edison watched them go, his emotions rollercoasting. "That . . . that was—"

"Fun, right?" Heather turned to him, an impish smile in her eyes. "Don't worry about her, she'll land on all four feet. She'll even find some perverse glee in it. The bigger they fall, the harder they come."

"And me?"

"You're the new Veep of Acquisitions and Expansions. If you want it."

"And you?"

"I like the fun stuff. Trust me, there's nothing so stimulating as a good takedown." She studied him for a moment. "I know you did it, Edison," she continued, almost in a whisper. "No idea how, but it was awesome. And exciting. The *fun* stuff."

Edison swallowed, lost in her eyes. "And us?" He doubted there was an "us." He glanced around the office. A hundred eyes stared at them, and a hundred eyes turned away.

Heather looked about as well, then returned to hold his gaze. She came a bit closer. "Us. As of this moment, us are colleagues. Not coworkers." She came closer still. "We're free to have personal lives," she whispered. Closer still. "I'd do you right here and now if no one could see us."

Edison swallowed, and almost reached out to touch her. "I think that can be arranged."

Notes

The power to become invisible has been a fantasy of humans for as long as there have been humans, and myths, fairy tales, folk tales, and fantasy yarns have used it for thousands of years. When H.G. Wells reintroduced the idea with science fiction trappings in *The Invisible Man*, (1897), the notion gained respectability and became a fave of science fiction readers and writers ever since.

When I decided to take a crack at invisibility as a vehicle for sci-fi comedy and to set it in the world of big business, the snarky phrase "empty suit" sprang unbidden into my mind and I was off and running. Trotting, at the very least. Well, maybe doing that vigorous walk race they still give Olympic medals for.

Friendship is a wonderful thing, but business pressures will strain even the strongest and longest friendships.

Double Effect

Gulf of Mexico, Brigands Key, Summer, 1968

Yazz Watson couldn't believe his own eyes, and wondered if what he'd spotted was a trick of light at the forty-foot depth, or a smudge on his dive mask.

When you work the sea for a living—fishing, lobstering, smuggling dope—you get what you get. Mostly, you work your ass off and the Universe still shits on you. Then there's days when you get lucky. Real lucky.

Like when you find lost treasure.

Like today.

He worked feverishly, clearing away the sand, finding more and more. The treasure had been disguised by a century under the sea. The silver bar was tarnished and caked with growth and might have been ignored by a casual diver, mistaken for a rock.

There was no mistaking the gold.

Shit had grown on them, of course. There wasn't no stopping that. Yet a glimmer here, a wink of sunshine there, gave them away. Yazz knocked the crust off, and six coins gleamed bright yellow, pure as they day they were struck.

Yazz scoured and collected, and as his air tank got low, loaded a bagful, gave a yank on the haul line from the boat above, and followed it reverently back to the surface, as his partner Jack, reeled the winch in. He broke surface, peeled his mask back, and climbed the transom ladder onto the deck of the *High C*.

He grunted out of his tank and vest, friggin' Jack not helping him out of the heavy gear. Okay, understandable; Jack was peeling open the bag, eyes gleaming, and let the folds of it fall away from the encrusted treasure, as mesmerized as Yazz had been minutes ago when he'd first found the stuff.

Yazz hurriedly pulled off his weight belt and fins.

Jack held up a gold piece, grinning, and tossed it to him. "By God, Yazzie! We've finally got it!"

Yazz caught the coin, pumped his fist, and sank to his knees. Tears welled in his eyes. "We done it," he murmured. "We really done it."

"You bet your ass we done it. We're filthy, stinking rich."

"Idle rich. Least, that's what I plan on."

They celebrated with a round of beers shaken and poured over each other's heads. Jack fiddled with his transistor radio, and managed to find a rock and roll station out of Tampa. Tommy James belted out "Mony Mony." Yazz and Jack danced and sang along, changing the words to "Money Money."

They had closed in on this site for five years now, having pulled up rusty iron chains, bits of china, tin cups, lead balls, the wrack and ruin of a shipwreck. Interesting historical stuff, all of it, and worth a few bucks to collectors. But they hadn't dared share an ounce of it with anyone. The attention would have ruined everything. Leak a word of success and a thousand fortune-seekers would be all over the site, and then the damned do-gooders would whine, wanting to put legitimate salvage into the "public domain."

They'd kept the whole project secret, and the closer they got to the wreck, the more secret it had become. Talk to no one, that was the first option; if that didn't work, lie about it. That worked pretty good, but even then there were a few folks real nosey about what they were up to. The worst of the lot was that weird little Nobles kid, the one that split his time fishing and reading fashion magazines.

The site remained unmarked, as had their whole trail as they had narrowed the search, mile by mile, yard by yard. They knew how to find it from years of experience in these waters. It lay nineteen miles southwest of Brigands Key, and northwest of Cedar Key, the only two points of reference visible being the tops of old Hammond Lighthouse on Brigands, and Cedar Keys Lighthouse on Cedar. They could triangulate the lighthouses pretty close—Jack was a whiz with compass angles—find one of their lobster trap markers, and go another five hundred yards.

Yazz drained his beer can and flung it overboard. He turned to Jack. "So how much you think *Maybelle* is gonna fetch us?"

Jack smiled. "Well, Confederate blockade runners weren't exactly Spanish galleons, you know. But they kept the South alive. They'd haul as much cotton or whatever as they could to England, fast as they could, and haul back money and weapons, fast as they could. *Maybelle* was on her way back, so she's got a heap of value still in her."

Yazz knew the story. The *Maybelle* had been easing around Brigands Key in 1862, when the Union steamer *Hatteras* came up out of Cedar Key, where it had burned seven Rebel boats, sinking four of them, and intercepted her and sent her to the bottom. Like most shipwrecks, she didn't go down where everyone thought she did.

"Yeah, I got that," Yazz said. "Based on what we been seeing, how much?"

"The records say she carried maybe $150,000 in gold and silver, and a heap of ammo and guns. Muzzle-loaders."

"How *much*?"

"This ain't a science. I reckon we might get a half-million in profit."

"That's all? You said a million before."

"Estimates change. Half a mill is still a lot of money, buddy."

"Yeah, I guess it's pretty good." Yazz felt his euphoria sag, like air being let out of a balloon. Half a million. That was a shit-pile of money, especially compared to the six thousand a year he pulled in fishing. Half a million. Divided by two was two-fifty.

Damn.

That wouldn't make a guy a genuine millionaire. Not even close.

Shake it off, Yazz, he told himself. *It's happy time.* "Hey, what you going to do with your half?"

"I don't know, buddy. Maybe we could buy a new boat, huh? I could use a little office for myself too. Yeah, and we could add somebody to help you out with the lobster pots. Sound good?"

Not so great, Yazz thought. Too much like it was already. "I was hoping we'd each live high on the hog."

Jack gave him a look. *That* look, the you-stupid-son-of-a-bitch look. "We need to reinvest in the business. Make it grow. Course a half-million's just a rough guess. There might be a lot more down there."

Yazz brightened.

"Course," Jack continued, his brow furrowing with worry. "There could be a lot less."

"Don't say that, for Christ's sake. Bad luck."

Jack picked up a piece of the treasure. "I've never actually priced this stuff out before."

Yazz watched him. He shook his head slightly. Why couldn't Jack just be straight for once? He leaned against the side of the boat and his hand came to rest against the long wooden oar secured there, just below the gunwale. He glanced at it, and a thought sprang into his mind; himself casually freeing the heavy oar, swinging it behind his head, a long fast arc, and smashing it into Jack's skull, a crunch of sound, a giving way, an indentation in Jack's head big enough to stick his fist in; an ooze of gray and red onto the deck.

Yazz snatched his hand away from the oar, and closed his eyes, trembling. Jeez, he thought. Too much TV.

He opened his eyes and drew a slow breath, and stooped to help Jack. "Here, let's get this stuff put away. It's gettin' late and we need to get home."

"You bet."

Yazz thought: you *can* be a millionaire, or at least a lot closer to one. He could feel the blood pounding in his temples.

They stowed the treasure in the forward hold beneath the bow and locked it. Yazz fetched another beer, took a sip and another and another, and set it on the wheelhouse console. He drummed nervously with his fingers on the wheel, watching as Jack sweated over the winch and reeled in the anchor. When the anchor cleared the water and rose dripping alongside the hull, Jack signaled and Yazz switched on the engines. Smoke puffed and the engines sputtered and growled, the sweet smell of gas and oil drifting over the boat. Yazz turned the *High C* in a long slow loop towards Brigands Key. He throttled up and the old trawler creaked and churned ahead.

Jack busied himself cleaning a few pieces. Yazz steered for the Hammond Lighthouse. He adjusted his speed to match the slowly following sea and they eased along as if riding a cloud.

His thoughts returned to money. Lots of money.

Yazz had partnered with Jack Duncan for fourteen years now. Both had remained bachelors, forsaking social lives for the business. That was a good excuse anyway. They'd started in their early twenties, busting their guts fishing. Always made a profit, sometimes really good ones, usually not. And the work never got boring. But fishing? Hell of a way to make a living, and the fisheries seemed to dwindle just a little bit more each year.

For the last five years, they had a new goal. They had gotten the treasure bug by accident when Yazz had found a single gold coin, minted in England around 1852, in twenty feet of water while he and Jack were spearfishing on Denton Reef, a long pile of rocks and rubble seventeen miles out.

They researched the coin, Jack taking the lead. He liked that booky stuff; almost graduated from college, studying psychology and philosophy and all that shit, and would have graduated if that one professor had not been such a damned rule-maker. Jack could do some good thinking, and handled the books and taxes. Yazz did the truck driving, the engine maintenance, the hull scraping. The grunt work.

Good old Jack. The smart one, Jack. Yazz shifted his weight, trying to find a comfortable position. Jack did have good business sense, no doubt about that. He had a knack for anticipating things, good and bad, knew who to see and not see, who to trust, who not to. Trouble was, he always let it be known that he was the brains of the outfit.

They had scoured Denton Reef for two years before admitting to themselves that the coin in that spot was a fluke, and that there were no other finds to be had there. Maybe that coin had ridden the back of a turtle to the reef. Whatever, the reef had coughed up all it ever would.

So the search fanned out from there. Logically, Jack figured, the source was farther from shore, and wave action had pushed it closer over the decades. Somewhere, within several miles west, lay a wreck that should be theirs. And bit by bit, piece by piece, they found a trail of evidence that told them they had to be on the track of the *Maybelle*.

Now they were rich.

Just not as rich as he'd hoped.

He glanced again at the oar, then at Jack. Jack had brains, give him that much. It'd be best to get the loot to shore, safely lock it away, and let Jack do what he did best, make deals and profits Yeah, that'd be the thing to do. Jack had the contacts. He had the touch. He'd get the best price possible.

On the other hand . . .

Could any possible extra Jack could wrangle outweigh the difference lost by splitting the money two ways? Was Yazz such a dummy he couldn't learn the dealers' ropes on his own. He frowned, turning the thought over. Sure seemed like his intelligence had been insulted.

Again the image. The oar. Jack's smashed skull. This time, Yazz let the image play on like a little movie. He could see heaving Jack's body overboard. No. Bodies float. Don't they? He wasn't sure. In the movies, yeah, and they float right to the cops. Wounds are exposed. Not good. What about sharks? The sun lowered out over the Gulf, beginning to set, stretching red and gold glows low in the western sky. Sharks liked to feed at night. Suppose Jack's body got dragged behind the boat on a long rope for a ways. A couple of yanks on the line would let you know the sharks were having a go of it. Chumming for shark with my good chum Jack, he thought, smiling. He could stay out until it happened, all night if needed. That wouldn't look suspicious—fishermen spent nights on board all the time.

What if remains *did* wash ashore, even after the sharks had a go at it? That wouldn't be a problem. The town didn't even have its own medical examiner, although the town council talked about getting one now and then. It wasn't like drunk fishermen didn't drown around here. Seemed to happen every four or five years. The town liked its booze.

The movie played on. Mopping the deck for blood, steering the boat into some mangrove swamp on the mainland south of Brigands Key, hitching to the mangrove, securing the sack of treasure to a branch and burying it in the muddy shallows. Returning to the mainland, rushing to the police with a weepy story about Jack getting drunk and stumbling overboard in the night and disappearing below the surface, despite Yazz's desperate, heroic attempt at rescue. Slipping into a deep funk of grief for several weeks, inconsolable in his misery. In a couple of months—no, better wait a full year—discovering sunken treasure, the wealth of a beaten rebel nation. Fame and riches. Interviews on TV about his tremendous loss, his resolve, and his final triumph.

Heroic, sympathetic, *and* rich. If that didn't get him laid, nothing would.

Yazz gave himself a little chuckle and shook his head, ashamed and impressed at the same time. It was clever, no doubt about that. All but flawless. But it was just playful thinking, something he was pretty good at. He couldn't hurt his longtime partner. They went back a ways, pals since elementary school. Jack really was a good chum.

Jack looked up. "Slow the son of a bitch down, would you? You been drinking and the tide's going out. Jeez, you can be so stupid."

Yes sir, Mister Duncan, sir. Yazz had piloted this bucket for years. What did Jack think he was, some big idiot?

He throttled back a bit, slowing the boat a couple of knots. He released the wheel, locked it into position. She'd maintain a straight line. He turned and eyed Jack, and slipped the oar gently out of its rack, careful not to rattle it against the hull. The weight, the volume, the heft of the oar, felt a lot different than before. It had new purpose. It was no longer an oar.

Jack cleaned and scraped bits of treasure, hunched over them astern, his back to Yazz. Good old Jack. Let's see what you think about this, good old Jack. He squeezed the oar in his hands, raised it over his head, and eased toward his partner. One quiet step at a time.

A deck board squeaked underfoot.

Jack spun, his hand flashing into his pocket and out again with a revolver. He leveled it at Yazz. The gun roared.

Yazz felt a bee sting the front of his shoulder. Another stung his back. He glanced down. Darkness bloomed wet under his shirt. He clamped his hand over the wound. The pain of the gunshot grew, and nausea swept like a wave over him. The edges of the world darkened. He slumped to his knees and stared up at Jack, disbelieving.

"You shot me!"

"Well, yeah. You were about to club me to death."

Yazz shook his head weakly.

Jack snorted. "You figured I couldn't tell what you were thinking? Ha! I put the damned idea in your head. We've worked together for years and I know you better than you do. That's why I run the show and you do the crap work."

"Your idea?"

"Sure. I knew you wouldn't be happy with a modest payday, not even getting to being a millionaire after all the work we put into this. So I lied. Hell, this wreck is going to fetch us four, five million bucks, easy."

"Five?"

"Easy. Probably six."

"Then why—?"

"Shoot, I want the money just as bad as you, buddy, but I'm no killer. I got me a conscience. Killing you and keeping the treasure, that's just cold-blooded murder. I couldn't live with that. But I tell you what, killing in self-defense, that's not wrong. Fact is, it's a goddamn moral imperative. Thomas Aquinas said so, long as you don't intend to kill. See, I was *hoping* to kill you, but not *intending* to. Philosophers call it double effect; you can maim or kill in self-defense, long as you don't mean to, and if some good can come out of it. Conscience absolved! Course, the police may not believe the truth and they sure as shit don't study philosophy.

"Now, there was this one school of philosophers that called 'bullshit' on them double effect boys. They was called "consequentialists," and they figured you don't get off the hook morally if the consequences of your action still end in some seriously bad shit for the other guy, because you can always find a way out of it. Sadly, I dropped out of school before we covered a whole bunch of that."

Jack kept his gun ready, and studied Yazz's wound from a respectful distance. "Consequences! I got myself in a little moral jam here. That wound looks superficial; it's bleeding, but not like I nicked an artery or something. Ain't likely you'll die from it."

"So go ahead and get it over with. This hurts."

"You still ain't listening. My legitimate self-defense didn't kill you because I can't aim worth a shit. Double effect don't clear my conscience if I finish you off, 'cause now it can be morally avoided. Man, this philosophy shit is tough." Jack sagged, quiet for a moment, frowning. He suddenly brightened. "But if I do something *good* for you, and bad shit happens anyway, I'm in the clear. What I *can* do is help you commune with nature, to heal your soul. Might be real good for you."

Yazz glared at him.

Jack kept the gun trained on him, and kicked a coil of rope toward him. "Tie this around your chest. Show your seamanship and make it a damn good knot."

Yazz obeyed numbly.

"You get a free ride behind the boat," Jack continued. "I'm going to tow you, is all. It's like skiing, only slower. I'll even give you a life jacket. I don't actually kill you, and that's a fine moral choice, it'll help me sleep. It's getting dark. Sharks ought to be real frisky soon. What happens in the water will weigh on their little shark consciences, not mine. Old chum."

Notes

While I was writing my thriller, *Brigands Key*, this story from years before kept creeping into my thoughts. I originally wrote it under the title "Good Chums" in the late 1980s. A couple of magazines wanted it but went out of business before they could publish it. Not believing the story was cursed, I rewrote it as a Brigands Key story. The hardscrabble cast, the insular society, the treasure-hunting, were cut from the same tattered, sweat-stained cloth.

Of the two Civil War era ships mentioned, only the *CSS Maybelle* is fictional. The Union warship, *USS Hatteras* was real, and indeed sank four Confederate vessels in the area. They still rest on the sea bottom, undiscovered and unclaimed. The *Hatteras* was later sunk by *CSS Alabama* in a pitched battle off Galveston.

Jealousy, domination, and alcohol are certainly a recipe for failed marriage. Sometimes the need to repair an unhappy union work goes far beyond what is usually expected.

Myrna

Fallen leaves crackled underfoot, and Jimmy Brant winced with each hesitant step. Probing gingerly ahead with his feet and stepping lightly did no good. Might as well wear a cowbell, he thought.

The night sky clouded and the darkness grew nearly absolute, robbing his vision when he stayed within the shadows beyond the faint light of the house. He felt his way along the wall of the barn, his right hand tracing its rough boards.

He looked up and shook his head. A light cold rain fell, and the wind that propelled it made him shiver. He looked back at the house. The warmth that filled the windows beckoned. He took a step toward it, and stopped. *I ain't going back in. Not yet.* He backed against the barn wall, drew a bottle from his back pocket, took a pull off it, and wiped his mouth on his sleeve. At least the rain would mask his approach.

He drew a slow breath. The sweet aroma of drying tobacco leaves inside drifted out and reassured him.

Tobacco.

He could've done real well growing tobacco up in North Carolina, with good land and the industry looking out for him, but this Florida dirt wasn't right for it. Years of hard work had brought nothing, and it looked as if this year might be the all-time stinker.

It wore him down. He now drove to town quite regularly to forget his troubles, drinking and laughing long into the night at Mike B's Lounge. Stiff drinks helped sort things out, so that he became painfully aware that his wife was screwing around behind his back.

Myrna had loved him once, he guessed. He still loved her, after all they'd come through. But this hurt too much.

Her blood ran part Indian, giving that quality of beauty particular to American Indians—hair black as night, eyes to match, and skin tan and smooth. Jimmy sometimes told others she had Seminole in her, but she bristled at that, insisting she was Timucuan. Her ancestors, she claimed, grew tobacco on this very farm generations before white, black, or Seminole ever set foot on it, and it had been in her family ever since. Jimmy indulged her little fantasy, figuring what the hell, although it was a fat chance her Indian blood ran anything other than Seminole. But the Timucua disappeared two hundred years ago. When he pointed this little fact out, all he got was "I know what I am."

The Indian in her came from her mother, Julia. Myrna inherited her looks and her farm from Julia, and not a damned thing from her father. Before he met her, Jimmy had seen Myrna and her mother in town with swollen, purpling lumps makeup refused to hide.

Her father, a pig-eyed, pinch-faced sailor, hated living on the farm. Nate Fielding ran it haphazardly, and barged through life mean and hard. He had few loves, most notably his thick shock of red hair, Irishman red, which he crowed about when he got to drinking and blubbering at the pool hall. Jimmy despised the man, and no one missed him after he lit out without a word a couple months after Julia died of pneumonia. Abandoned Myrna just like that. She was fifteen then. Jimmy married her when she turned nineteen. Four years ago.

Business got tougher and growers gave up and moved away. Jimmy's farm—it was *his* goddamn farm—turned in regular losses after that first good year, but he'd turn it around. That hadn't happened, and he hated when Myrna started telling him how to run it.

All the while, she screwed around with Wayne Penney.

Jimmy figured that out. He'd seen Penney eyeballing his wife, and lately the bastard had been going out of his way to talk and joke with her at the grocery store, at the bank, at Charlene's Restaurant. Jimmy had eyes. He could see.

The rain settled in, a cold, sad all-nighter. He leaned against the barn and remembered their life together, mostly the rough spots, like that night she came home with more goddamn new clothes. There had been words, a fight, some hitting, some bruising . . . but nothing that justified her catting around.

He had let on as how he would be shooting pool in town until real late, and went and showed his face there. No Wayne Penney, just as expected, but he knew where to find him. He gulped down a beer, and stopped off at Mike B's to buy a fifth of whiskey.

Jimmy drove back toward home, taking pulls off the bottle all the way. He parked his pickup out on the road and stumbled half a mile in the dark to the house. The house lights shone warm and yellow from the windows. As he neared, he got down on his hands and knees and crawled to the bedroom window, his heart pounding. He stood, clenched his fists, held his breath, and peered in.

No one there.

He punched the wall, and turned away. He saw a flicker of light through a crack in the lapped wall boards of the barn.

* * *

He eased along the wall outside the barn, listening, listening, while his wife carried on with Penney inside. A lump rose in his throat and he wanted to cry, but he forced it away. He had to do what was needed. He had no choice. He hated to hurt people.

But Myrna hurt *him*.

He reached the pump shed that jutted from the barn wall, and gently opened its door. It squeaked defiantly and he froze. A rack of plumbing tools hung on the interior wall. He switched on his flashlight and scanned the tools, settling upon a heavy pipe wrench. He eased it from its hook, switched the flashlight off, and moved out into the rain again. The wet steel of the wrench reflected a tiny glint of light. He swung it once, twice, batted it against his open palm. It felt good, even scary, and he wondered if maybe it was too much.

No. Too late for second-guessing.

The barn door stood ajar, just feet away.

He heard muffled voices from inside. He stopped and cocked his ear. No use; the drumming of the rain smeared the words.

He squeezed the wrench handle and stepped in through the doorway. He opened his mouth to shout.

Myrna knelt near the opposite wall, alone, her back to him. The electric bulb glowed overhead, and swung gently in the night breeze. Shadows swayed with each swing of the bulb, making the interior seem alive.

Myrna was speaking. Not in English; in something he'd never heard before. A phrase—speaking in tongues—occurred to him dully, and he thought back to feverish summer revival meetings, the faithful falling to their knees, trembling in the spirit, speaking in tongues.

But those people spewed gibberish, making it up as they went, or were just confused idiots. The words Myrna spoke were foreign, but seemed to make sense.

She knelt by a small hole in the dirt floor. Beside the hole lay a little box of gray metal, its lid open. A small clay figurine lay beside it, a little man-shaped thing the size of a fifth of whiskey. A little whiskey man, Jimmy thought, and he reached impulsively for the bottle in his back pocket and took a drink.

A braided coil of something—hair, maybe—encircled the figurine's chest.

He picked out one of her words. *Hinino.* He'd heard that one before. Myrna once said it meant "tobacco," claimed it was Timucuan.

Her words began to take elusive shape in Jimmy's mind, like a radio broadcast fading in and out.

" . . . no haste . . . time is not . . . will get out."

And then Jimmy heard—no, felt—another voice, distant, as if spoken through a wall: *Please let me go, let me go let go*

Jimmy glanced around the barn and behind him. The guy must be hiding somewhere. He squeezed the wrench tighter. It didn't sound much like Wayne Penney; maybe she had other lovers, too.

"When sentence is served," Myrna said.

Jimmy felt his skin shiver. She *was* speaking to the figurine. He shook his head; that couldn't be right. Must be the whiskey.

Please let go

The voice again, like wind in the pines.

"Sentence is six years gone. Ninety-four more."

Let go

"Ninety-four more. You should have thought of that. Good behavior, you might get out in ninety-two. If I'm still here. If not, the spirit of my people will be, and will keep you company."

Please please

"You killed her just as surely as if you'd shot her. Didn't you think I'd tell her what you did?"

Please let go I'm sorry let go

"And you didn't stop even after you killed her. You wouldn't stop!" Myrna paused. "Maybe you'll have company someday soon."

Please

"You're a pig."

Jimmy's heart thudded and he could feel his legs weaken. His breath grew clipped and rapid and he struggled to control it. Six years. Six years. His thoughts raced back into the past.

He stared at the figurine. Braided red hair coiled about it. Where had he seen hair that bright red before? Red hair . . .

Like her father's.

Jimmy stepped back. He felt dizzy, touched his head, laced his fingers through his own hair.

Myrna lifted the figurine. "Break time is up." She placed it in the box.

No please so dark please no please let go please . . .

The cry snapped off as she closed the lid and locked its hasp. She dropped the box into the hole. "Good night."

Jimmy backed from the barn, spun, and ran stumbling for the house. He slipped on the wet grass and fell face-down into the mud, scrambled to his feet, and burst into the house, the screen door slapping shut behind him.

He tore off his muddy clothes and threw them into his closet, grabbed a towel and wiped himself down. He tossed the towel in with his dirty clothes and threw himself into bed and pulled the covers over him. For a second. He kicked off the covers and sprang from the bed, rooted through his dresser drawer. He found his stocking cap and pulled it down over his ears, stretching it as far as he could.

A squeak came from the front door.

Jimmy dove back into bed, and pulled the blankets up over his head. He squeezed his eyes shut. Words crept into his mind. *Maybe you'll have company someday soon.*

Myrna came into the bedroom. "Oh, Jimmy. I didn't expect you back so early."

"Me neither. I was tired, is all."

"Is everything all right?"

"Just tired."

A pause. A long one. "I was just out in the barn looking for a hammer to hang a picture."

"Oh. Okay."

"You're shaking."

"I don't feel too good."

Another pause. "Too much to drink?"

"No. Yeah. I think I'll stop drinking."

"That would be good. What's with the stocking cap?"

You're not cutting my hair off while I sleep, you bitch!" I got cold. From the rain."

"Well, good night." She flicked off the lights. "I'll be up awhile."

"Good night, Myrna."

* * *

Jimmy waited in his pickup outside Harley's Barbershop at seven the next morning. Harley pulled up and opened his shop. "Little off the top and sides, Jimmy Boy?" Harley asked.

Jimmy pushed past him and took a seat. "All of it. I want my head shaved."

"Shaved! You kiddin' me, right?"

"Just shave my goddamn head. It's a new look. Nobody asked for your thoughts on style."

Jimmy stuffed a pinch of tobacco under his lip. "You got it, Jimmy Boy."

* * *

Around Jefferson County, the Brants became known as a fine couple. The ladies would spot them and nod their approval as Jimmy got the door for Myrna. "That Jimmy Brant sure is a fine young man," they said. "Ever since he got off the bottle. Myrna is a lucky girl, if a bit undeserving."

For a change, the farm turned a profit.

Myrna and Jimmy shopping. Myrna and Jimmy at church. Myrna and Jimmy at the Independence Day fireworks.

Myrna and Jimmy. Such a fine young couple.

* * *

"Get you a glass of lemonade, honey?"

"No thank you, Jimmy, I'm fine."

Jimmy set his hoe aside and wiped his face with his sleeve. "Think I'll get myself one then. Awful damn hot today."

He left the vegetable garden and went to the kitchen. He poured his lemonade, and thought back over the past year. Things had been good for the farm, and for himself and Myrna. A little money in the bank, a quiet life. Very stable. It was good.

No, he told himself. It wasn't. She leashed him up like a dog. He never went out with the boys, never skipped off for some fishing, never touched a drop of liquor, not even beer.

He lived like a monk.

"But this ain't living," he mumbled. He remembered that rainy, whiskey-soaked night. His life changed that night. Seemed like for the better for a while. Not so much anymore. It seemed now so distant and unreal.

Was it real?

He wondered.

* * *

Jimmy dug feverishly. He knew where the box would be, if there even was a box. Myrna would not be back from the store for a while.

He suddenly stopped digging at two feet. Nothing here! He closed his eyes, recalling the scene. It came slowly, hazily, but clear enough that he knew he was digging in the right spot. There was no sign this spot, or any other, had ever been disturbed.

His doubt in the memory grew.

Maybe it had all been just a whiskey nightmare.

* * *

Days. Weeks.

Jimmy lay sprawled on the couch, nursing a can of beer in front of the TV, eating potato chips. He crushed his empty cans and arranged them in a circle on the coffee table. He laughed at the TV when it amused him and launched potato chips at it when it didn't, and stabbed it repeatedly with the remote.

The door swung open and Myrna struggled in under the weight of three bags of groceries. She set them heavily upon the kitchen counter, turned, and glared at Jimmy. He turned and mumbled at his set and stabbed it again. Myrna spun away and went to fetch the rest of the groceries. Jimmy popped another beer.

When the groceries were all put away, Myrna approached. She snapped the TV off.

"The hell you think you're doing?" Jimmy said. "Turn the son of a bitch back on."

"Jimmy, why can't you lift a finger around here? You're acting just like you used to."

"I do plenty. I got this farm turned around, didn't I?"

She touched his arm. "You were so good to me this past year. I thought you'd started loving me again."

"Course I love you. That don't mean I got to be the woman of the house."

Myrna's eyes glistened. "You're trying to drive me down again."

Jimmy watched her for a moment, swatted the potato chips aside, sending them everywhere, and sprang from the couch. "Christ, woman, you drive me nuts! I'm going to town."

"Please don't, Jimmy. We should talk."

The screen door slapped behind him.

"Please don't, Jimmy," she called again.

* * *

He laughed and roared and drank, first time in a year. He shot pool with a vengeance, relishing the *clack* of the balls, his consumption of beer improving his aim and then bushwhacking it. Damn cue was crooked. It became a snake after a while and he abandoned it for another, which turned out just as snakelike. He lurched against a table, shooting, missing, drinking. Jukebox honky-tonk filled his ears and molded itself around his brain, becoming a muffled din, a slab of sound. Lights grew brighter all around.

Another round of drinks, all around! Roaring good fun. The boys all shooting and drinking. Harley there, not barbering, but laughing and pulling at him, saying come on, Jimmy, time to go, too much to drink. And Jimmy shoving the fat little prick away, falling flat on his face, no pain, a little blood, roaring funny. Lurching out to the parking lot, climbing into the truck, gunning the motor, backing over the sidewalk, knocking over trashcans, blasting out of the lot, spitting gravel and dust, fishtailing, following that hypnotic dashed line down the highway to home.

Stumble into bed.

Sleep.

* * *

The sun warmed his face in the morning, slanting through the window. No, not morning anymore.

He looked about. He heard Myrna rustling about in the kitchen, and he smelled ham frying. He stretched and the clouds of memory dissolved, and he remembered the night. Parts of it anyway. He smiled and rubbed his eyes. What a night. Hadn't had as much fun in ages. The knuckles of his right hand were scraped and swollen.

He nervously touched his scalp. His head remained slick and clean-shaven, and he sighed with relief. He'd stuck with that little bit of insurance, in spite of his growing certainty about that whiskey night. No point in giving the squaw a chance to scalp him.

He felt an urge in his bladder and got out of bed. The room wobbled and he banged into the bathroom door and held onto the frame, waiting for balance and for his head to clear. It did, and grew a small dull ache.

He relieved himself and went to the sink. He rinsed his mouth, and looked into the mirror. The eyes were a little bloodshot and stubble darkened his face. He rubbed his hairy chest.

He caught his breath and looked down at himself.

His hairy chest was smooth.

Clean-shaven.

From the kitchen, Myrna hummed, high and bittersweet.

Notes

"Myrna" came about through my fascination with lost cultures—in this case the Timucua of North Florida—and the spiritual ties to the lands they inhabited. The title character may or may not be the last living descendant of the Timucua. She believes she is and demonstrates it with conviction, and that's what matters.

In times of siege, notions of good and evil disappear, and only thoughts of survival remain.

The Valkyries of Leningrad

January, 1942

Twilight wrapped Sergeant Johann Olbermann of Germany in a funeral shroud, melding color with shadow, turning red to black. Wetness seeped through his winter coat. He clamped his hand down upon his bleeding shoulder, his thoughts racing with the last and greatest mistake of his life.

The shattered, charred farmhouse, the object of his fool's errand, lay just steps away, dark against the new fallen snow. Beyond, more wrecked and abandoned houses littered the outskirts of Leningrad, a no-man's-land between siege army and defenders. The German line lay four hundred meters behind him, its claws sunk into the earth, its big guns behind, silent of late but poised to rain death upon the ancient city at a moment's notice.

Johann and his patrol had studied this farmhouse for three days now, each day coming just a bit closer, planning, whispering in debate, and finally deciding. The little house remained somewhat intact, more so than others, and likely had been abandoned in great haste. There would be modest items to be stolen. Blankets. Good woolen socks. Vodka, if luck smiled on them. The stillness and tedium of winter siege lulled them, and his men urged him to make a move. In the gathering darkness, they could make the farmhouse, plunder it, slip back to the German line in a matter of minutes. The approach was sheltered in ruin and shadow. If questioned, they would claim a Russian patrol had entered it. Such engagements occurred all the time. And they were soldiers, here to take St. Petersburg, here to win a war, not sit it out. It would be heroic. At the time, it seemed almost rational.

His patrol moved like ghosts through skeletal trees and houses toward this one. Twenty paces from the house, a Soviet machine-gun spit death, arcing through them like a scythe through wheat, bullets sending up gouts of snow and blood.

* * *

Like the Kaiser's army in the Great War, like Napoleon's in the last century, the *Wehrmacht* swept east across steppes and farms in a relentless wave. It reached Stalingrad in the south, Moscow in the center, and Leningrad in the north. Three vast prongs of steel and fury, just as planned.

Any fool could recognize the great flaw in the plan, the endless Russian landscape and the ever-lengthening and vulnerable supply lines. But the generals devised a solution, oh yes. The army would feed itself on the foodstuffs of the lands conquered. Leningrad, the grand old St. Petersburg, renamed by the communists, would fall by July of '41, and would sustain them once they'd taken it. But July bled into August. September. October. And the bitter Russian winter engulfed them, and froze the blitzkrieg, the lightning war, in place, a handful of kilometers from the city.

With the city untaken, the Führer issued his frustrated decree, to blast old St. Petersburg from the Earth, to leave nothing. And the big guns roared without stop, and the dive-bombing Stukas screamed down. And still the city remained. Then came the new orders: waste no more men and equipment. Starve Leningrad. Accept no surrender. Make them die. All of them.

And the Russians died. By tens of thousands, of starvation and cold. Leningrad became the City of Hunger. The food, all gone. Livestock, all gone, butchered and eaten. Household pets, all gone, eaten as the starvation settled in. Birds and rats, all gone. Eaten.

Whispers of cannibalism seeped from the city through captured Russians. The barbarians were not at the gate; the barbarians lived within and preyed upon each other.

* * *

Johann failed his men, murdering them with stupidity. The squad had already been shorthanded at seven and now only he remained. All six lay dead in bloody snow behind him, the burst of machine-gun fire having come rat-tat-tat directionless from the gloom. A bullet tore through his overcoat. Two struck more than cloth, one passing through his shoulder, another striking his knee. He threw himself against a shattered stone wall of the farmhouse, unsure of the direction of fire. The pungent smell of gunfire lingered, laced with the smell of urine and blood.

The bee stings of bullets welled into slabs of pain. Dizziness washed over him, the world tilting and clouding. He shook his head, tried to clear it, and the world returned to a manageable slant.

Wetness gathered on his leg and shoulder. He moved his arm, wincing. The leg resisted. He gingerly touched his knee. Pieces of bone gave and shifted.

He reached into a coat pocket and withdrew his flask of Russian vodka. He took two pulls off it and returned it, needing its balm to stave off shock and pain.

The firing ceased, his enemy lay silent and waiting. Studying. Deciding how to finish him.

His mind darkened and drifted.

* * *

Assignment to Army Group North had been Johann's fervent wish and he'd received it. If one must serve, it should be in the north, in the country of the Norsemen.

When he was a little boy, his father led him on long walks through the forests and fields, gesturing and regaling him with tales of the old Norse gods, of Thor and Odin and Frigga. Little Johann listened, wide-eyed, peppering Father with questions. The stories brimmed with heroism and valor. The old gods ranged far and wide, smashing enemies, ruling the seasons. And Norsemen followed a code worthy of the old gods, one that demanded their best in the fight. If their best wasn't enough, they still earned the approval of the gods, winning entry into heavenly Valhalla to dwell there for eternity.

His father went to the Eastern Front in 1914 and never came home. Father's last letter said:

Johann, my brave beautiful son, do not worry. The war will end soon and we will again walk together in the shade of the woods and bask in the sun of the seashore and spin tales of the Norsemen.

But then a soldier arrived, bearing a different letter. An official one. His mother read it and fell to her knees, shaking with sobs. Johann ran to the barn and cried until he decided that Father at last dwelt in Valhalla.

The Valkyries, the ancient men of the North knew, hungered for the battlefield, drawn to the clang of metal and the cries of anger and pain. They descended like angels upon the fallen, gathered them into their arms, and carried them off to Valhalla, to a paradise of the warrior class. For the brave, life demanded much but eternal reward awaited.

That first war did end, badly for Germany. Then came the next war, and Operation Barbarossa, and the Wehrmacht swept like a relentless wave into Russia. Now, the glorious stories of the Norsemen were just stories. He learned that lesson in battle, first in Poland, in France, and now in Russia. Tales of valor and bravery seduced starry-eyed, stupid recruits and gibbering politicians. In battle, you die or survive.

The stupid die.

* * *

The pain of his wounds grew into a monolith of agony. He took another drink of vodka, shook off his daze, and tried to think. He dared not move for fear of giving away his location. But if he remained here, he would die of cold and blood loss within hours. Perhaps minutes. If he could make the farmhouse, he might survive the night with the last of his rations and a fire, and pray for rescue in the morning.

Think. Think it through. Machine-gun fire obliterated his squad. He focused, trying to recall the instant of the assault. He remembered the staccato sound, the tat-tat-tat, clean, uncluttered. The sound of a single machine gun. No other rifle fire punctuated the fight. That meant there just one gunner, with perhaps a gunner's mate. He prayed it was one. The gunfire came from his left.

The enemy remained hidden, unmoving, though they'd cut down every man of Johann's patrol. To be that cautious, they must suspect that he still lived, and would wait him out. Let him die.

A light snow began to fall. Good. Any natural movement masked his own.

He needed to locate his enemy.

He felt about where he lay, and his hand settled upon a brick from the shattered wall. He gripped it and shifted his body just enough to see through a cleft in the low wall, keeping himself hidden. He looked out at the snowy ground, and heaved the brick as far as he could, the exertion wrenching him with a new hell of pain.

The brick struck the snow with a geyser of white and clattered off rocks. He choked back his pain and fixed his attention upon the line of trees to his left.

A ghost of movement caught his eye, a shooter swiveling, taking the bait.

Johann eased his rifle about and took aim. He drew a breath, held it; and the shooter turned to look in his direction. He squeezed the trigger. The rifle barked, jostling his bad shoulder, and the figure slumped over.

Johann gasped, drawing in air. Dizziness swept through once again. He kept his rifle raised, studying the dark hiding places. Nothing moved amid the gentle snowfall.

Sensations. Needles of cold stung his face and hands and crept into his soul. The pain of his knee and shoulder grew, feeling as though someone dragged barbed wire through him. Blood leaked from his wounds, taking warmth with it. He studied his trembling hand.

Valhalla would reward him sooner than planned, he thought. To forestall that imaginary paradise, he must be warm and secure, and able to bandage himself.

Waiting and watching for other Soviet shooters wasted time and life. If others hid in the shadows and he moved, he would be shot down. Surrender amounted to suicide; the Russians would not waste food and warmth on a prisoner amidst the starving and freezing people of St. Petersburg.

If he waited, he would die slowly but die nonetheless. At least moving offered a chance.

He shifted away from the line of trees and dragged himself along the rubble wall toward the farmhouse. The expected explosion of gunfire never came.

A rustle of sound came from within.

He stopped and lay still, listening.

The world tilted lazily, first in one direction and then in another. He tried to shake his head clear, to little avail. Dizziness swelled into nausea. His stomach spasmed and he shivered.

Darkness flecked the edges of vision. He blinked it away. If it closed in, he would never waken. He tried to stand but his legs refused.

His mind drifted. Father exhorted him with tales of Thor and Odin. But all Johann could think of were the Valkyries—the choosers of the fallen—and the journey to Valhalla. The beautiful maidens sweeping down to Earth to the strains of Wagner.

Movement again, in the corner of his eye. He turned.

From the shadows of the farmhouse a figure emerged, slowly, and stopped. He tightened his grip on his rifle. The figure advanced three more steps.

A woman.

She looked this way and that, her eyes large, sunken, suspicious. A tattered gray dress and overcoat hung from her skeletal body, a scarf drawn about her head, a cloth bag draped over her shoulder. She gazed at his fallen men. She took a step.

Valkyrie, his mind whispered. My friends have given way to the long night of the North, have slipped their mortal bondage. War is ended for them, the warrior's death has taken them, and Valhalla awaits, the justice and reward of the gods for the brave. The Valkyries are here to take them.

Two more women in rags emerged.

"Valhalla," he gasped.

They stared at him. One pointed, her bony hand trembling. "*Nemetskiy*," she said in a cracked voice. "*Nemetskiy!*" Her voice became a hiss. "German!"

The Valkyries staggered from the ruins. Not the beautiful maidens of yore, but gaunt figures, eyes staring from sunken eyes. Lips shrunken against teeth. Faces like skulls. Their clothes in rags hung upon them. Shadows of humanity, frail living skeletons. Madness glinted in their eyes.

The desperate, starving masses of old St. Petersburg, of new Leningrad. The rumors confirmed. The livestock, gone. The pets, gone. The birds and rats, all gone. Nothing left but emaciated human beings with emaciated children to feed, in any way that presented itself.

The Valkyries of Leningrad crept closer, wraiths in the gathering twilight, silent as the snowfall. The nearest drew a butcher knife from her bag.

The Valkyries chose from the fallen and drew near.

Johann closed his eyes and awaited Valhalla.

Notes

Founded by Peter the Great in 1703 on the shores of the Baltic, St. Petersburg, the glorious capital of Tsarist Russia, has endured change and horrors on a scale few other great cities have seen. When the Tsars fell in 1917 and the Bolsheviks seized power, the city became Petrograd. With the death of Vladimir Lenin in 1924, it became Leningrad. And with the collapse of the Soviet Union in 1991, the city once again became known as Saint Petersburg.

In June, 1941, Hitler launched Operation Barbarossa, the largest invasion in history, and the German blitzkrieg rolled across the vast steppes of the USSR. The northernmost prong of the offensive was aimed at Leningrad, and reached the outskirts of the city before grinding to a halt as the bitter Russian winter set in. Blitzkrieg became siege, and the siege lasted 872 days.

Leningrad was cut off, and descended into nightmare. Food ran out, and mass starvation gripped the city. An estimated 1.5 million people died.

Amid desperation and death, cannibalism took root.

This became the dark white stage for "The Valkyries of Leningrad."

Heaven and Earth. What they mean is really just a matter of perspective.

Under the Whelming Tide

Whilst thee the shores, and sounding Seas
Wash far away, where ere thy bones are hurld,
Whether beyond the stormy Hebrides,
Where thou perhaps under the whelming tide
Visit'st the bottom of the monstrous world . . .

—John Milton, "Lycidas" (1638)

Excitement grew like a living thing within the ship as it hurtled through the endless void of space. The Aethir living within the vast ship, thousands of them, for two thousand generations, knew it only as Great Vessel. And a vessel is just that, a container, a ship, something serving only to carry them.

It was carrying them home.

Giddy with anticipation, the Aethir greeted each other with unabashed hugs and smiles and laughter and claps on the back. The Aethir were returning home, to the Heaven promised by the Masters, to the planet of their origin.

They had entered its solar system.

The Aethir pressed to the great triangles of windows, awestruck. There, sunward, a tiny blue speck hung in the blackness of the void. They were so close now they could actually *see* Heaven.

They were returning to Earth.

* * *

Alone with her husband in the Library of History, Daneeth studied the shimmering images Tonven had selected and listened to him with growing despair. She shook her head; she loved Tonven but this heresy would get her and her unborn killed.

She glanced about to make sure they were alone, and placed her hand on his. "Tonven," she whispered. "Please. We can't think of these things."

"We have brains."

"You know what I mean. This . . ." She waved her hand at the flickering images of the Aethir in the air before them. "This hardly seems the time to undermine our salvation."

"There's no other time. In another sixteen sleeps we will arrive at Earth."

"At Heaven, you mean."

"Yes, Heaven. Heaven on Earth."

"Don't you think it's a little late to question Heaven?"

"I'd have questioned it a thousand sleeps ago if I'd been ready but I've just been piecing it together, bit by bit." He paused, and his eyes avoided hers for a moment. "I lacked courage. I feared my own conclusions. They seemed so . . . bizarre, and I couldn't be sure."

"But now you are?"

Another pause, longer. "One can never be absolutely sure of anything."

"How sure are you?"

"Enough to be afraid." He gestured toward the images. "Look close, Daneeth. What do you see?"

"Us."

Tonven nodded. "Us. As we are now. Don't you wonder about us as we once were? How the first of the Aethir were?" He paused. "How different they were from us?"

Daneeth watched the images. The Aethir filled the images by the sixteens, by sixteens of sixteens, all so beautiful and slender, so full of grace. She placed a hand on her swollen belly, then both hands, and felt the miraculous small movement of their child within her. Soon the child, a tiny girl, would be born, another of their beautiful kind. "Of course they were different," she said. "All things change."

"That's the problem." He motioned with his finger, and the visions of Aethir shimmered. "Look back across generations, Daneeth."

The tall, beautiful Aethir began to change with the reversal. Generations flitted past in the span of mere heartbeats.

The Aethir changed. Their long slender fingers shortened, by half. Their arms, legs, torso, necks, all shortened too, and grew thicker. Impossibly shorter, impossibly thicker, brutish in their new dimensions. Shrinking as the time of tens of thousands of sleeps receded. Shrinking to a mere half of the height of the Aethir, and growing in girth by more than double. Their skin, so tan in color, a caricature of the purest white of the Aethir, and so vulgarly bulging with muscle.

The images stopped regressing.

"That's us. That . . . *creature* is us. That is what the first Aethir looked like."

"It's . . . well, ugly to be sure. But everyone knows these pictures, and how we changed over ages."

"But what caused this change?"

to act upon, and I remain your humble servant." He executed a respectful bow and stepped back, his eyes downcast.

"Well put, Mister Monitor," Tonven said.

High Magistrate Soola looked from Ghed to Tonven. "You understand the charges, Tonven?"

"More or less."

"You do not wish to recant, or to plead insanity?"

"I do not."

She regarded him for a moment. "This is your opportunity to do so. We do not—*I* do not—particularly wish this affair to go any further."

"If I did so, you wouldn't hear what you need to hear."

The High Magistrate sighed. "Very well. Monitor Ghed?"

Ghed coughed delicately into his slender fingers and looked in turn at each member of the High Council for what Daneeth guessed was meant to be dramatic effect. "You know the charges, my Magistrates," Ghed said. "This man of the Aethir, this Tonven, has spread great untruths, solely for the purpose of sedition and fear-mongering. He has stated that—"

"Enough," Soola said with a dismissive wave. "The man can speak for himself without you to filter it. Tonven, tell us what you will."

"Thank you, High Magistrate." Tonven stole a glance to Daneeth. "I have considered this problem for thousands of sleeps now. I won't bore you because time is short. Am I correct in saying we arrive at Earth after just eight more sleeps?"

Vox, known to fancy himself the only true technocrat among the Magistrates, cleared his throat. "More or less, eight and three-eighths."

"Unless we abandon this plan," Tonven said, "we will not live to see nine."

"Nonsense," snorted Vox.

"Nonsense," repeated Ghed, emboldened.

Soola glared at Ghed. "Perhaps. Perhaps not." She returned her attention to Tonven. "Continue."

"I've long had doubts about who we are, what we are. Why we are. So some thousand sleeps ago, I began to attack these doubts and research our histories."

"Already I take offense, young man. Everyone knows our origin story and our history. These have never been hidden."

"I do not mean to imply that the truth has been intentionally hidden from us, or even lost. The records are glorious and detailed." Tonven turned and faced the man slouching at the end of the semicircle. "Magistrate Deriss, you are the greatest historian among the Aethir. Tell us of it, and I'll tell you what we're missing."

Deriss straightened and beamed. "Why, I will be happy—"

"Do keep it short, Deriss," Soola said. "No one here wants to die of starvation."

Deriss's face sank. "Well. There's so much . . ."

"Then I'll prompt you, Magistrate Deriss," Tonven said. "Who are we and where are we from?"

"You know that already."

"Pretend I don't. I want everyone to see the picture anew."

"Well. I shall attempt an abbreviated version. In the beginning, the Masters came to Earth and—"

"From where?"

"They were always here."

"Here? What is here?"

"Here. Within Great Vessel. They were always here."

"I doubt it. They came from somewhere else. Not from here. From one of the billions of worlds in the galaxy."

"And so the heretic speaks," Monitor Ghed mumbled.

"They were ship-bound," Deriss said. "They claimed so themselves."

"Yes, they *were* ship-bound, probably for thousands of generations, just as we have been," Tonven said. "But they came first from one of the myriad worlds."

"They never claimed that."

"After so long in space, they probably no longer cared."

"But we care. We want to return to Earth, the Heaven. Why would the Masters be so different in their desires?"

"They *were* different. So completely different from the Aethir we can't begin to fathom their thoughts, their psychologies. And they felt no need to explain because it would have been pointless. Suppose for a moment that they did care where they were originally from. Why then did they never return, if they were so similar in thought to us humans?"

Deriss fidgeted. Daneeth thought he wanted to shrug, but that would be a sign of doubt. Unsafe doubt.

"I'll tell you why," Tonven continued. "Because they couldn't return. Like us, they had been too long, too many generations, in space."

"How can one be too long in space?" Soola asked. "It's a natural home."

"Remember your teachings, Magistrate. You know how the first Aethir looked."

Soola regarded him for a moment, and traced a small circle in the air with her finger. An image flickered into existence. A First Aethir, a woman, short and stout. Another gesture, another image, this one a man. More gestures, and dozens of unique individuals, men and women, boys and girls, stood about, moving, accomplishing odd tasks.

"Now us, please," Tonven said. "And at true scale to these first Aethir."

The images shimmered, so like the images Daneeth and Tonven had viewed just a few sleeps ago. The first Aethir, short and impossibly stout. The modern Aethir, graceful, ethereal wisps, towering by more than double over the first Aethir.

"Ah," Tonven said. "Modern human and ancient human. Aethir all, and yet so vastly different."

"Not so different," Deriss said, leaning forward. "Same features, same eyes, same noses, same mouths. Five fingers on each hand, five toes on each foot."

Tonven nodded and raised a hand, fingers extended. "Five. Five plus five makes ten. Another example of how different the psychology of the Masters was from that of the Aethir. Did you ever wonder why all our maths, all our figures, are expressed on the number eight?"

"Eight-form is the simplest, most logical, form of mathematics," Deriss said.

"To the Masters it was. They possessed two digits on each of their four appendages, and eight stalks upon which they carried themselves, each stalk also with two digits. Naturally, they expressed figures in eights. If we had developed our own culture, we would have expressed in groups of ten."

"Then why don't we?"

"Because we were handed eight-form math and told to use no other."

Deriss settled back and studied his hands as if for the first time.

"Remember the teachings," Tonven said. "We changed drastically from the first Aethir. I suspect that the Masters also changed drastically from the first Masters to live aboard Great Vessel."

"Perhaps," Vox said. "The histories are vague on that point. However, you conveniently forget that the Masters themselves taught that all species, on all worlds, change slowly over time."

"That's my point. The Masters changed. We changed. We aren't like those first Aethir, and neither will we be like the Aethir that still dwell on Earth, if any do."

"But if we change over generations, and all species change over generations, then the Aethir of Earth will have also changed. They will be just like us!"

"I don't think so."

Aethir. "But the images don't lie. They tell a story, and this is the only explanation for these images that makes any sense."

Soola let out a long sigh. All eyes turned to her. "Have you anything more to say, Tonven?"

"I could go on, but I've summed up my thoughts for you."

"And still you do not recant this fairy tale?" Vox said.

Daneeth moved closer. "What will be his fate if he does not?"

Monitor Ghed glared at her. "Quiet, girl. *You* are not to question the Magistrate."

Vena placed a hand on Daneeth's forearm and squeezed. "A conviction, by majority vote, carries expulsion into the void."

Daneeth felt her world, her love, being stripped away. "Cast out into space? That is instant death!"

Soola said, "It is harsh in the extreme, but it's a law held sacred since the last of the Masters passed away. Discipline has kept the Aethir from passing as well."

"It's barbaric!"

"It's the law."

Daneeth trembled. "Tonven, please, my love, recant. I can't raise our child by myself."

Tonven shook his head. "Unless we abandon the notion of this supposed Heaven, you won't have to." He looked at Vena. "Represent me now as I wish."

"Magistrate," Vena said, her voice breaking, "Tonven restates his position. And I add my voice to his; I am convinced by his logic. You may prosecute me as well. If he has just a chance of being right, you must change course and study this issue until it's resolved with certainty. Anything less than delay is tantamount to a crime against humanity."

"We may well indeed add you to the casting-out, Vena," Ghed said.

"That's enough, Ghed," Soola said. "Tonven's musings border on paranoid mental illness, but Vena has a point."

Hurix, the most ancient of the Magistrates, cleared his throat and pointed a shaky finger at Tonven. "I for one have made my decision. I see no reason to beat a dead Master any longer."

"Hurix, vulgarity has no place—"

"Spare me, woman, and call a vote."

Soola tapped her long fingers nervously. "Very well. You all know the charges of heresy and maliciousness, and the defendant is clearly in control of his faculties and competent to have been placed on trial. Vena, is there any closing statement you'd like to make?"

Vena trembled. "I . . . we wish to state once more that Tonven is a loyal Aethir and believes what he is saying. And now so do I. In the least, I urge the Magistrates to delay Heaven. Heaven can wait."

Ghed muttered something inaudible.

Daneeth trembled. "Vena, that is no defense! My husband stands to lose his life!" She turned to Soola, and wiped a tear from her cheek. "Tonven has not been himself. Clearly he has great passion and beliefs. That's why I fell in love with him! But passion leads to conviction and stubbornness. Tonven does not say these things out of malice, but out of love for his people. You cannot find a lie in that. No one has ever caught him in a lie because he says the things he believes, right or wrong. Please, I beg of you. Let him live. In a few more sleeps all will be forgotten as we enter Heaven. Joy will reign over the Aethir. Do not make my beloved perish for his thoughts. Lock him away, muzzle him until the blessed moment arrives; by then all will be right with the world. Please. Please!"

"Crime and the law do not make adjustments based upon circumstance, dear child," Vox said. "Call the damned vote."

Soola looked at Tonven. "Your last chance."

He grimaced and shook his head. "High Magistrate, I cannot recant the truth."

Soola nodded. "We now vote. A simple majority will determine guilt. As High Magistrate, I vote first as prescribed by law. I find the defendant not guilty."

Vox slapped the table. "What? You cannot be serious."

Soola ignored him. "Hurix, your vote?"

"Guilty."

"Deriss?"

Magistrate Deriss looked down at his hands. "Not guilty."

"Vox?"

"Guilty!"

"Serena?"

"Not guilty. This whole trial is a corruption of our ideals."

Daneeth's heart surged. Three to two for acquittal so far! She looked at Tonven. He kept his eyes on the floor, and trembled slightly.

"Tess?"

"Guilty."

"Zissen?"

"Guilty."

Four to three in favor of conviction.

Only Tovi remained. Daneeth held out hope. The most reasonable person in Great Vessel held her husband's life in her hands.

"Before the final vote," Soola said, "I must point out that a tie vote constitutes an acquittal. Guilt requires a majority. Tovi, your vote?"

Tovi closed her eyes. "This is the most difficult vote I have ever cast. I've heard compelling arguments from Tonven today. They ring true. Yet at the end of it all, guilt or innocence in our system is not always a function of truth, nor whether we should wait, nor whether guilt or innocence will even matter when we reach our destiny after eight more sleeps. Rather, it is a function of whether a violation of admittedly antiquated laws has occurred. And in that regard, Tonven is guilty."

Vox and Hurix simultaneously shouted approval. "Then it is done!"

Blood drained from Daneeth's face. Her vision darkened, her beloved condemned to die, her world dying with him. Faintly, distantly, she heard Tonven imploring Vena to catch and steady her.

Vena took Daneeth's arm and eased her into her seat.

Soola said, "It's settled then. The court has delivered a verdict of guilt."

"And justice must be immediate," Hurix said.

"Into the void with the heretic," Vox said. "And not soon enough."

Soola said, "Settle down, old men. The law says that, in a verdict of guilt, if the High Magistrate sides with the dissenting opinion of innocence, he or she may replace the prescribed sentence with an alternate. I have decided to invoke that law. Tonven will not be consecrated to the void. I hereby sentence him to probation, without penalty or restriction, until the end of his days, or until the Aethir return home."

A rush of relief and joy swept into Daneeth, and she caught her breath. *Tonven would live and be free.*

"No!" Vox screamed. "This is an outrage. I won't stand for it!"

"Magistrate Vox," Soola said, "might I point out that you now come dangerously close to sedition yourself? Shall I open a new trial here and now to determine if indeed you do?"

Vox opened his mouth, thought better of it, and sank back into his seat.

"And our arrival on Earth?" Tonven asked, his voice flat and devoid of hope despite his reprieve.

As if in answer, a slight change in the floor of Great Vessel could be felt.

"That will not change," Soola said. "We have begun the braking. Descent into Heaven has commenced."

* * *

Excitement rippled throughout Great Vessel. The moment of destiny had arrived, the moment of prophecy and promise. The ship had braked for eight straight sleeps.

The populace had hung on every announcement from the Magistrates. Great Vessel had passed the outer planets of Earth's planetary system. Each milestone revealed itself just as the Masters had promised. They flew past the outer gas giants, one with shining rings of ice; past the largest with its vivid bands of color and red spot like a benign observant eye; past a small planet of red; past the brilliant glowing whiteness that was Earth's lone moon.

And there before them grew the third planet from the star, blue, green, brown, and white, the indescribably beautiful planet Earth. Daneeth watched it, mesmerized by the beauty and mystery. It took her breath away, this shimmering planet of life and bounty and sweetness.

Great Vessel approached, slowing ever more, and dipped into the upper atmosphere, and descended.

The entire population, many sixteens of sixteens of men and women and children of the Aethir gathered in the vast hold of Great Vessel. The mighty ship, after nurturing thousands of generations in space, would gently kiss the fertile ground of Old Earth, and the people would at last be home.

Daneeth had gathered with all the others, giddy with the infectious euphoria. Her fears, stoked by Tonven's own fears, had evaporated. She felt their baby kick and squirm, and she caressed her bulging belly. Her sweet baby girl would be the first born of the first generation of the returned Aethir.

She looked at Tonven standing beside her. His eyes were drawn and gray from lack of sleep. She smiled, took his hand, and squeezed it gently. He forced a smile in return.

Next to him stood Soola, beaming, her grin infectious. "We believe we are landing in a region of advancement," she said. "Great societies abound there, and great numbers of people. I'm glad you could be with us, Tonven."

Almost imperceptibly, a slight bump and shudder were felt in the floor of the ship. A chorus of cheers rang out all about them.

They had landed on Earth.

"See, Tonven?" Daneeth said. "We are here and all is well. All is perfect."

Tonven gave a slight nod.

Through the great rows of triangled windows, Daneeth saw the dust of landing drift and clear. She gasped.

As far as the eye could see, magic and beauty surrounded them. She had seen the archival images of Earth and knew what to expect, yet it still had defied her imagination, outstripping her expectations many times over. Plants, much like those grown in Great Vessel, but in limitless variety and size and numbers, abounded. The ground stretched away, rippled and uneven and beautiful, and in the distance towering heights of ground—mountains—reached into the brilliant blue and white sky. To her right in the distance, a great plain of blue—a sea—shimmered and stretched to the horizon, dappled with golden light from the sun.

And people—*humans*—gathered by many sixteens on the hills and watched and pointed. Some appeared riding on the backs of great four-legged beasts. Many fell to their knees and bowed. Many more turned and fled. None came closer.

Tonven said something, inaudible below the buzz and cheer of the thrilled Aethir. Daneeth asked him what he had said.

"Look at them," he said. "They haven't changed."

Soola squinted into the distance, and a look of horror flooded into her face.

A hiss of air. A seam, like a broad malignant grin, appeared in the hull of Great Vessel as the vast bay door slowly opened.

The simulated gravity of Great Vessel vanished in an instant.

Screams pealed all about.

Daneeth felt the weight, the horrific pull, of the home planet throughout her entire body, as if each tissue, each fiber, each cell of her being were bearing down. Agony seared her. Her lungs felt sodden and gorged, her head shot through with pain, and she struggled to hold it upright.

She heard a snap, and then another, as first her left leg and then her right, buckled and broke under her sudden weight, too thin, too frail to support her. The splintered femur of her right leg broke through her flesh with a splatter of blood. She stumbled and collapsed to her knees.

Soola lay nearby, writhing in agony. All about, the Aethir collapsed in great heaps, their screams filling the air.

Tonven collapsed last, and slowly, as if he'd known what was to be. Tears filled his reddening eyes, and he whispered, "I failed you, Daneeth."

She felt the child within her, their child, sink through her abdomen, its great sudden weight pressing down, her thinly boned pelvis cracking under the strain, her body unable to resist the great demanding pressure.

The destiny of the Aethir fulfilled, Daneeth closed her eyes and prayed for a quick end to the crushing pull of home.

Notes

Among evolutionary biologists, study and debate continue about the rate of evolutionary change. Charles Darwin envisioned slow, gradual change. In 1972, Stephen Jay Gould and Niles Eldredge offered a modification to gradualism with "punctuated equilibrium," arguing that significant change in a species occurs rapidly when that species is subjected to environmental change. During periods of little environmental change, species change slowly. Bear in mind, "rapidly" and "slowly" are relative; it would still take many generations for the emergence of a new species of human like the Aethir.

This story snatches a population of ancient modern humans—the Aethir—from Earth, drops them into a spacecraft, and sends them hurtling off on a never-ending voyage through interstellar space in an environment much different than that to which they had evolved.

Another notion is that of a population with incredible technology at its disposal, yet remaining childlike in understanding it. We expect extraterrestrial visitors to have giant 1950s B-movie brains, able to break down the complexities of the Universe into bite-sized equations. But why? What if they were taken from their homes as a pre-literate and prehistoric group and kept at that level? Perhaps after the Masters passed away, the Aethir began to finally grow and study math and science. So I placed them at perhaps a medieval level of knowledge. A Renaissance man like Tonven, piecing together a working knowledge of the Universe, is seen as both genius and heretic, a Galileo of his culture.

About the Author

Ken Pelham's debut novel, *Brigands Key*, won the 2009 Royal Palm Literary Award and was published in hardcover in 2012. The prequel, *Place of Fear*, also a first-place winner of the Royal Palm, was released in 2013. Pelham co-founded the Alvarium Experiment, a groundbreaking writers' consortium specializing in speculative fiction anthologies. His nonfiction book, *Out of Sight, Out of Mind: A Writer's Guide to Mastering Viewpoint,* was named the Florida Writers Association 2015 Published Book of the Year.

Pelham's nonfiction book, *Gumshoes, Fangs, Rockets, and Spies: How Fiction Genres Evolve and Change Our World*, won the 2021 Royal Palm gold award for history. Check out that book's companion timeline:
www.tiki-toki.com/timeline/entry/758542/THE-EVOLUTION-OF-GENRES-A-Sideways-Look-at-Literature/

Brigands Key
Death sweeps in off the Gulf of Mexico . . .

An ageless, impossible corpse at the bottom of the sea. A lethal plague. A ruthless murderer. A monster hurricane. Archaeologist Carson Grant comes to Brigands Key to escape the limelight and repair his shattered reputation, and finds himself instead staring down an apocalypse.

Place of Fear
Deep in the rainforest of Guatemala, a missing scientist, long given up for dead, languishes in a lightless prison cell. Fueled by a powerful, unknown narcotic, his senses are on fire; he can feel them expanding far beyond human bounds, even as the drug tears at his sanity.

Carson Grant, learning that his friend is alive, mounts a frenzied rescue before the appointed time of execution. While a cutthroat band of looters, seeking easy riches, closes in for the kill, Grant stumbles onto the remnant of a mysterious hybrid civilization intent on destroying anyone that threatens to expose it. Trapped and desperate, Grant entrusts his team's survival into the hands of a young Maya cop and his beautiful, haunted sister.

Out of Sight, Out of Mind: A Writer's Guide to Mastering Viewpoint
One of the most difficult writing skills to grasp is that of writing from the viewpoint of fictional characters. What distinguishes the novice from the pro?

The go-to manual for writing in viewpoint, *Out of Sight, Out of Mind* teaches through example how to spot and fix errors of literary point-of-view.

Great Danger: A Writer's Guide to Building Suspense
Why do some novels keep you on the edge of your seat, flipping pages as fast as you can read them, while others you trudge through? What is it about the page-turner?

In a word, suspense. The author entices you, hooks you, and lands you. But how? It's not by accident. Learn the tips, tricks, and techniques of building suspense in fiction. In this concise guide, you'll learn what makes suspense tick, why we like it, and how to turbocharge your writing with it.

Ken Pelham is a member of International Thriller Writers, and lives in Maitland, Florida. Visit him at *www.kenpelham.com*.

Made in the USA
Columbia, SC
25 August 2022

65221750R00176